Amande's Bed

Amande's Bed

John Aberdein

THIRSTY BOOKS : EDINBURGH

First published in 2005 by Thirsty Books
an imprint of
Argyll Publishing
Glendaruel
Argyll PA22 3AE
Scotland
www.argyllpublishing.com

The author would like to thank the Scottish Arts Council
for a bursary which enabled him to devote time to writing
the first draft of this book.
Warm thanks to family and friends for their unfailing support
and to everyone who offered ideas and criticism during
the writing process.

British Library Cataloguing-in-Publication Data.
A catalogue record for this book is available from
the British Library.

ISBN 1 902831 84 5

Origination: Cordfall Ltd, Glasgow

Printing: Bell & Bain Ltd, Glasgow

For Sandy Boots,
fisherman and friend

eve

the most of scotland spread out

His mother woke several times that night, over-sweaty to sleep now with memories stirred. Finally she upped and padded from the bed-recess to the scuffed porcelain sink. She poured herself a cup of cold water, standing and nursing it, her candlewick robe over her nightslip. Dee water it was, Dee water that had come eighty miles from the roof of Scotland into the tenement.

Circling it in the cup she stood, taking wee houps, as her mind flowed from the summit over red jewelled gravel in the quiet mosses.

They said if you stravaiged the bald plateau rim, you might see the most of Scotland spread out, rough-folded, like a purple Bartholomew's brown-green map.

But clouds materialised from the west, the only day they were up there, and spilled over Angel Peak and Cairn Toul, filling the Lairig Ghru. She had to lift her puffy feet from the infant Dee and tempt them back into gray Co-opy stockings with the heel darns. Andy was shouting her through the mist. *Madge!* He'd gone doitering after ptarmigan, his left fist stocked with granite flints. She tugged both boots on. *Madge?* Laced one of them up. *Aye, I'm ower here—*

First full year of the war that must have been, the first summer, *passionate leave* her C.O. called it.

Lino cold on her soles, she padded back to the bed.

She lay on these hills, she lay at sea: her hair trailed, she lay on her back. Then something bad, snouting at her depths. It pushed into her like steel in water.

But it's Christmas the morn's morn— It bullered, throbbed like a U-boat, black.

She slid a long hand out for her husband, Andy. O, Christ! she tensed, hoping the pain that thrust would draw back, subside.

But every night it took long, longer, an awful long time.

fit dae they ken o the revolution?

The sea was filth, yet it drew you. It was cauld, grey, slick with undulated sewage. It came at you, heaving out of a blankness. His Dad said folk that worked on it were tinks, tinks of the sea. They drank gallons, maybe of seawater, their boats weeping with rust.

– Tinks, just. Tinks. Nae organised. Just a bunch o Torry Tories.

– Tinks are suddenly Tories? said his Mum.

– Aye are they. Skitin alang wi their *sink or swim* – never join a union, buy one *Daily Worker*, or put their cross for the Communist Party.

– My, my—

– Just clamber fae their ship aclart wi scales, an stiter stinkin tae the nearest pub.

– Ye dinna ken the hauf o it, they're fine. Look at aa thae skeely filleters.

– Aye, said his Dad. Them that get the jandies fae rats' pish in the fish slime. Filleters? They should be oot on strike, nae wallowin in it.

– Well, tak Fittie folk.

– You tak them—

– Open yir een! Mugs o marigolds in their knee-high windas, a gowpen o yella sand flang on the fleer, and aye blue sea, on three sides, lappin. A Venice o the North is Aiberdeen—

Father's laugh broke in at that. Ye've something there, ye're mebbe hauf-richt. If our sea was blue and our sand nae flechy. But the point is—

– O, nae doubt. There's bound tae be a point.

– The point is *Fit dae they ken o the Revolution?* and mother gave her smile back, pained so often now.

– Maybe as much as you ken about the wifie next door.

And father said *Ye ken fine that's nae true*— He plucked out a loose cup-hook from the damp wood over the sink, slammed the door of the flat, and stomped the dark lobby out to the shed.

And mother said sharp *Peem, were ye listenin? Up on a chair and get me doon twa pund o sugar oot o the press.*

Even on a chair you bare reached up to the topmost shelf. You used a packet of hard macaroni to draw the sugar bags out, and wheechle them to the edge.

Then under the bed she went and fetched the deep pan to boil toffee that she knifed into squares.

Which wifie next door? Wifie Herd? Wifie Dargo? Wifie Morrison? There were wifies all over the shop. Anyway the point was, the point was—

The point was, clamped in Inkster's iron desks, you'd never do a project: *Fishers.*

Romans you did: short swords, hook noses, straight endless roads.

life's too short, eh?

– And a Merry Christmas to you too, sir. When it comes.

Heading for the exit they stepped off the tartan rug, then waded through blue carpet, a sponge of blue. The tall one reached the revolving door. Lofting his crocodile briefcase, he pressed on the polished flange of brass. The door began to revolve. The stockier, jigging in sideways late, got his heel clipped, *Fu—!,* and the whole jing-bang juddered.

Out on the steps of the North British Hotel they came, out onto North Bridge, where a queue of black cabs purred and waited. He chose to walk. But bare a step when the on-ding came, down came the undammed rain.

– Jumping Jehosophat—!

– Bugger it!

– And lil black fishes.

Royston and Cran were the Time-and-Motion men.

Rain to dodge and time to kill before the north train, they approached a Goth of a monument.

– Like devils' cake, said the tall one.

– Do whit? said Cran.

– This freaked-up pile, said Royston. Like devils' cake, black.

– Come again?

– Baked and burnt for that deluded Limey. Stuck in his half-buried tent, storm like a thousand wolves, raving for hot grub, anything, pemmican.

– Ptarmigan?

– Till he froze.

– Wha froze?

– Scott.

– Wha bluidy Scott?

– Then the black gangrene. When they hauled off his gloves his fingers fell out.

– Pull the ither ane.

– His huskies ate them—

– His huskies ate bollocks. Scott was a writer. *Wri-ter,* said Cran.

– That low on fingers? Tough call.

– Listen a minute, it's nae nothin tae dae wi explorin. Scott, see, Scott Monument. Novels—

– Novels? In the name of the big monkey, you get a monument for that? Novels?

– Dinna look at me like that, I dinna read them, Mr Royston. Life's too short, eh?

Royston looked up at the sooty curlicues.

– They had piles o them in Thin's thonder when I was in buyin exercise paper, Cran said. Whit dae they cry them? *Rob Bluidy Roy, Guy Mannering, Ivanhoe—*

They entered and paid. Then they began climbing, Cran fitting slip-on shoes to pre-worn grooves in the steps, and saying the syllables, a mindless pacer, as the stairway narrowed.

Sir Wal Sir Wal,

Sir Wal-ter Scott,

Sir Wal Sir

Wal

ter

Scott.

wee pause

reprise

like jaded gongs

– Now, children, you can go now, in your rows. Happy Christmas.

– Hap-pay Chris-muss Miss-Ink-sturr.

– Front row.

She let the front go first, the smellies, glad to see the back of them. Now she could wrinkle a smile at clean-faced Iris Gray, filing past her with pigtails swaying.

In 1916, she had been summonsed through that same door. The headmaster standing like King Gillette, his crow-wing gown lank. Her mother in the shadow behind him. Cold in the stone corridor, watching mother's mouth move, taking nothing in.

Gas, she had said for some strange reason.

Gas.

Peem and Tarry kept an eye on Inkster, as they came down between the double desks, kicking the japanned tubes like jaded gongs. School on Xmas Eve, typical. As though their brains would parch with too much holiday. They were dry anyway. Revision till ten, an hour's division, a break for the settled milk. It gave you a thick moustache of cream, then was blue and warm.

– Fit's next, Tarry?

– Slessor.

– O no—

And in she'd come in her flowery smock, and out had come the pug-eared hymn books. Slessor arranged herself at the piano: Inkster went and sat behind her desk, on the splay-leg bentwood chair.

Sleeping in heavenly joy (rise)

Sleeping in heavenly joy (fall).

He watched Inkster cough and play one-handed for her hinged tin of lozenges.

i think that's sandpit mary

So on that very last half-day of school Peem cut and grabbed his small black bike from the bikestand. He dried the rubber grips with his hankie. Then he flung his leg extravagantly over and pumped down Nelson, slewed across Kinger with wettish brakes under the bows of a No 1 tram (guessing how taut the driver's fists), clattered atop Urquhart cobbles (tum sloshing like the word *galoshes*), then hissed along a tarmac curve, till he thumped forks onto the Bumps between golf links and beach.

Last summer Tarry had dragged him down to the Bumps after lost balls. Golfers whacked and yelled *Fore!* – and a fat white bee would fizz into the gorse. Should a ball be properly lost and honestly found, you got sixpence. If you picked one up on the roll – a clip on the lug. But a couple they'd come on in a dip were still bouncing. For her part she was thrashing her legs wide – trying to get away. A blonde wig had fallen askew in the struggle.

– I'm nae sure fae this angle, but I think that's Sandpit Mary, said Tarry.

– But she's nae in a sandpit.

– Nae this time. She's usually the ither side o the harbour, at Balnagask. Must be playin awa fae hame.

Humped over peeled handlebars, he drove the sliddery tyres to race at the next rise, high on the pedals, banging his cotters, riving from side to side.

But the day was weetcauld: no chance of couples. The fleet would be wallowing home with their last shot before Christmas. Maybe he could head down the harbour, brave a bluffert or two of foul spray on the great North Pier.

socifuckinology

Rain was breaking over Edinburgh in waves from the north-west, darkening the freestone buildings, gusting and spitting from gargoyles as they climbed. Royston and Cran wound up the last tight awkward stair. There was somebody up on the platform, some young man, back to the pillaring, bowed by the elements. He had his book out – *Suicide*.

– Aye, aye. Grand book ye have there, said Cran.

He glanced up.

– Manual? said Royston.

He shook his head.

– Novel? said Cran.

Shake.

– Socifuckinology, said the student.

Then they looked down on Princes Street, where they'd just finished giving Jenners its T & M, its Time-and-Motion, as per commission.

Big store, down on its uppers. *Crème de la crème*, very genteel. They'd arrived and caught them for the Christmas rush.

– Rush? said Royston. Say again? Did I hear you correctly? *Rush?*

– Ye see it, said Cran.

– Makes the Erie Canal look like Niagara. Geezers here wouldn't know throughput if it jumped up and bit them in the ass.

– Mebbe no.

So they applied stopwatch-and-clipboard to all the sales staff in turn.

– You wouldn't believe it in a book, said Royston to the manager, in front of his owner. Average time to accost a client and turn one sale?

– Accost? We like to think we make each customer welcome.

– How long are they welcome?

– Ten minutes, perhaps.

– Double that – twenty.

– Well but surely—

– Your top guy for sure is Mr Sillar. Tugging at wooden drawers, writing out receipts in backhand longhand with a fountain pen for chrissake, folding and refolding and patting farewell to each item of garmenting on his glass counter, hiding the goods in oodles of tissue and brown paper and a mile of sisal, he chats to every goddamn client about pesky ministers, best boarding schools, Morgans, scandal, rugby—

Morgans? said the manager. Surely not, that would be in Dundee.

– Wee sports car, said Cran, wi the wire wheels.

Royston spread on the manager's table a three month acceleration set of service interaction targets: 11 minutes, 8 mins, 4. The manager murmured *Not that kind of shop*. But the owner said it had better be, the chainstores were spreading, *sharp and jewish*, new ones starting up.

– It's *piskie*, Cran'd said, afterwards.

Piskie ministers. Some in Edinburgh, they worship bishops—

– Believe it.

– The others hae nae time for that. They get on fine. They worship themsels.

Cran rolled his eyeballs down the Gardens, hopped them across the railway lines, and up at the famous Castle with its crusted apron of rock. He nudged at Royston and pointed.

– Wait till one, there's a gun. Cannon.

– Where?

– The Castle, whaur else?

– When?

– One.

– A joy. Who do they shoot?

Cran snorted.

– It's for aa ye invaders. Wait ye here, ye'll get a hole whaur your dinner should be.

– Ouch to lunch indeed, Mr Cran.

– Ye'll be lucky if it's jist your belly they blaw awa.

– Yanks don't invade.

– Eh—?

– We just take over.

Cran shared a grimace with the student, as Royston spun. Tracking him on the staircase spiral, Cran jigged and concertina'd his thin-suited knees all the way down.

The rain came sudden. Peem threw bike aside and dived into a machine gun pill-box. Churchill had warned all East Coast folk they might be first, Hitler slamming landing-craft hard on the pleasure beach and spewing his troopers up through the spear-grass. So they put blank blocks and Bren gun barricades, higgled along the two mile Prom.

A *Press and Journal* lay raffled on the floor. On the front page a scuffed photo of the Provost, Lord Provost Rust with his gold chain, wabbling out of his Daimler. Peem deciphered a damp crumpled headline:

'N^T N^KED INTO THE
CONFE^^^^E CHAMBER'
Britain Must ^^^p
A-Bomb Bev^n S^ys

Confee Chamber? The place felt miserable.
Drop?

He was scared of the window shaft for a stick-grenade. It could come rattling in and tumble and wait, like a tensed maul. Then smash – into smithereens.

He'd be nothing – blood.

He moved to the shaft, across the raffle of paper.

Chin on the ledge he watched the ocean, collapsing towards him in gurls and heaves, straining his eyes till the rain would pass.

come on, billy, get aff

Their fawn shoulders got wet in no time as the wind shoved them back along Princes Street and down the brae, the steep ramp, into Waverley Station.

– Better wi ma bluidy auld trench coat, said Cran.

– Drench coat?

– Trench coat, I says.

– Sure. They explained you served in the weekend army.

– Nae totally weakened. Terriers, eh! We used tae train on Rannoch Moor.

Royston dug out his coins and inspected them.

– Used tae ram oor bayonets in hingin dummies, till the flock burst oot. No for a *Scotsman*?

Royston proffered a silver florin for a copy of the *Financial Times*, pink and thick, plus a pack of strong smokes, Capstan Full Strength.

– Dummies?

He got brown cents back.

– Flock?

Royston looked up at the green glass eaves of Waverley Station. Sources pushed humphs of steam into the air, dank chugs of smoke, and long indicative whistles.

Cran tiptoed, jumped, to scan over the throng.

– Aye, dummies. That's us ower there, Platform 19.

– Rule 1, said Royston. Always stick with a native.

Off the Aberdeen train the carriage doors were hanging, on their strop. They checked that the North British porter had lodged their cases with the guard. They walked along the concrete platform till they came to First Class. Royston led aboard and began sidling along the corridor. He came to a blockage: some skinny guy in a jerkin, a blonde dame neat in uniform. The guy had her double-bolted against the panelling, his bony paws on either side pressed flat.

– Come on, Billy, get aff.

– Pardon please, could you budge over—?

– But Ah thocht Ah wis hame wi ye tae Fife.

– Pardon please—

– Naw, Billy. Ye're comin tae nae Fife.

– An inch, fellas—?

– Aw, Dinah!

– Write tae me ower Christmas, okay?

– But Ah didna ken whit tae dae.

– Ye're still the guid man.

– Do travellers—

– Rubbish man, ye mean.

– Retain rights in this country—?

– Ah luve ye, Dinah. Ye ken Ah luve ye.

– Naw, Billy. Naw.

Billy shut both eyes and pursed his lips. He kept his groin well back, short of touching her.

– Comin thru—!

Billy shot forward, their hips butted, twice, he coughed on her nose.

– Christ, Billy, really! We're through wi fumblin aboot.

Bundled in his arms, she glanced down the corridor one way and, more awkward, the other. There was no help, there never could be.

Royston slid a compartment door open, and Cran reslid it shut. Ample. They had a six-seater all to themselves. Cran shook out his fawn overcoat, folding the shoulders inwards, then lengthways in two, and nestled it high on the chrome hammock. Royston placed his crocodile briefcase on the spare seat beside him. He had elected the carriage's external window, gazing forward, so Cran sat on the corridor side, looking backward, on the scarlet plush.

Fancy antimacassars had been fastened over the headrests, against greasy hair and falls of dandruff, crocheted *BR. British Railways. Brylcreem*. He pressed his head back, nice and quiet on the train. Cran peeked at the tableau still in the corridor: that skeleton jailing his hot nurse. A special softness under uniform—

The whistle blew, there was a last decisive slam.

The Aberdeen train jerked like a snake immediately weary, that slowed through Princes Street Gardens, a shallow Glencoe, and moulded painfully into the dark bowels of Edinburgh, its six mottled 20 watt bulbs pitiful in their fittings. A fart of eggs rose through their compartment as they ghosted past a criss-cross-criss of headtorches. Some workers, amongst the fallen faeces and the rats, bent about their business, restoring loosened brick.

– See there, Mr Royston, oot there in the tunnel?

– I can hardly look anywhere else.

– There's a bodge-job needin a wee study.

– Whole two-bit country needs one, Mr Cran.

Then they were lost in a gust of smoke.

the ae warst woman

Gazing at the gurl of waves, Peem minded the woman's sang he'd heard come roll from the Fishdock Saloon. Often enough Uncle Hugh would dirl out a bothy ballad, full of orramen and kitchie deems and a dose of their shenanigans.

But this had been his first sea ballad, unco and strange.

– Gie's *Sir Patrick Spens*, some bloke had piped up.

– Auld hat! cried some other bloke. C'mon Mary. Gie's *The Laily Worm an the Machrel o the Sea*.

Whatten long for a title! But they hushed up for all that.

I was but seven year auld
When my mither she did dee—
My faither mairried the ae warst woman
The warld did ever see.

For she has made me the laily—

Mary gave a wee cough.
For she has made me the laily—
She hoasted.

For she has made me the laily worm,
That lies at the fit o the tree,
An o my sister Maisry—
The machrel o the sea.
At *machrel* she nigh brought up.

Somebody breenged in past Peem from the street, in a blue serge jacket with flapping pocket, the door guffing out fag reek. A hullabaloo got up inside the saloon, and a hash of tankards hit the bar. The nyaff would surely get the heave, his skull a nova in the glass where it said *Younger's*—

Pale Ale

Younger's

Pale Ale

But the door flapped slower, the nyaff got somehow absorbed. Mary got her tubes sorted, and Peem picked out the next of her weird verses.

An every Saturday at noon
The machrel comes to me,
An she takes my laily head
An lays it on her knee—
She kaims it wi a siller kaim,
An washes it in the sea.

Minding a coorse queer song like that often slid him off in a dwaum. His eyes would narrow, and his mouth would play, a smile like his mother's, some would say. He would see nothing of the world around him for a while, and probably never hear *Awa in yir dwaum,* *again* till his father repeated *YE'RE AWA IN A DWAUM!*

Stolid faces slid into view, scores of parcels under arms, wrapped in tan or coloured paper, sellotaped and squared with string. Naturally the platform was packed, it was Christmas Eve.

The tableau broke. Cran didn't see the final farewells, for he pulled his corridor blinds down smartish to deter boarders, and harkened the Haymarket shoppers as they shuffled on past. It worked, nigh on. But then shoes clipped to a stop in the corridor. As the heavy door slid back, there stood the young and fair-haired nurse.

– First Class obtains here, said Royston.

One sideways stride took her round Cran's lumpen knees and patent feet. She arrowed an arm into her dark green duffel-bag, and fished out a book for the journey.

– Obtains whit, whit does it obtain?

– Lady, are you First Class?

Her calves tautened as she flipped the duffel high in the luggage net, then thought she'd need help later, else stand on the seat, she'd made a mistake. She unbuttoned the neck of her black coat, and made to unbutton, but didn't unbutton, the breast. Plunking herself down on the broad window seat, two away from Bulky Boots, and opposite Mister Pushy, she hooked one lock of hair behind an ear, and lowered her eyes into her orange novel, *The Cruel Sea* by Nicholas Monsarrat. She'd no be moving, no for any Yank.

Then she looked up.

– Aye, I'm first class, thanks, fine. How are ye, yersel?

Royston had unfolded the pink acre of his *Financial Times*. He poked his head round and spoke, away from the girl, towards his junior.

– You Brits sure do choose some damn funny colours for newspapers. Dunno what Senator McCarthy is gonna say.

21

Cran shrugged.

– I'm serious, partner. Nodding towards the nurse. This pinko tendency could spread.

mervellous thing

The waves rolled on their clash and clatter, like folk in a pub. A wind flicked through the newspaper, and stirred the ghosts of the six-sided pillbox.

Things hadna gone weel on sea nor land for Cherlie.

His wife. Amande.

His Free French lass, bonny, braw, tormentin – that'd come way across the sea, and sat aside him his last year at school.

His French refugee lass he'd run eftir in the playground, day and nicht, till one day, eftir they'd just left the school, they went thegither tae the beach. Haary hure o a day it was. They harkened the gulls greetin owerheid, inland fae the gaitherin storm. They spied mongrel dogs couplin, brak aff their couplin, in the scroggs and bents. Syne a blatter o cauld rain cam on, an drave them doon intae a pill-box. The Allies had pushed their flat-ersed boats and Bailey brigs across the river Rhine that very day. Sae there was sma enough need now for ony Home Guard or machine gun pill-boxes. The floor was a sotter o propaganda, an gey coorse tae smell.

They'd startit up against the wall, pressin thegither for warmth, but she said he was weet.

Preence, ma Preence Sharlie, your trouser is très weet.

Weet, aye, ma breeks, aye. And sae's your skirt, your dress, your jupie thing, Amande.

And weet also ma quelquechose—

Fit's a quelquechose fan it's at hame?

Ma petite con, Monsieur Gowk! Tu par moi, quickement!

Sure that'll be aaricht, darlin?

Oui—

Fa's wee?

Non. Pas du tout! Give me a, how-you-say, gweed roddin, mais retienne vos spunks.

Fit for, like? Sookins—?

Really, Sharlie, you are the very rude man!

But there's mair spunk in a Torryman's bugs than cod in the hale North Sea. They were mairried afore five month had passed. She'd nane o her ain faimily wi her on the day, her brither was a Hurricane pilot doon in Kent somewey – an he culdna be spared. Soon Amande had three bairns – *like slack elastic* aabody said *the knickers are never on her*.

His auldest, Haze, a lump o a lass, she was dozent enough. But the dark-haired loons were a different kettle o fish, folk said: as scherp as his brithers, Doddy an Jed.

Syne Randy Mandy's breedin aa dried up.

Birth control, mervellous thing.

out between the diamonds

Scabby outskirts, South Gyle, rolling country, Dalmeny next. Good to get away from the capital, her training done. She thought of Billy at Haymarket, tears in a man.

– Smoke, ma'am?

She lost it before she could rerun the unsatisfactory dream.

– Capstan?

It was Mister Pushy, trying to suck in, trying another tack.

– Ta. I dinna bother wi these.

– Really? Guess in your line of country you'd be glad of a puff, now and again.

She thought, No a puff like you.

– Why in ma line o country, would ye think? said Dinah.

– Worry and fret, worry and fret.

– Ye winna catch me frettin, less matron gets up ma back.

– Got to keep the fillies on the pace.

– Oh. Ken aa aboot it, dae ye? Ken aboot hospitals here, then?

– It's Ern actually. Big Ern they call me, said Royston. And you?

– Dinah, if ye must.

– Charmed.

– Dinah, mind. Dinna caw me Diana. Dae ye ken hospitals here, I'm askin?

– If you insist, I ken, know, Chicago.

– Never mind Chicagos. Ye should try our isolation ward.

– With you? A delight.

– No muckle delight. Kids greetin an bawlin the hale nicht.

– Who do they greet?

– Means bluidy cryin, said Cran, looking up from his travel guide of East Coast Scotland.

– O, tears after bedtime. Sure, we all got our little troubles.

Royston lit a fag with his silver lighter. Dinah put her head down to her book, then asked out straight.

– Chicago. Is that whaur Al Capone?

– Yeah. All kindsa slaughterhouse, cannery, the biggest.

– Whit dae ye dae for a livin then, mister, can hot air?

He put his head back as though to smile, and blew a ragged ring. They were drawing out of the small halt at Dalmeny, past some prickly hawthorns, out between the diamonds of the great red bridge.

– Time-and-Motion, to tell you the truth.

– Nivver heard cheep o them afore.

– Taylor's the operator. Taylor Universal. You will be aware of us?

– Me, naw, I hardly think so. Sae what does Mr Taylor hire guys like ye for?

Cran looked up from the gazetteer he was hiding his face in.

– Upgrading efficiency.

And sae that day the trawler *Dépense* was lang overdue, oot an back intae Aiberdeen, last o the scratchers, boats that draggit their pokies up an doon the barren grund nae thirty mile oot fae the fishertoon, nivver near the Faeroes nor Icelaun, plates hoatchin wi rust, engine room like a Glesga steamie wi burstin valves. An that day they'd a sma enough shot in her hold as they limpit hame, swung wide and swallawed by the north-east gale. Onywey they'd missed the market, her furnace splutterin wi a slush o weet coal. The Aberdeen sandbar was brakkin white across, wi an ugsome snarl. But there was nae help for it, they could hardly ride it oot in the bay in aa that wind.

Prop gland's leakin murnit Doddy.

Last o the fuckin coal! yallochit Jed.

Aye, aye, greet awa— thocht Cherlie, clenchin the spokit wheel.

Cherlie bade ootside the brakkin bar, till he judged his run. A lull wis it? He made a breenge, but reek fae the boat's black lum cam darkenin roon the wheelhoose winda. Aye, they would nearly hae made it but for that blindin fae cheap weet coal, the clapped-oot pistons, fae the brakken stack. The *Dépense* broached at the boddom o a troch and, lyin broached, she was flung by the furlin wave, sideweys intae the harbour mou. Syne she scrapit agrund, in the jaa o the auld grey brakwattir.

Let that be the price o ye— thocht Cherlie, steelin himsel for fit micht come.

She was left on twa teeth o rock, neither agrund nor floatin, but duntin hersel wi each passin wave, holin hersel wi the biggers. The gaberdined Coastguards soon ran doon, and oilskinned blokes in a panic. A mere hauf-lenth she was aff, the *Dépense*, they needna fire rockets but simply flang raip, coil eftir coil till her, the wind uncoilin ahind.

But nivver a billie would come oot the wheelhoose, the rescue raips dreeped slack.

Come awa! Come awa! went the Coastguards. But Cherlie, Doddy and Jed just clung far they were.

Come awa! Come oot, ye gangrels! went aa the leal. White phisses inside that ticht wheelhoose, an orra scuffle, the three o them rivin, wrasslin. Syne jist the ane left staundin, gruppin on till the stalled wheel.

Come oot! Come oot, for chrissake! went the final megaphone, as belfries o spray pealed ower the brakwattir.

Cherlie stood braced in the wheelhoose, they culd see his white phiss, but nae his twa brithers lyin humped at his feet. He thocht lang, lang on Mandy – legs aye open like a deep-wattir trawl. An he was scunnered wi trawlin.

The raips an lines o helpfu men lay strandit across the *Dépense*.

He didna see, he couldna see, but O he heard her comin—

The Mitherwave.

Wi a muckle smash the Mither gaed whoosh aa ower them, peelin boat an brithers clean aff the rock, whummlin them doon deep channel.

Sweet fu— thocht Cherlie.

scenery came for him

When it came to the Forth, they'd learned their lesson, the guide-book assured, about jerry-building. 5,000 men it took in all, working in shifts for 7 years. They planted and clenched 6,500,000 white-hot rivets. For cladding they daubed on 60 tons of dull red paint.

57 of them died also.

Fell mostly, Cran imagined. Struck on the skull. Or crushed.

Clicketty-CLACK, clacketty-CLICK. Royston put aside his paper. The noise echoed inside the bridge, inside his head, his seat vibrated. Through the window smear, the lattice of railings, through the great angular tubes, he glimpsed downwards. The choppy waters of the Firth of Forth narrowed as he glanced up west, scuds of rain hiding whatever was back there. But looking ahead, through the flicker of each red pillar, he got cubist impressions of a vessel, or vessels. The superstructure of a Navy high in dry dock, turrets in steps, the long grey guns. Clacketty-CLICK, clicketty-CLACK, Clacketty-CLICK, clicketty-CLACK.

RICK-RIICK-RIIICK—

Royston pitched forward, his right palm whanging the dame's forearm, as the train thrust down on hard-braked bogies. Her novel flew.

– For ony pity's sake, said Cran. Some clown's pulled the cord—

But Dinah was past him, first in the corridor.

A carriage door lay banged open. She ran along and clambered down and out onto the wet ridge of ballast. Along the way stood the engine, *shoosh-shoosh, shoosh-shoosh*, pistons arrested, bull in a pen. But her eyes were for Billy, scissoring over the railings, an ant in a huge red web.

– Billy!

Rain washed in scuds behind him. Billy's left knee buckled, he grabbed some bracket at the very edge. Out in his summer jerkin, he clapped its gappy zip together, and felt its collar flipper at his neck.

– Naw. Naw, Billy!

Then the squall passed like a hurled veil. Billy stood on the last girder. He looked down at the broad-faced Forth and its poxed Inches, studded irregular with concrete and gulls. Could hear her, worried now, *tap-tap* on the boards towards him.

The Rubbish Man, trembling a bittie.

– Easy, Billy—

Like at the Public Baths, high on the springboard once. The attendant below would yell at first-timers *Lowp weil oot!*

– Steady, Billy. Come on tae Fife—

On a springboard if you overpinged – back coming down, you'd whack on the jut.

– Nae problem, Billy. Honest—

Dinah said after, that he half-turned.

– BILLY!

Scenery came for him in a bright, black rush.

naebody sees aathing

– Sae what did ye actually see? said Peem's Dad.

  – Aathing—

  – Naebody sees aathing, said his mother.

  – Did though.

  – Not, said brother Hughie.

  – Did sut.

a box of codling bongoing round

BANG! took him from his dwaum. Nazis must have sneaked ashore—

BANG! Nah, maroon for the lifeboat.

A shiver as he was hit by a driv of rain. Peem leapt onto his bike, and bowled along the tarmac Prom. Outby he could see grey seas leaping, white-tipped with fire, half the height of Stevenson's lighthouse. He scudded past the neat low houses at Fittie. Just as he heeled, along came a scurry of coastguards, three of them, holding their caps down, hard on his wheels.

A lone mast stood gyring, a hundred yards ahead.

Cuffed by the wind, he still got there first and walloped himself up on the pier wall. God, a trawler. Hard-on, half-off, she seethed and sawed on ledges of barnacles. A puckle gulls hauled through the wind and came Stuka-ing down, as a wave swashed over the deck and sent a box of codling bongoing round. Some pair of blokes was in the wheelhouse, riving at each other's ganseys, twisting by the throat.

The coastguards flung a rope across. The sea just washed it off. The coastguards swooped the line back in loops, and reflung. But for ropes and lines they'd little heed, now a third had joined that wrestling.

A dark-haired tinky loon came pelt along the pier, and up on the pier wall parapet.

– *Daaad*—!

Down three flaky rungs the loon dangled out and shouted. Trawler awash to the gunnels, her scuppers creaming. *Hey, nae-users, come oot o that!*

Gulls upsheered as a coastguard caught him *Mad wee shite!* and hauled him back.

The lifeboat poked round Pocra Quay, blue, with a band of orange, just as the sea darkened from seaward.

– *Daaad*—!

The trawler *Dépense* was taken big, duffed from her ledge and scourged into deeper channel. Wheelhouse, red bruised keel, bitten propeller, all slipped from sight, till only her truckle wires sliced through the water.

– Jesus God, wis that—?

Till all that was left was a swirl.

– Ye kent fa—?

The tink recruited a gob from his small insides, and spat.

And folk came grieving out of Fittie, and folk came wailing down from Torry. Wifies wandered the pier. Peem tried to dicht the gob from his shoe with seaweed as two of them came by.

    – O, ma boys. Ma puir boys.

    – Perdu.

    – Aa three o them in a single whuff.

    – Perdu. Perdu.

    – Nae jist *perdu*, Mandy. Deid—!

Dripping handline slack was being recoiled uselessly back, the drips brief pearls.

    – Ach, said the hauler.

    – Yach aye, said the coiler.

    – A fool wey tae stert Christmas.

    – Non! They are no *fols*, the Frenchwoman said.

    – Just means *dirty*, missus, the third man replied.

eat up yir macaroni

– Aye well, never easy, his Dad said, when Peem finished his tale round the kitchen table. It's a peety for them. A peety ye had tae see that, Peem. Let that be a lesson.

    His Mum just shook her head.

    – Eat up yir macaroni.

    – We had macaroni on Tuesday.

    – Well, that's foo lucky ye are. Ye winna hae it the morn, it's Christmas Day.

Dinah inched her heart to the edge, and gazed over. Three gulls, loosed arrows, were fanning away off the surface. They looked not white, opal.

It was long past the splash.

When they arrived, the plain clothes, they took her out of the hubbub up to the guard's van.

Rank smell, as they drew her over to a wicker trunk.

– Take the weight off your legs.

A threshing arose from inside, within.

– Easy, lass. Homers.

Then the guard laid his head outside, peering upline, till his eyeballs stung with wind and cinders.

Dinah sat in the cramped toilet a long time. At one point the door started to open, and she leapt up, shoving it shut. She moved the snib. Outside it would now read *Engaged*. Hunched over her knickers, over her knees, she swore at her gripped shins.

Ye swear like a nurse, he'd said to her once.

The lid rose with her a little. She leaned on a tap, and read the bossy wee plaques.

Ne pas pour boire. Kein Trinkwasser.

A buff curdle of egg and Flakes whacked round the bowl.

– Got any gum, mister?

– Be my guest.

– Ta. Thanks.

Cran stooped, and picked the orange paperback up by its wings.

– We thought you scheduled to descend at Fife, said Royston.

– Descend? said Dinah.

Chewing slow, she closed her eyes and dozed.

Law agents were gassing with his sidekick somewhere. She had a speck of something on her coat, on the dark button of her gaberdine. He inhaled, paused, then picked a shred of gold from off his tongue.

He blew a lasso.

The train huffed north, through red clawed furrows, blown sketches of coast, at length across a whorled river. A grey stone set slid by, the puffs grew slower.

Royston peered at the board and mouthed.

– *Joint Station*, yeah. *Joint Station*, that about says it.

– Says what? said Dinah, pretending to wake up.

A pigeon swooped then hightailed – up through girders.

– Here already?

One shoe levering on the plush, she hoicked her duffel-bag clear, then stepped back down. She tugged an alloy comb through.

– Bye, Mister Ern.

– Ern Royston.

– Ta for the gum.

– I sure do hope—

But she was off down the corridor.

christmas

The darkness ticked into Christmas.

She cooried into Andy's back.

A bell birzed, door bell. She moved up half on an elbow, and keeked at the green glowing tips on the alarm. Happening too often now, these maintenance call-outs. The acid test, Andy had joked. Acid bit through exposed wiring.

BIRZE-BIRZE.

She shook his pyjama shoulder, till Andy grumphed.

– Time's it this time?

– Five past—

– Three, I hope?

– Five past four.

– Bloody swicks!

They had it down to an art, the night foremen – mingy swine.

He threw his legs out over without first turning and giving her a kiss.

No 7/6 bonus now, just ordinary overtime.

He put on his leather slippers.

That would be three half-crowns they wouldn't have for Hogmanay.

He went out to their little hall, then out through the common lobby, thence to the front door.

– Fit did ye say tae the man? said Madge.

– Tellt him tae tak an atomic taxi.

– Fit for?

– Sae as tae get here afore four, next time—

Why was it coldest just before dawn? Peem drew to his chin the blue flannelette, the armyish blanket and hen feather quilt. He was feart to put his head further under, in case of the three drowned men.

Not that they were alone in death, he'd nearly died too once, of scarlet fever. Even the name, *scarlet*. Sober serge men had come into his bedroom. His brain a furnace, tongue thick as a trunk, mighty elephants wheeching round the walls. *Just here to help you,* said his mother. *No!* he'd skraiked when he saw their brown stretcher. *Traitors!* He wobbled to his feet, lugged up the bolster and swung at them from his sickbed. *No—!*

The City Hospital, two hundred yards away, might as well have been two hundred miles. His mother never came in to see him, ever. Just stood outside, just made mouths in the glass. Nurses brought him slop food, saps, the ruins of bread in warmish milk. He had to pee in a white porcelain chanty, he did it yellow so that it really showed up. He said *I want ice cream to cool ma tonsils.* Nurse said *The National Health Service doesna run to ice cream.* What was that supposed to mean? *You'll be getting them out, soon enough.* He tipped the pot when he stood up, it got stuck to his bum and one side lifted. A slew of yellow pee went into the seams of the planked floor.

– Peem!

The white V of her bosom, you could look down into that V from the top of the stair. Everybody liked her, Miss Florence. Bent over his infant desk, her bosom in passing pressing, helping him respell. Mannie Harrow, it was easy for him. He was tall and thin, blue-jowled, like the cartoon of Chamberlain. He looked down her jumper just walking past. Mannie Martin with the pox face, it wasn't so easy for him, shorter.

– Time you were up! shouted his Mum.

He flipped the top bedding aside, down to the sheet, and looked at the wee wigwam his mannie made. If he was really ill again, at the school, Miss Florence might have to take him home. To the wrong house.

– An hae a keek oot the winda when you're at it.

How did she know he was at it? Women didn't know.

– Come awa, noo.

Stevenson. He got to bide in his bed till he was better. Didn't have to get up to rotate porridge with a spurtle. Just wrote his fevery poems, and stories about countries. Or islands. Why was it always coldest, just before dawn. No, he'd said that one. If you weren't careful, you went back in a circle.

– Peem!

There was a rasping from outside.

Under the paper blind, there was a pool of condensation on the sill, and a dead fly. Why were there always flies in winter? He jerked on the endless string, the roller blind went up squint – the dulled bedroom was undercut by dazzle. He jerked again and it tore. Snow, smooth and billowy, across the breast of the road.

Out on the road, Hughie, rasping away, sliding a spade under horses' oranges. Being hot they sank through. He was scraping up a good selection. He lobbed the oranges over their paling, so as to ruffle the skeleton of a rose. *Roses need a gweed dung* his Dad aye said.

The window was fugging. Tongue lodged, Peem fingered out *boS tfaD*, then knuckled sharp for big brother to see—

Quick bend and straighten from Hughie, his arm drawn back. White thud, an exploded blossom—

Once more and the pane might crack, so he nipped ben to the kitchen.

A schlorich of stinking kale lay sprawled in the sink.

How could he Pepsodent his teeth?

His mother, in her apron.

– Where's Dad, Mum?

– Whaur dae ye think, loonikin?

– Call-oot?

– The back o four.

– What was it though?

– Sulphuric Acid Plant.

Good your dad was so vital he got called-out at night. Who else, doctors, firemen. The works made artificial fertilisers, out of guano came in from Peru. Or Chile. There was an Ammonia Plant as well. A Nitric Acid Tank.

– What is there kale in the sink for? It's disgustin.

– Because, bonny lad, you'll be skirlin for dennir, lang afore tea-time.

– Inkster says *dennir*'s the wrang—

– She does, does she? Had a few four-coursers hersel, by the look. Well, never mind that. Has Santy been?

He ran back to the bedroom. Palpated the lumps in the grey school stocking. It wasn't a bike then. A wee box, likely a Dinky. Couple of soft tangies, a chocolate soldier, several Brazils in tough-to-crack shells.

Maybe Dad was getting a bike for him, maybe the call-out was only a ghoster. He'd be bringing a bright bike home.

– Well? Fire?

He knelt down at the hearth. Three *Daily Workers*, his quota, knotted, and just one match. The *Workers* flared, then charred.

– Ye'd be better tryin it wi a pucklie sticks.

He'd never sold them all, now he hardly sold any. Many ye got, Dad? A quire. Peem wondered if they twisted his arm, a quire was madness, a hundred and twenty, or if Dad just wanted to be a hero. *Stakhanovite*, that was a word Frankie Groat used. *Stakhanovite*.

A Stakhanovite worked to keep the revolution going, twelve, fifteen, eighteen hours a day.

He gazed into the rebuilt grate, that waited a tongue of flame. He flared his nostrils at the second match. Real sulphuric—

– Okay, watchin a fire winna mak it burn.

Mum passed him the thin wooden spurtle, dripping the early stages of porridge into the tawny revolving mixture in the pan.

– Watch and nae let lumps—

She hung over the crib by the bed-recess and hauled Tammy out and across her lap, tweaking a knot free on his hard plastic overnappy, exposing in turn the outer terry, the inner muslin, the sookit bum, the soft beige nuggets.

– C'mon ma wee lamb.

Ammonia stung your eyes.

Peem faced the mottled wallpaper above the gas stove. He had a couple of Biggles to finish. *Good Old Biggles*. It was set in the desert, the days of Rommel. *Biggles to the Rescue* was waiting under the bed. But after breakfast, Tarry and Raymie were sure to rap at the door and drag him out in the snow to make a long slide, a chute for the unwary.

– Watch and nae let burn!

He caad the spurtle through the porridge, making oval O's, feeling the pan-bottom thicken to a fur.

– Mum, did he tak the Panther?

Then he minded he'd seen the thick treadmarks where Dad must have wheeled her across the crispness, under the gaslight. He should have waked, waved *Ta-ta* at the window, just in case. Goggled, pushing the blue brute along, cutting the earlier tracks of the call-out taxi, before jumping on to gather momentum from the brae. Kick-down, away—

Miss Florence with her golden locks, twined behind and streaming.

– Peemie!

A bubble popped and left a hole and rings.

Hughie burst in the door and plumped down at the table, red in the face and pleased with himself.

– That's me.

– Cleared the hale path noo?

– Good as.

– Better be good when your faither comes hame. Peem, keep steerin it.

– I am—

Annie's shiny face swung in. Hanging like a monkey off the doorknob, she slowed heels of her pink slippers on the brown lino.

– Annie, ye'll hae that haunle aff, ye vratch.

– Maam, Megan's nae happy.

– Nae happy, nae happy. Come awa an tell me aboot it.

– Megan's got German weasels.

– German weasels? Have ye tried her alang tae the doctor?

– Doctor'll be aff tae the Bahamas, said Hughie.

– Doesna like doctors, Mummy. She's a scaredycat – hidin in the lavvy.

– Well, would ye tell her please, I'm burstin?

– Bet your spurtle willna stand, said Hughie.

– Will sut—

– Will not—

– Sut—

– Right, seein it's Christmas, you young anes can hae your porridge in your pyjamas.

– I dinna want it in ma pyjamas, Mummy.

The immutabilities of porridge. White tablecloth, with a waterproof breakfast one on top. A big bowl of porridge and, close to you, a small lotus bowl of milk. You flew with your spoon to the furthest away porridge. You had to claw up most of a spoonful, osprey up some milk, then take your prey whole. No jam, no mixed-in cream or other concession.

Annie was off her porridge because of Megan.

– Noo here it comes, fleein, Mum offered.

To Peem the laden spoon seemed like a Lancaster banking and speeding with Merlin engines across the polythene, to bounce a lump of pale porridge out of its bomb bay into her mouth.

– Look, Anniekin. Flutterby's comin.

– Not a butterfly. Not got colours. 'S a moth.

– Gad's sake! said Hughie.

– Up wi ye? said Peem.

– Fa left this muckle lump?

– Lumps are good in porridge.

– Nae this big.

– That's the sheep's eyeball.

– I'll gie ye eyeball—

– Hughie!

The fire wasn't glowy enough in the mornings to make toast, the coal was still black and wheezing. They Storked loaf. Stork was made out of whales and chemicals. They never got Robertson's marmalade, because of the golly, the black-faced badges.

– Mum, is there jam—?

– Finished. Wash faces now. An nae just a cat's lick!

– Maam, can I tak Megan tae the shops wi me? Her granny's needin somethin fae the chemist.

– Aaricht, dinna mak her late for school.

– Nae school the day—

– Nae even for Megan?

But there was no formal education for dollies, not even imaginary ones, on Christmas Day, and none now till after the New Year. Snow had come and the snow lay thick, above a week. The teachers would be lying full to the gunnels with booze.

Teachers? Ower muckle money and ower little sense, the lot o them folk said.

january

just a wee smallich

Peem checked the beautility sideboard. Six ovalled nip glasses, six stemmed sherry glasses, six thistle-engraved glasses for advocaat or port, and four shapely schooners for Carlsberg or MacEwans.

One of the Carlsbergs was gone, and two MacEwans. The Bertola Cream was down near a quarter, the Bells was worse. Hughie got allowed a wee Bols for the first time, being fifteen. The port hadn't moved. *Ye dinna hae tae drink tae enjoy yersel* his Dad aye said.

They had taken in the New Year in their own flat with the Hirds, stepped lightly up to their place, swapping a dram there, *Just a wee smallich* his Dad had said, then zigzagged up to the Crichtons where there was good black bun. The Morrisons across the way didn't drink or anything, being Jehovah's. Paterson, *puir whey-faced besom* Dad called her, wore a close-pulled mutch and had bristles. Auld McMorency was totally immured, and even her spinster daughter passed you in the lobby but once or twice a year. They'd hardly give you *Hello*, the McMorencies, they'd never speak to dirt from tenements, simple as that.

So it was bed by the back of two. Then Uncle Hugh arrived in the afternoon, took a wee sherry after a great prigging, and squeezed a tune from his red button accordion, *McGinty's Meal an Ale* rattling along fine.

> *They were howlin in the kitchen like a caravan o tinkies,*
> *An some were playin ping-pong an tiddley-widdley-winkies,*

Bridget was with him, a teacher. Some teacher, aye ready to

gabble in Gaelic if you gave her the chance. But Hugh hammered on with his bothy ballad.

For up the Howe and doon the Howe ye never saw such jinkies
As McGinty's Meal and Ale, whaur the pig gaed on the spree.

That was the Doric. You weren't supposed to come out with that in the school. But Bridget said never mind *Jocky-come-lately Doric, it was the proper Pict-Gaelic Aberdeen used to be speaking,* before the place got overrun by Saxons, Vikings, Visigoths and Huns.

Bridget was a Scottish Nationalist, that was her story. She had a depressed scar on the side of her neck and her hair up in a bun. Maybe they took her tonsils out from the outside. She used to wash Peem standing up in the sink, viewable from the backie by all the neighbours fetching in coal. But that daft caper was nipped in the bud when he turned ten. He'd run out the back and go clambering over the barbed rose-clippings to hide in the concrete air-raid shelter, or go bang on Tarry's door till the worst of her visit was past. Bridget had to content herself with irrigating his sister.

She was getting long in the tooth and it was obvious she wanted a bairn of her own but Uncle Hugh was sweirt to marry, though they'd been going to tennis and Kirk together for ages. Why, Peem wondered, still go to the Kirk if he was a Communist? He must have signed as a spy for God or Stalin, probably one of those *fellow-travellers.*

Anyway Bridget was game for a song, unaccompanied. It started *Tha mi sgith,* very bouncy. *Ha me ski*, you had to say. It meant *I am tired.*

Then she chose the swoony one, *Boatman.* She'd written out the Gaelic, had Singy Bridge, plus a translation facing, for Peem in a little notebook.

Fhir a' bhàta, na hòro éile,
Fhir a' bhàta, na hòro éile,
Fhir a' bhàta, na hòro éile,—

That just meant *O my boatman*—

Then the slow last line *Mo shoraidh slàn dhuit's gach àit' an téid thu.*

Even without translation, that seemed to reach a good bit deeper, a lot further out.

Of course Uncle Hugh had been a Marine in the War. A Commando, like in the comics. You could say either Marine or Commando. They blackened their knives. A Marine Commando.

He liked words ending in *o, Mikad-o, Meccan-o, Gepett-o, Ghett-o.*

Commandos could creep, slit your throat in the dark.

this is nae paris

– Peem!

– What?

– Messages!

– Mum, can Hughie nae go?

– Hughie shovelled the snaa again the day.

– An spoiled it—

– An Hughie didna tear the bedroom blind last week.

– I never meant tae.

– Hughie doesna like shoppin. Nae like you. I'll write ye a notie.

– Mum, dinna be horrible. Is it the butter side or the sugar side?

– Baith sides, ye'll need twa bags.

– Mum!

He got his black wellies, new soft leather flying helmet from hanging up in the Hall, and pouched the coins and notie. Exact money, bound to be.

In Urquhart Parade, the quiet bombed tenements. You didn't think they were bombed all the time, just empty. The granite just stood, block on block, the upper lathwork lay in rips. Was anybody killed, there wasn't any blood. He could ask Dad, but Dad never liked about the War and would change the subject.

He stopped for a moment. Snow soothed the splintered lath, and lay in millions on the sills.

– Aye, aye, Peemie loon, let's see your listie—
Everything was diminuable, even a long list.
– I'll need it back, Mister Jackson, I've tae go tae the ither side.
– Ach , I'll easily nip roon the ither side for ye.
– It's okay, thanks, I've plenty time.
– Suit yersel— Foo's Madge?
Madge, eh, funny to hear his Mum's name.

The Northern Co-operative Society had set out a threefold counter system. At the long wooden counter you purchased sweet goods, dry goods, tea and flour. At the long blue-veined marble counter you sought your butter, ham, and eggs. At the windowed kiosk you paid for everything, and reported your Co-opy number.

Aproned assistants hurried hither and thon. Scooping orange lentils into stout brown bags, balancing them on solid scales against a range of brass chessmen, pleating them shut. Dropping six buff eggs cannily into thin white bags and twirling the ends shut. Slicing bacon with a huge stainless wheel encased in a red guard, cradling each rasher as it fell, and layering it out on greaseproof paper. Taken as a whole it was all called *groceries*, yet there wasn't a single one you could call a *grocery*.

Ofttimes it was a pest queuing three times, when you wanted back to play. As your pinkie traced the marble veins, as you harkened to black tea rustling, as you wired with the guillotine through cheddar, it wasn't difficult to understand some of the big words Mannie Martin plied you with: *emporium, dividend, cornucopia.*

He liked *cornucopia* best: like a goddess with her bosom full of poppies, lupins, sheaved with oats.

His classmate, Iris, gave him a glance from the dried goods queue. Peem half-lifted half a hand. Bapface.

There was that new woman, near the front of the queue, her that flitted from Torry. Up above Guffie's the Butcher with the dark-haired loon.

She was from foreign, *an ill-farrant foreign hure* some of them cried her. Supposed to be French. But bonny too, a bonny figure, like the glass that sat on the Morrison's mantle. Jehovah Morrison would flip the glass upside-down as he tried to persuade you. *The sands of time are running out, the world is coming to an end. See! See how quickly!*

Jehovah's so-called *hour-glass*.

Four minutes. For eggs.

– Bye, Mrs Casey. Now, ma dear, can I help ye?

The Frenchwoman opened her hands elegantly, the palms facing each other.

– I wish, please, one packet of café.

– Just tea, ma dear.

She flung her palms to the roof in quick impatience.

– Café it is that I want. I have many coupons.

– Mercy me, this is nae Paris. Only tea, missus, coupons or nae coupons.

– Pouf, thé, coupé!

And she drew an index across her throat.

– Is there ony mair thingies?

He translated himself, for her sake.

– Thing-*ies*—? *Mair* things—?

The Frenchwoman burned at him.

– Winna be a minutie, Mrs Dargo.

– Aye okay, Johnny—

– Monsieur, Monsieur du Magasin, I piss in your thé.

– O, aye—

– You don't listen to me?

– O, I'm hearin ye, wifie.

– I piss in your Scottish thé!

– Naebody's stoppin ye.

– You don't care?

– It's a free country.

– Where nothing is free—

– No, but ye div get your divvy wi the Co-opy, divn't ye?

She turned, her string bag empty, and made for the door.

But Peem liked her in that moment, all that waving of hands about, she knew how to stick up for herself. Mostly everybody he knew kept themselves well haudin-in.

Then he got served, at the butter side. A half of marge. Six eggs, their fortnight's portion. But only streaky bacon left, *Affafatty* Mum would say, so there was indeed change.

Affafatty. Affaaffaaffaaffafatty.

He could have abandoned his meagre messages and followed her. Just to see where she lived. He knew where she lived. Just to see how she walked, then—

He tried to pick her tracks in the snow, but they were all overlapped.

He popped into Strathdee the Baker. With a penny of brokeners he kept a clan of starlings ahead of his snowy boots by flicking crumbs.

Royston reckoned without the full force of Hogmanay, though Cran had warned him. They were in the Town Council offices, in a high-ceilinged room with two canvas-back chairs, a round-leg table, dark olive cabinet and a tin cylindrical bin.

– How many goddamn Hogmanays do these people celebrate?

– Oh, just the one. Ye've got tae see the New Year in—

– It's in, for chrissakes! It's January four.

It was not as though they'd achieved much in the week between Christmas and New Year either. Cran had warned him of that.

– Aathing's higgledypig, this time o year, he'd said. Plus aa the snaw—

– *Higgledy-pig, Hog-manay*. This place is getting a *bore*. Why are we here at all, remind me?

– Ye ken fine. Plenty folk fleein about soon. It's aye a thrill in Aberdeen, the January sales.

Today at last they were able to get Time-and-Motion's staples out, stopwatch and pen, and spring-loaded clipboard, that put them at advantage, and others ill at ease.

A council official had given them a street map of Aberdeen with tram routes marked in red. The routes made an arthritic red spider, whose striped body was Union Street.

They started at a place called Castlegate, that looked like a nerve-centre, and travelled on all the routes in turn, counting whatever can be counted: the number of stops, the length of stops, the number and gender and approximate ages of passengers mounting and dismounting, plus the top speed and average speed, on each of its routes, of each of the species of tram.

Though there were only two species: the blunt and the streamlined. Three if you counted the open-tops that sailed down the Beach Boulevard in summer time.

The old blunt tram was simple: hexagonal ends, driver in his bow cabin, and a gaping single entrance at the stern.

The new streamlined tram was like two tall torpedoes welded in the middle. It had two bows but no stern, a Janus tram, with a cabin for the driver at each end, and pneumatic doors on port and starboard side.

Tram tactics at a terminus, say Bridge of Dee, Bridge of Don, Sea Beach, Hazlehead, were perforce very different.

The old blunt tram had a loop she bogeyed round, a loop of rail she negotiated at half a knot, till she faced the way she'd come.

The long supremo was magically and noisily different. At a terminus, the driver moved his handle to the Zero Power option, sallied from his first cabin the full inside length of the car, entered an identical cabin by an identical door, and sat facing the way he had come. The two conductors meanwhile were striding along, upstairs and down, clacking the backs of the hinged seats over from 10 to 2, so to speak, so that fresh passengers could plunk down happy, facing their journey's end.

For though some may prefer to gaze on where they have been, mulling petty history, massaging incident into myth, and accidents of change into malign catastrophe, yet most prefer to read the future, preferably twenty seconds in advance, by gawping and gyping out of a broad-paned window, at lurid posters in the passing shops, at the attempted suicide of tram-racing dogs, and for early signs of their destination, so as to stand up swaying well in time, elbowing the skulls of seated fellows, and jabbing an anxious index at the red button, recessed in the tramcar's roof, or proud on a steadying rail. Else, undescended as an infant's testicle, they might sweep past their stop, the driver happily recovering schedule in a smooth electric glide.

Royston and Cran sat on the lengthways seat at the door and counted and timed and remarked. They had a cardboard pass so conductors didn't pester them, but conductors did. Conductor Ron Casey downstairs on the No 4 was a case in point. Heading up Union Street with his tram wedged with grumphy grannies plus a polio lad on calipers, he nodded pointedly to the notice that said *Please give up your seat for ladies, the elderly and the infirm.*

But could you work clipboard, stopwatch and pen while hanging off a leather strop? Manifestly not. Time-and-Motion's men sat tight.

Ron Casey grunted.

Cran stood up.

The Woodend tram got as far as Queen's Cross and there she stuck, wheels skittering. The points were iced.

The driver climbed down stiffly with a sack: he shook a handful of salt on the frozen points. Then he opened his satchel and poured a cuppie of tea from his slender Thermos. He delved for the small Cod Liver Oil bottle of milk. His wife had forgotten it.

Royston looked down at the stopwatch in Cran's palm. The stopwatch already said 4 minutes 50.

– He'll be waitin the salt tae work—

The driver climbed back into his cab, and down with another coarse sack. A sprinkle of grit, for grip. He topped-up his tea, and screwed back the loose stopper using a makeshift greaseproof-paper washer.

The stopwatch said 7 minutes 40.

– Now what, in the name of the big monkey?

– Hing on. Hing on, Mr Royston—

– Don't tell me. He's waiting the grit to work!

– Na. Tea's probably too het for his mou—

– Pour it out on the goddamn points then!

But somebody spied on them too.

– So that's what Yanks call a day's work?

Royston looked up at the strop-hanger, in her uniform.

– Hey, miss, you again.

– Aye, me indeed.

– Diane, you look real swell.

– Dinah tae you—

– Dinah. Apology. Did you get into nursing hereabouts?

– Dotting back and fore at the moment. Relief. I've been given a shift to Woodend this week, they're desperate, but I'm needed back at Casualty pretty soon.

– What news of Edinburgh, what about Fife?

– Naw, I canna go back, it was across the front o the papers. My stepfaither's livid—

– Your stepfather?

– Miner. He works under the Forth.

– Where do you live, then, nurses' quarters?

– Naw, I dinna qualify, only temporary.

– So?

– Digs.

– Digs?

– A room and breakfast.

– You'll need more than that to keep you going. We should—

– I'm fine.

– And did you, may I ask, have they—

– Naw, poor Billy's body's never been found.

– Deeply sorry to hear that.

– They questioned me for twenty minutes, dae ye realise, the CID, said Cran. Whit could I tell them? I said you seemed tae be haein a wee disagreement on the train, nothin physical though.

– That's right, said Dinah. Nothin physical.

– Ye must miss him an awfu lot.

– Ye'd surely think so. A guid man. Hey, is this my stop—?

On their return journey Royston saw her still walking, eyes down amongst her slithering feet, out towards Woodend. He leaned across the tram and banged on the glass to attract her.

Casey hit the red button twice, the tram whined and accelerated.

vanguard of an invisible convoy

On the 5th of January the school started back, the pavements ranged with depths of slush, gamboge with dogpish at lamppost and corner. The end of slides, the end of snowballs. Slush was horrible on your cuffs.

– Boots, said his mother.

– Obviously— said Peem.

– An dinna be sae cheeky.

He turned along Urquhart, sloshing along. The street door of the tenement next to Guffie's the Butcher opened just ahead. The bonnie big French wife was shooing the dark-haired loon out, the one who'd spat on his shoe.

– Va, go. A l'école, mon brave.

He tried to winkle past her in her big rose-covered wrapper.

– Merde. Jed, si tu plaît!

She cuffed at him as he ducked, then drew back quickly and slammed the door. Peem came slooshing along. Jed wheeled on him.

– Hey, radge-face—!

– Fit?

– Splash me once, an ye're fuckin for it.

Peem crossed the road to the bombed house. He wanted to shout *Have ye seen the bombed house?* But it was daft. How could you help seeing a bombed house, if you lived across from it.

A gutter each. They would walk on wellying, like four ships. Vanguard of an invisible convoy, they were minesweepers, sweeping the approaches. Your foot could be blown off, you'd be off school for ages.

– Mines! he shouted.

– Dinna spik shite— said his convoy partner.

the wee blue eyebath

Dinah flew out of her digs at the bottom of Crown Street in a tear. 7/6d a night she was paying, so she always made sure she gobbled the whole breakfast. Rice Krispies with sugar and poached egg like a jaundiced eye on soggy toast. The tea was hot so she fired in plenty milk which made it taste like nothing on earth. She didn't finish it. Then through the brash of slush up Crown Street, the Ferryhill tram had been cancelled, and she was due at Woolmanhill, a mile away, in ten minutes.

She saw a small queue on the canvas seats on both sides in the corridor: a collar-bone girl, a cut hand, a greenstick wrist, a man with a cotton moon to his eye. A change from the self-diagnosing drunks at Hogmanay, *I've splutten ma heid*, or kids with a teddy's eye in their ear after Christmas.

In her coat pocket was her third attempt at a letter to Billy's folks, out in Sydney. They hadn't found the body yet, it was nigh on a fortnight. She hadn't sealed it.

– Trainee Nurse Wylie, you are late again.

She went straight to the cloakroom, locked herself in a cubicle, read it and tore it up. *You'll have heard I was with Billy. He had given up his studies, I told him not to. We were planning a trial split, not for long—*

They couldn't afford to come back till there was a body, the police had told her. There was no phone for them in Australia. It took four flushes, she noted grimly, before it sank.

Then she went to help Cotton Moon man.

– Whit have ye done tae yersel?

– Nithin. A seagull shat in ma ee. It's nippin.

– Oo, it would be. I'll wash it oot wi borax crystals.

She fetched from the cabinet the wee blue eyebath, it looked like a plastic miner's hip-bath.

– Better—?

– Tons, fantastic. That's fit ye get for bein sae optimistic.

– Sorry—?

– For lookin up. I dinna suppose they pay ye muckle in here?

– It's the National Health, and I'm no a consultant.

– Well fanivver ye mairry an hae a hoose o your ain, I'll gie ye a wee tip.

– Whit's that then?

– Dae ye ken foo tae mak a Venetian blind?

– Aye, but I think ye're gonna tell me onywey. Is it—

– Poke ees een oot wi a sharp stick.

mum would hand-wring

– Mushy-slushy, your breeks are splushy!

– Shurrup ye!

– Mak me!

The dark-headed loon thrashed after Heidcase as far as the school railings, with Raymie, Tarry and Craigser splashing in tow. A car was drawing up the cul-de-sac. Isobel, Veronica converged. Bapface stood by the dyke watching them.

– Rare car that, said Raymie.

– Aye, ye dinna often see a sardine tin wi a wheelhoose, said Tarry.

Below them, Mannie Bain was squeezing out of a black Ford Popular. Briefcase handle clenched in left, and stick with rubber protector tucked under arm, he stooped and jiggled at the car-door with his key.

– Christ, fit's he got on his feet the day?

– Plastic pokes.

– Cellophane bags.

– Wife must be fed up cleanin his shoes—

– Hasna got a wife.

And up the half-cleared slushy steps he came, towards the plateau on which his fortress stood.

– Good morning, boys.

– Morning, sir.

Tarry's flathander, half-curtsey from Isobel, two splayed fingers to the temple from Casey.

– Find the janitor for me, hurry.

– Where, sir?

– Hurry—

Staff hung around in the wet stone corridor, stamping their feet without lifting them.

– I see Mr Martin has not graced us with his presence, said the headmaster. Taking advantage of a little ice with it, no doubt. Miss Florence, good to see you back now looking so well. How was Europe?

Then the pupils were summonsed to the big green door by the rude tongue of a handbell.

The lavvies had burst, the place was swimming.

– Now two things, said Mr Bain. First of all, we have a new boy today, Jed McClung, joining Primary 7. From the other side of the river, from Torry Primary. Put up your hand, boy, so we all can see you. Boy at the back beside Casey, put your hand up. Immediately! Secondly, some of you may have noticed that the school today is a little damp. I am therefore closing Nelson Street School for the remainder—

– Hooray!

– And therefore, I want you to get clear of the playground and straight home.

The boys at the back peeled off like fighters, chances of straight home – nil.

– THIRDLY—!

In school clothes, their only available, they would thrash and chase till dinner, some past gloaming. His Mum would hand-wring, and spread them to steam on the wire fender or, if full, over the skeletal wooden clothes-horse Dad had made.

Straight to jamas and into bed with a book. By morning your vest would be toast.

a halo of ice-blue horns

There was less trade at Casualty as the day wore on, now that the thaw was in. Dinah had a long interview with the sister. The sister was busy. Dinah would have to log each new case, each returning outpatient, at every chance, at every break, and what she did for them. Done for them, she mentally amended.

When she got to her digs to the bottom of Crown Street, there was a second letter from her folks in Fife sitting in the hall. They complained her notes had only been brief, apologies for missing Christmas, stuff about needing time.

She let herself into the one-rug room and plunked her wrap of chips on the french-polished table. It was stained anyway. She turned to the gas ring. Using a single Swan she created a halo of ice-blue horns.

After a cup of tea, Dinah reckoned her digs. It was a big slice out of her wages, 7/6 a night, and the place had a foosty smell, like the bottom of Crown Street had been rotting quietly behind its heavy hinges for centuries. Nondescript rug, an airless quilt, the only thing missing was the aspidistra. The broad cold window was jammed: unhoistable by its wee brass rings. She nearly heeled her hand through a pane, trying to dunt it up. That would have severed an artery or two.

But she'd been forced to pay a month in advance, she'd have to stick it a good while yet.

nibbling lucky tatties and composing dirges

That evening he was restless. He came back through in his jamas.

– Dad, can I hae a bigger bike?

His knees were about knocking his rotten teeth out on his first bike. But for his birthday last year he'd got that wooden garage instead, which he knew fine he was getting because brother Hughie and Dad had been out in the shed since whenever and hiding it under a sack.

Hughie had made a good job of painting it, except for the orange runs on the side-ramp, and a lemon puddle on the rooftop carpark. Peem had four cars now, four Dinkies, with eleven tyres between them, a problem of rationing, and he toyed to make things fit, trafficking on the front room carpet.

Or he parked them fast on the lemon roof, creasing the paint puddle, and had a solo game of paper and dice, Cricket or Destroyers.

– We're no made o money, ye ken.

– But Dad—

– Dinna deave!

Deaving was one of the things never to do, along with *being unreasonable, saft in the heid, scunner, minker, dwaumer, Greetin Teenie* or *tink*. There was small room left for manoeuvre.

– Dad though, can I—?

– We'll mak a plan.

Ach no, plans were terrible. Somebody aye had plans, plans to keep your bedroom tidy, plans on whose turn it was to dry the dishes, plans on whether to go to the plot twice or thrice a weekend, breached plans on scrubbing teeth, proposals to read a hundred books, keeping a record in a ruled feint notebook. Even plans imposed to write to aunties, be they in London, Bieldside or Belgrade, at the very least monthly to give them all your news.

What news was there, except he didn't have a bike to fit him.

– If ye raise half, we'll gie ye half for your birthday.

– But Dad, it's twelve pounds.

– Aye, six pounds fae you an six fae us, then. How much pocket money dae ye get?

– Sixpence—

– Well how many weeks is that, if ye dinna buy sweeties and aa that galshach?

Galshach was a Gaelic word, that was where all the Gaels lived now, *Am Galshach*, nibbling Lucky Tatties and composing dirges.

– Come on. How many sixpences in a pound?

– Twent— forty.

– How many sixpences in six pounds, then?

– Twa hunner an forty.

– Some race atween yir new bike an yir auld age pension, said Hughie.

– Shut up you, said Peem.

– That's it aa worked oot, then.

– But Dad, it's five years—

Less at the sugarless desert looming ahead than at the insouciance of planmakers, Peemie began to greet.

– Dinna bubble, Dad laughed, raking a ruffle in his son's hair. Here's ma hankie. Dry your snotters.

i shall write to your father

School did go back properly on the 9th, only Mannie Martin wasn't there, and they still got Inkster, she should have been retired before the Flood, a face cracked like a canyon and a brain to match. Harrumphing in her print sack, face and neck one net of wrinkles, fawning on her favourites and sucking Meggezones.

They got an intelligence test.

Stallion, bull, mare, cockerel. Circle the Odd One Out.

Odd One Out, there were aye different ways of looking at that. It wasn't bull anyway. Could be cockerel. Legs.

Then she went on to parallel lines.

– Parallel straight lines are straight lines such that they, no matter how far they are produced in either direction, will never meet. Define parallel lines, Tarr.

– Parallel lines are straight lines so that they, no matter how far they are produced in either direction, will never meet.

Bapface was sketching the loops of some intricate web on the back of her jotter.

– *Parallel straight lines. Such that—*

But hadn't got round to a spider.

– Parallel lines, Endrie?

As Peem stood, Iris glanced up at him from her pencilled web, pigtails aswing.

– Parallel straight lines are straight lines such that, no matter how far they are produced in either direction, they will never meet.

– Your second *they* should be first.

Eh—?

Miss Slessor came in for the last half-hour and planted herself down at the pianoforte she called it, diving into an introduction. They had to stand up from their desks to sing hymns, catching the lids by collective accident and clattering the seats back. After the free percussion, the introduction got reintroduced, and Miss Slessor nodded them in decisively.

All things bright and beautiful,

All creatures great and small,
All things wise and wonderful—
Tarry, with one twitch of his glasses, was a great modifier.
God made and rode *them all.*
Peem had to stifle. God in a white beard *riding*, eh!
Whatever *riding* was.

Slessor slanted her eyes at Jed, his dark hair up in a quiff now, probably listened to Radio Luxembourg.

– You, boy, name?

– McClung.

– McClung? McClung what—?

– McClung nithin, it's ma last name.

– McClung, Miss, you must say. I shall write to your father to teach you manners.

– Ye'll hae a hard job.

– Why, may I ask?

The class drew in its breath.

– Ma faither drooned a fortnicht ago.

– Oh, I see. How did he come to, ah – sorry – drown?

– Fisher.

– I didn't know we had fisherfolk. Fish, what did he fish for?

– Whales.

– How surprising. What kind?

– Ye dinna want tae ken.

– No, but it might be of some interest to the class.

– Micht be—

– So tell us, then.

– Sperm.

– Ooooh! the class breathed out. He said *sperm*.

– O, and by the way, Master McClung, what was that you sang a minute ago?

– Nithin—

– Nothing!

– Ah nivver sang nithin—

– I didn't sing anything—

– That's acause ye were bangin on yir piana.

The class laughed.

– Awa, Sperm. Tarry nudged with respect, on the way out.

– Hiya, Spermy!

The good girls hurried on past.

but the night life?

Royston and Cran were sitting in the bar of the Royal Hotel, just off Bridge Street.

– Short on travellers, post 1800.

– 1800?

– Hours.

– Well, the rush-hour's past.

– But the night life?

– Aberdeen? There's nae that muckle tae come oot for.

They dumped their papers in the room. Quick facewash, then troop downstairs. They always had one before the meal, taking turns to pay for it.

– Same?

– Aye.

– Same, barkeep.

They were the only ones in the dark-panelled bar, perched on stools. The barman footered around with a dented measure, spilling a couple or three drops each time he decanted into a thistle-graved glass.

– There ye are, sirs. Will that be everything?

It was whisky-and-soda for Cran, for Royston a Whisky Mac.

tell tale tit

The fire was red embers. Tammy had been on the breast for a good half-hour. He was fine pleased. Maybe she should be further on weaning him, but Tammy was for none of that. Baby Heinz tins of puréed carrots, beef boiled to extinction and general mush, he let that go by, or spat it out in long brown falls, down his feeding napkin. Plus screaming.

He aye kept sookin until he'd got the good of a breast. Then Mum put him on her shoulder, hard-patting his back, heading through to the front bedroom.

– C'mon, ma wee sookie.

– Dad, tell us aboot the War.

– There's nithin glorious aboot war, Peemie.

– Specially if ye werena fechtin, said Hughie.

– Aye very clever. We were aa fechtin one wey or anither, an it was gey horrible, I'll tell ye.

– Well tell— said Peem.

– Tell tale tit, your mother canna knit, said Annie.

– Well it was like this. Jump up on ma knee, Annie. Stop howkin your elbow intae ma neck, Peemie! Hughie, go an get us a fine gless o wattir.

Mum came back in, and looked at the fire. She went out again with the empty scuttle.

there ye go, eh?

– Aye. Didna used tae be nae hotel here, said the barman.

– Guess not, not if you go far enough back, said Royston.

– Used tae be the leatherworks. Tannery oot the back, an this was the actual leather works.

– Sae whit did ye used tae dae in the auld days? said Cran.

– Me, O fitba for Aiberdeen till five year syne.

– Football, did you say? said Royston.

– Aye, left wing.

– No short supply— said Royston.

– Aye, good supply. Pottie Donald that used tae work in the paint factory was left half, fit a tackles he put in. He just used tae blooter the ba up tae me, and the crowd would ging aff their heid.

– Are ye cried Wishart? said Cran.

– Aye, Freddy Wishart.

– Scored in the Cup Final?

– Aye, that's me. We still lost though. I got tooken aff at hauf-time. Groin strain. Leather ba, eh, fit a wecht, specially fan it wis weet! Took me aa ma time tae kick it, nivver mind cross it, Hampden Park is that flamin wide. I wis nivver the same again.

– I'm not untroubled with my groin myself, said Royston, as a matter of pure fact.

– Aye, sir, there ye go, eh? Heavy ba's— a bugger.

Royston gave him a look.

– Yir tea should be cooked noo, if ye want tae ging through, said the barman.

a scuttle of coal

– Richt, the three o ye, sit at peace.

– I am at peace, Daddy.

– Richt, ye see, far I got stationed, it was awa up in Greenland an it was blinkin cauld. Really, really cauld, and I was set tae guard this big aerodrome, see. An aa I had was a rifle, acause in these days it was the early days o the War and we didna hae that muckle o guns yet. Ae rifle per aerodrome, and just the ae bullet.

Well this nicht, fit a nicht it was, I was oot wi a thick coat on sentry duty, guardin the runway in case o spies. It was near on midnicht. Nigh on midnicht, an as quiet as onything. The searchlicht was muvin slow, an sometimes it caught ma breath driftin up. Syne at last midnight came. I was just aboot tae gang aff watch, fan— dae ye ken fit I heard?

– Nuh, tell us.

– Well comin fae the far end o the runway, I heard an affa snufflin. Near, an nearer, an mair near it got, O an affa snuffly, shuffly thing. Can ye guess?

– Foo big?

– Mebbe a—

– A dragon, said Annie.

– Na, never a dragon. A polar bear! Stracht for me, and fan it reared up tall—

– Were ye scared, Daddy?

– Scared? Nae time tae be scared. I squinted alang ma rifle, the beast just forty feet aff, gallumphin stracht for me, an pulled at the trigger. Oot came the speedy bullet an skiffed through its hair—

– Fur, said Hughie.

– And on it came!

– Did it get ye, Daddy?

– Wait now. The beast was thirty feet aff. I felt in ma pooch for some auld gunpowder an trickled that quick doon the spoot o ma rifle—

– Wow, said Peem.

– Twenty feet aff now, fan I pickit a white hailstane aff the runway an rammed that doon the barrel as well. O, the muckle beast was a ten feet aff, its paas raxed oot tae get me, an its jaas were opened wi—

– Stop it, Daddy!

– Wi bad breath, said Hughie.

– Wide. Sae for the very last time I pulled that same trigger—

– Nae much choice—

– BANG! The powder meltit the hailstane, the meltwattir jetted oot the barrel, froze in the Greenland air intae a great lang icy spear, and stuck the bear here, richt here on the broo. In that spear went! And doon, doon the polar bear crashed at ma feet.

– Aye, sure—

– Daddy, is it dead now?

– Wis it deid? said Peem.

– Deid, na. Just an attack o wattir on the brain—

Mum was coming back in, with a scuttle of coal.

– Noo scamper awa tae your beds!

– Ye shouldna hae deen that, said Dad.

february

wish young lady

Dinah was on her umpteenth round of the East End. She'd got the length of looking in a paper shop along King Street for the tenth time.

> *Pram for sale, will exchange – bike with steadiers.*

> *Battery radio, excellent. One careful owner, now deaf, £10 o.n.o.*

> *Flat for to share, one chambre. Wish young lady. Three pounds. In the Urquhart Parade.*

But it was a bit late to search it out and visit it that evening.

must be

February was a lean month. Miserable Inkster with her endless IQ tests, long division revision, her patent Odd One Out.

– Square, rectangle, triangle, quadrilateral. Which is the Odd One Out?

– Must be quadrilateral, Miss Inkster, said Veronica.

– Why, Veronica?

– I ken maist o the ither anes.

flat on a blood-stained tray

Dinah didn't hang about. She skimped her reports and finished prompt. Borrowed a bike from big Sheena, and wobbled off through Woolmanhill via Gallowgate, Causewayend, Nelson Street and King Street. She pedalled across the tramlines at a good angle, and caught the tang of the sea as she rattled down Urquhart Parade.

She laid her bike against Guffie's window. There was a hard plastic price-tag flat on a blood-stained tray. There had been an offer on mince. Pound of mince for 1/1d, a free mealie pudding thrown in.

The butcher smiled out, raised a stained hairy forearm at her, squeezing the crook of his elbow.

She wheeled her bike along to the granite wall.

She read the japanned plates screwed to both jambs and chose the first floor bell, above the name *Demaison*. Pulled on its futile knob, though the door lay already open. She passed a headscarved woman in the lobby, but when she climbed the stairs to the first floor flat, she couldn't get anyone in.

he, she or it

Next day it was onto parsing and general analysis. Parts of speech.

– *You* is the second person.

– Please, miss.

– Yes?

– Shouldn't it be *you are the second person*?

– Don't try to be clever, Robert Tarr. *You* is the second person. *He, she* or *it* is the third person.

– Miss.

– Yes, Endrie?

– All of them?

– Yes! *You* is the second person. *He, she* or *it* is the third person. *I* is the first person.

Well, you knew that.

So Stinkster marked them down like dopes in the parsing test, she said she couldn't read their writing, and immediately she reset the class, Peem down to 8th, Tarry away to 19th.

Iris had laid a freehand web on the back of her jotter, but still got to be top, Inkster always blind to a bright girl's failings.

en avance to pay, okay?

Spermy was out somewhere. Amande sat in the kitchen parlour, with her visitor.

– Perhaps you are not liking paper of the wall?

– No, the wallpaper's fine. A bit scuffed. It's just—

– Perhaps you are not liking the petit lit?

– It's lumpy, aye, but no, it's maybe—

– I still wait the insurance, you know.

– What for? The wallpaper?

– No, for my husband, who drowns.

Dinah looked at her. Went pale.

Offered to stay.

Amande nodded.

– En avance to pay, okay?

naois like worms comming to get you fart

Mannie Martin, at last, put in an appearance. Shambling into the classroom with his pockmarked smile. Brown prickly jacket, oxford brogues with the broken laces. But not today. Long laces – things were looking up.

No hymns or hellos, he wanted them to get their jotters opened fresh, and a pencil. Pencils were more for earwax, geeing up tortoises.

– Let's get you off your t-t-t-treadmill, he said. That was what did for him, Oscar Wilde.

– Ask a while, sir?

– Oscar Wilde. His t-t-t-treadmill. Seize the day!

– It's the thirteenth.

– Sir, please, sir—

– Yes, Casey?

– Ma pencil's broke.

For some reason Mannie kept a stock of stubs in his jacket pocket.

– Catch!

He asked them to rest – at ten past nine. Foreheads on arms.

– And shut all your eyes.

– Only got the twa, said Spermy.

Came a dunt, a couple of dunts, a scuffling.

– And k-k-keep them shut! he breathed, from somewhere high above them.

Then THUMP, the floorboards trembling.

– Open them.

– Already open, said Spermy.

The rumour-mill.

– Used the chair tae climb on ees desk.

– Used the milk crate tae climb ees big cupboard.

– Took a flyin jump, onywey, said Tarry.

– Aye, wish he would—

– Right, da-date in the margin, *13th Feb-Febuary, 1956*. Heading, *The Noise*. He blocked the title on the board. Now. In se-se-sentences.

– Does it have tae be in se-se-sentences?

Casey, a would-be conductor like his Dad.

– Get on!

– Awa an toss, I'm nae writin sentences.

That voice? McClung? The one they'd told him to ignore, the son of the fisherman.

A sucking of pencil-leads to make them blacker, then they set off across the page. Raymond Dargo's snapped immediately. Pressing too hard. The makings of a reporter.

– Dae it in ink, sir, can I?

– Of course.

– How can I, ma inkwell's empty?

– Sh-sh-sharpen your pencil, then, we haven't got time.

The ink was kept in giant carboys, like chemists' supplies.

– That's me— said the voice. McClung.

– Surely you could try a bit more?

– Foo can I, I'm finished.

– How many sentences?

– One.

– One?

– Plenty.

– Joyce, yes, very Joyce.

– Hey mister, fa ye caain JOYCE?

– I mean ve-very Ulysses.

– Hmm, bluidy well think so.

– There's no need to—

– Please, sir, sir, can I leave the room?

Isobel Harley, a housewife shortly.

– Yes, and the continent.

– Eh? He's screwy, she said to her pal.

– Worse than that, said Veronica. He's aff ees heid.

The massed scribes sighed, collapsed, hoofed and rattled at the desk in front. He could read some out, suggest a comment, organise a vote.

He chose Veronica's first.

– Now she might need some help with her punc-punc-, with her punctuation.

– Dinna worry, sir, we'll soon help her.

– Wi her *punc-punc*, said Casey.

– Peem, you do the honours. St-stand up. Here, you read it out.

– Else we'll be here aa day, said Casey.

Peem hinged his seat back and stood up in the carved desk he shared with Iris at the top of the class. Change of teacher: change of ordering. Tarry was one away in third, Spermy trolling around at the bottom, down at the front.

Peem received the blue-backed item from Mr Martin and cleared his throat, twice, keeping the jotter up really close, so none of the twenty six could put him off with a gargoyle face. It wasn't easy, reading out loud, half of them staring and hissing *Swot*.

The naoise

Theres is no such thing as silenc, spesialy in are class even in the grave you would here naois like worms comming to get you fart *and poeple walking on your head with flouwers* faaart *that is why it is good writing about naois it shows you what it is like and you get a bit of piece without* failed fart *the tyeacher shouting and climing frunitur like a loonie that is all about naois.*

Fa-art, phaaaart, *fart-fart,* a freemasonry of farting.

Mannie Martin flung a red stick of chalk to rattle Casey's cage.

Not that it was only him.

– Bring it out, Casey. Go-go-good, Peem. Good, Veronica. I quite liked that. It takes off.

– Lets off you mean, sir.

He took a risk and turned his back on them. Patched elbow cocked, he scratted on the board.

Metamorphosis—

A fart for that.

– Re-re-read it oot, Mister Ma-Ma-Martin!

He kept on writing.

Metamorphosis, he wrote, *is a magical change of shape, for creatures, objects, or ideas.*

– Now Peem, I have a note here. Could you take it along to Room 1, please? There might be an an-answer—

Room 1 was – Miss Florence. He walked along the planked upper floor of the school and down the stone steps till he reached the Infants Department. He used his middle knuckle to tap three times on the bottom glass pane, which moved. Somebody was doing a story for them inside, and that somebody was – Miss Florence.

Leaning on him, her breast—

He knuckled three times, the pane tinkled. Perhaps she wouldn't even remember. The bottom panes patterned with a spray of ferns. Perhaps she'd be angry, having to stop her story. The top panes were clear and you could easily watch her – if you were taller.

Then he found he'd crushed Mannie Martin's note. As he uncrushed it, he saw a tail of words appear, so he opened it further. Then he ironed it against the wall, and refolded it.

He made the glass rattle. God, she'd stopped reading. Footsteps came and the door-handle moved.

– Why, Peem! It's so nice to see you.

Nice.

– Is there a problem?

– I think your door, the window's coming loose.

– Yes.

– Putty—

– Putty? Is that why you've come? You're concerned about my window?

– A note from Mr Martin.

– O.

– Think he said I should wait.

– Better come in, then.

She turned to check none of the infants was taking advantage, and tossed a blonde bolus of hair back on her shoulder.

– Use your plasticine.

Lacking ideals, they palmed it in oblongs.

She uncrumpled the note to decipher.

– Do you know what it says?

He coloured up.

– No, Miss.

– But you don't know what it means?

– No, Miss.

The stuff was wild.

BE BEATRICE

My Seven Circles of Heaven

Meet me Ponte Unione

7pm

DANTE

She bit at the edge of her right fore-nail.

– I should never—

Peem shifted his weight.

– Tell him there's no answer.

dirt or noise, tak yir pick

Big brother Hughie bumped it under the sideboard to make the glasses rattle. He roared it round the kitchen. Peem and Annie leapt up on the chill rexine chairs. Easy chairs. He zoom-zoomed at them.

– Bite yir taes!

The square-head second-hand Hoover was a Mekon from Dan Dare.

Peem glanced at his Mum's back. She wasn't even saying anything.

Bowed over the tatties in the sink, she pressed a hand to her belly and halted. Too many eyes, poisonous green bits.

– Waaaa—

– Hughie, that flamin Hoover!

– It's dirt or noise, tak yir pick.

– Fit's wrang, Mum? said Peem.

– O, nithin, nithin at aa. I get these grimmers noo an again.

– Will I get Tammy?

– Aye, lift him a minutie, I'll feed'm later.

It was good the Hoover, though. Dad called it *J. Edgar* when jokey.

more ^ machinery we need humanity

Saturday evening they all went out to the Party social, quite an excitement, held in a bareish hall in Lemon Street. First, after the fraternal greetings, was a Charlie Chaplin. The Party secretary had ordered *Limelight*, but landed up with a half-dozen reels of *The Great Dictator*, a bit disjointed, there were supposed to be twelve.

They sometimes argued in the house if Chaplin was a proper communist, or how Anti-American.

– He can be a bit winsome, said Dad.

– There's worse crimes, said his mother.

– A bit daft, a bit downtrodden.

– Clowns are meant tae be daft, said his mother. Nae like some folk.

– I see your point, I think— said Uncle Hugh.

Not only did *The Great Dictator* come in bits, there was a poor connection in the Party speaker. One minute Chaplin was a persecuted Jewish barber, next he was Adenoid Hynkel, who waltzed with an inflated globe and wept when it burst. Dad laughed at that bit, and Peem looked across at him, but Mum just shook her head.

Suddenly the barber was mistaken for Hynkel, for they both

had a toothbrush moustache. So the barber got to make big talk, at a mass rally. Peem was taken with the barber's speech, such as survived the crackles.

We want to live by each other's happiness, not by their misery ^
more ^ *machinery we need humanity* ^

The reproduction was terrible.

^ *more than cleverness, we need kindness and gen* ^
^ *the good earth is rich* ^
^ *dictators die, and the power they took from the people will* ^

Then a huge blurred chunk, before the finale.

Look up, Hannah! The soul of man has been given wings and at last he is beginning to fly.

Lines came slanting down the picture as the credits rolled.

– In Commie films why is it always drizzle? said Hughie.

After solid applause, there was tea out of a kettle, plus rectangular boiled ham sandwiches. Triangles were bourgeois.

Then the Chairman, Theo, Dad said he was a sculptor, announced that the second film, which had come up from London HQ, *Post-War Reconstruction in Russia*, with an introduction by the late Comrade Stalin, was fairly damaged about the sprockets, and couldn't be shown. There was a small *Oh—!* but otherwise a pretty disciplined response.

– So, said Theo with the pointy beard, the next song will be a dance.

Uncle Hugh got his squeezebox out and gave them *Linten Adie* to get a chorus going, some lad with a fiddle up and gave them a reel, *The De'il Amang The Tailors*, Theo and his wife Marcie danced it two-handed, and soon Dad was pushing at Peem.

– Go on.

– Stand up, ye must. Sing now.

Gonna lay down my shield and sword, no, sword and shield
Down near a riverside— no, Dad!

– Tak a gweed breath an start again.

Gonna lay down ma sword and shield,
Down by the riverside,
Down by the riverside,
Down by the riverside—

The only one he dare glance at was Uncle Hugh, who regarded him with hope.

Gonna lay down ma sword and shield,
Down by the riverside—
Ain't gonna study war no more.

But then they all joined in with the chorus on the last line and he was able to sit down with a great flush, glad that Stalin had damaged his film.

Maybe there were sixty folk in the bareish hall, enough for the raffle to come out in profit. His mother had never joined the Party but she still took along a half-pound of fudge. Dad slipped in a large piece of silver, half-a-crown. She looked at him.

– Haud on a minute, can ye? he said. The Party Executive's haein a pow-wow.

– Fit aboot? said his mother.

– Fitewashin.

– Whitewashin?

Walking home with the pram and everybody, brother Hughie about twenty yards ahead, Peemie asked for chips.

– That was great, there, his father said.

– Well he's nae wantin horrible greasy chips on top o sandwiches.

His mother was an expert on what he was wanting.

– He can hae a suppie milk when he gets in.

He was definitely the third person.

It was really dark in the places where the gas-lamps were out. They came round the corner of Rosin and bumped into Spermy.

– Hey, hiya— said Peem.

– Hay's for horses, div ye nae ken?

– How is he? These days? said his Mum, when they were past.

– O, fine.

– Puir loon, she said. An as for his mother—

She looked at his Dad.

Dad gave no signs of having been looked at.

There was about a thimbleful and warm.

Dad went out to the shed with the torch because there was no moon. Peem heard him come back an hour later. Mum gave him an awful row.

sir, dae ye luve miss florence?

Fresh milk came jingling along Urquhart at some ungodly hour.

Then it turned up your smooth tarred street.

– Woe, Peeteeer, woe—!

The schoolbooks printed *Whoa!* very posh. Daft way to speak to a horse.

The Clydesdale halted outside his window, whuffing steam in the February air, and stamped a feathery hoof.

– Woe, Peeteeer!

Peem wasn't sure he knew the milkman's name, they sort of assimilated him to his horse. *Here's Peeteeer comin.*

Nostrils flared, he hitched on the canvas bran-bag, and whomping in went the great white muzzle.

But at school you got condescended to. Third-pint bottles. Wedged cardboard lids, cloyed on the underside with cream.

Iris got to give out the bottles just before break, because she was first finished. Goody-Goody Bapface. Raymie Dargo went up and down the rows like a millionaire, shaking a box blazoned *500 Straws*. They started on a nod from Casey and raced to the bottom, the boys, like a fleet of dredgers, until all their straws sucked flat.

– That's nae fair, sir. McClung took twa straws.

– And—?

– Can I tak twa next day?

Outside, as you played chasies, it slopped up in your guts like a sea swilling along breakwaters.

Today Mannie Martin was on Geography. Apparently Scotland was moving and used to be buried under a deep ice-cap. O not in the Ice Ages, that was only like yesterday.

– No, it wasna, sir, yesterday was bonny. Ma Ma got aa her washin oot.

– But 600 million years ago when Scotland was dow-dow-down in the Antarctic.

– Please sir, how do you ken? Were you there?

– Less cheek, Casey.

– Sir, how big is a million?

– Very big, Veronica.

– How big is 600 million then?

– As big as you could imagine.

– Sir, dae ye luve Miss Florence—?

– We-we're not discussing that just now, Isobel.

– She's too young for ye.

– That's nae true though, is it, aboot the Antarctic? said Raymie.

– True as I'm standing here, and Scotland's still moving, we could soon be up in the Arctic if we're not careful.

– Are Arctic Wafers cheaper in the Arctic?

Scotland was doing all this work, darting about the globe. So no surprise that out to the Plot it must be, the whole tribe of them, willing or unwilling, and plenty to do with the autumn digging abandoned for wet weather.

They cycled out on Saturday, out the road to Cults, past set-back bungalow and walled mansion, Mannofield cricket ground, the Waterworks, turn down and over the humpback brig, down the avenue gaunt with beech and empty of chestnuts, and finally in by the gate.

There must have been scores of them, rectangular plots, pieced together in their various stages of cultivation, harvest, fallowness and neglect. The one next to theirs had been neglected for three seasons, a criminal waste.

– There's some new kinda bloke at it, Dad.

– Aye, well he's some job aheid o him. Awa up to the sheds an get our tools, Hughie.

Dad hung his anorak on one of the stout poles that anchored the wire that supported the raspberry canes.

– Aye, aye, chiel, fit like—? he shouted across.

The man came out from behind a screen of weeds and string and poles and tall brown grasses.

– O, it's yersel, Ludwig. Didna realise ye were eftir a plot. Fit a sotter! What an absolute mess, eh?

– Hello, Andy. No, it's good makings for me. I want my plot since post the war.

– Well, ye've your wark cut oot there, Ludwig. Are ye needin a haun? I've gotten an auld scythe up in the shed.

– A hand, no. A scythe, yes, very good.

– Peem, run up an tell that brither o yours tae pit the scythe aboard the barra as well. An the schairpenin stane.

– Aye well. Better get doon till it, Ludwig. Think there's a schouerie o rain on its wey.

– Big schouerie—

– Fan the grass gets weet, watch an nae let the scythe skiff roon an cut ye.

– Dinna nein worry, Andy. I be very doubly careful.

aiberdeen's trams should be reid

Royston and Cran spent the weekend in their hotel room typing their first report. The ten thousand pieces of data. Analysis. Recommendations.

They went down for a dram on the Saturday night.

– Trams, eh? said the barman. Fit are they like?

– Well, there's nithin too duff wi the drivers, or hauf-hung-tae wi the rollin stock, said Cran. Maist o it—

Royston looked at him.

– Translate.

– Dinna like them colours, though, said the barman. Green-an-fite, minds me too much on Celtic. Aiberdeen's trams should be reid.

poke at dee, pox by don

They went down again at Sunday lunch for a pick-me-up. There was someone on a stool in the corner.

– Foo's your trams farin noo? said the barman.

– Not good, said Royston. There are throughput issues, passenger flow, income optimisation.

– Aye, that's trams for ye.

– The standing passenger permit situation, it slows embark-ation. It conduces to customer panic when disembarking. It hinders fare-evasion intercept. An estimate eight per cent revenue drain, per uncollected fares.

The man in the corner looked across and smiled.

– Eight per cent? said the barman. That's fit we would jist caa *spillage*—

– And then there are three variants of tram: pre-war, post-war and open-top unconvertible. A one-design template would rationalise on spares.

– Nae mair bastardisation, said Cran.

– Ye mean fire the auld trams oot? said the barman.

– Sure thing, said Royston.

– Fit a waste, said the barman. Wouldn't ye say, Harry? C'm here a mintie, Harry. This is Harry, he's a lecturer at the University. Ern Royston an Jock Cran – Harry Bowyer.

– What is it you lecture on, Harry? said Royston.

– V.D., said Harry.

– Pardon me?

– Pox, said Cran. Venereal disease tae you.

– Are your lectures, em, popular?

– Ye get the odd one or two.

– Is the pox big in Aberdeen?

– I would say. There's a particularly virulent strain o gonorrhoea going the rounds.

– The rounds?

– Aye. Condoms are no proof against it, this strain could penetrate a Wellington boot.

– Crivvens— said Cran.

– And the time between exposure and symptom onset is very short, even within the timespan of a No 1 tram journey. Poke at Dee, pox by Don. Or vice versa, of course. Use that as a footnote in your report?

– So far as I am advised, Taylor Universal has no brief to study the efficiency of the oldest profession.

– O, pros are not the problem, in the main. It's the enthusiastic amateur that spreads the word.

– Mind you, said the barman, tae be fair – that is an affa lang run, the No 1. Must be nigh on five mile, it's Aiberdeen's airtery.

– Or something— said Royston.

march

bend at the knee

Being early March, harvest wasn't in that muckle swing. Dad got Peemie picking *hungry-gap*, curly kale. It grew in tough frilled bunches, like hussars' plumes.

– Fa was that mannie again ye were spikkin tae last time, Dad?

– Ludwig. He works doon in the baggin plant.

– Whatten plant is he baggin, Daddy?

– O, Annie, ye're aye the one for the questions, aren't ye? Just the usual. Aa the stuffie tae mak the fairmer's neeps an oats an tatties grow fine and big, ye ken.

– Whatten stuffie?

– Superphosphate, high nitrogen, the stuff we mak at the works.

– An sulphuric acid— said Peem.

– Ah, well, sulphuric acid's just part o the process, we dinna sell it.

– Why? Does it burn ye?

– Aye, if ever ye see a man wi broon holes in his overalls, dae ye ken fit that is?

– Moths, Daddy.

– Aye, big sulphuric moths. Come on noo, the pair o ye, back tae wark, we canna stand here gassin aa day. Brusselers, fa's pickin the Brusselers?

– But why is he German? asked Peem.

– I canna answer for the mannie's origins. He's an auld POW, that's aa I ken. Ditched his Heinkel close tae the beach, and bade on eftir the War. Come on.

Brusselers were like emerald pagodas. One puff of wind – Pisas. The top sprouts were like marbles, the lowest blowsy and done. Peem helped with a few, then Annie insisted to pluck the rest on her own: Megan to hold the bag.

Hughie was pinging stones at hopping robins. He wouldn't fiddle-faddle with vegetables, Hughie.

Dad passed him the steel spade, the Neverbend.

– Noo this is earth an muck, nae a flaff o snaa.

– So?

– So it's heavy, isn't it? Dinna ging bendin your back.

– I'm nae bendin ma back.

– Tak a haud.

– Ah've got a haud—

– A proper haud!

Peem, behind dry raspberry canes, hugged at himself.

– Bend at the knee, an let the tool dae the wark.

aberdeen trams optimisation report

They went along to the Council Offices at 10 am on Monday morning, with their *Trams Optimisation Report*.

But the Lord Provost didn't like it, he told them straight. And strode out of the meeting, only his belly preceding him, into his official Daimler, with the fluted silver radiator and the golden Bon Accord flag.

They had to redraft it.

puffs of pale haar

When the weather improved and the various snows and slushes had disappeared along gutters and down branders, and as soon as the air swung in from the south-east and warmed up a fraction, then you got fog or haar.

Dinah could seer it swirl along the road from her first floor window. She put her head out. When she was little, her folks used to take her on holiday, every second year – they saved up his miner's wage – to the West Highlands. It was usually the dipping season, when the sheep got dosed against maggot and tick. Now the tenements in Urquhart Parade looked like a long curved fank, enclosing the flocks and puffs of pale haar moving up from the sea.

There must be mild air somewhere, stirring. Amande was still in bed, she'd been down the stairs till late the previous night, whereas Dinah was tired from Casualty and went to bed early. Often they'd go for days and barely meet.

blueprint

Royston and Cran set off from the Palace Hotel through the shrouded streets. Royston had in his briefcase the report for Lord Provost Rust.

Blueprint for the Sixties – Municipal Tramways & Busways Options Report. If that passed muster, they'd have a couple of days off.

– Soon be launching the next crusade.

– No afore time. Political interference gets on ma tits.

– Back to simplicity, a private outfit.

– Namely?

– Scottish Fertile. A sub-division of IPI.

– Aye, if ye canna mak dough sellin powdered shite tae fairmers, what can ye dae? Ye ken how hungert they are.

– Hungert?

– Greedy.

– Who, Imperial Phosphate?

– Them an aa—

– I repeat, Mr Cran, capitalism is not the same as greed.

– Different as twa sides o a dirty dollar.

- That pays your hire.
- An your fat salary.

all no more than a set of stuff

Through the dense grey haar in his bone-buttoned shirt Peem walked to school. The world came to him strange and fragmented, a gaping door, a cracked rone, half a tenement steepling over him, bartizan of a dubious castle.

He passed: the big grey gable where they flung spongeball in the carless street.

He passed: the sweets outlet, where Wifie Ploomie sold Sherbet Dabs.

He passed: Crabbe the Bookmaker, Buster Crabbe.

He turned right at the grocerish junction with its three corner shops. The first thighdeep in hessian sacks of half-washed veg. The second vending rolls, baps, Titbits, Woodbine in fives.

The one on this side had a good-going Club, a Clubbie. Its propped chalkboard announced *Only 299 Savings Days till Christmas*.

Folk are easy gulled had said his Dad.

But his Mum had come back *So?*

So they shouldna be.

Aye but we are.

It was that tone of his mother's she used more and more.

He passed Guffie's the Butcher, and under that gas lamp, where last year a motorbike loon impaled himself high on the cross-bar. He glanced off an emerging lorry and flew through the air, it was Tarry that saw it. Blood filled and then cascaded – out of the top of his boot. He pushed himself off, he disimpaled. Then slumped against the post to die, pressing in his puddens as they spilled.

His mother still wanted to run a petition, round the doors if she could find a minute. They absolutely must have a *Halt* sign. *Halt At Major Road Ahead*. The trouble was, neither was majorer, both seemed eachy-peach. The Parade busy but cobbled, the Road quiet yet wide. Drivers would half-brake, then barge across, and largely get off with it.

– Mair need o a *Halt* than a revolution, his Mum had said.

– We canna waste time on petty reformism.

– Ye waste plenty time in that shed, if that's far ye go.

No answer.

He passed the bare roofless shell of a bombed tenement, battened downstairs with corrugates of iron. Three pale ring-doves, in a high blackened alcove, taking their chancie to nest away.

Rooketty-doo. Rooketty-doo.

They'd come colonising from India, Theo the Sculptor said. He called them *collared doves*.

Everyone else called them *doos*.

Rooketty-doo. Rooketty-doo.

Glimpsed through the haar, it was all no more than a set of stuff. Like Cousin Airchie's boxed clockwork trainset, that you toyed with for a while, then put back carefully. Like the repeat menu every week you had to make disappear from your plate, else you got no pudding, which semolina times you didn't want anyway.

So he strolled along his usual road, Urquhart Parade, it was called, after Sir Thomas Urquhart, Mannie Martin said. Urquhart translated a man called Rabelais into Scottishy English. Doubled his length, Mannie said, and died laughing. He'd promised to read some today.

Mannie fetched a book from his coat pocket.

– Of course Rabelais was French, said Mannie Martin.

Of course.

– Spermy's mither, she's French, said Veronica.

– A French hure— said Casey.

– Better nor your fuckin mither, ony day, said Spermy.

Mannie ignored them.

– Aye she fucks better, said Casey. That's fit aabody says.

– Rabelais! shouted Mannie.

– Fancy givin her one? whispered Tarry.

Peem looked at him.

– Rabelais! Now, take this down. Heading, top line: Dictation. D-I-C-T-A-T-I-O-N.

– *The Great Dictator*, whispered Peem.

Tarry looked at him.

– Date March 18th.

– It's the 19th, sir.

– Okay, it's the 19th, the 29th, the 99th, what can it possibly matter. Seize the day, if you've the slightest of sense. Seize the day!

The hair was starting to fly.

– Sub-heading: Sir T-T-Thomas Urquhart. U-R-Q-U-H-A-R-T.

Spermy refused.

– Nuh, I'm nae writin that. I have tae bide wi aa these shiters in Urquharter, that's bad enough. I dinna hae to write aboot them an aa.

Mannie Martin plucked the volume up in his hand and let it fall open easily.

– *I have comma said Ga-ga-Gargantua comma by a long and curious experience—*

– That's nae you started, is it? said Casey.

– *I have comma said Gargantua comma by a long and curious experience comma found out a means comma to wipe my bum—*

– Sir, that book's disgustin, said Isobel.

– *to wipe my bum—*

– I'm nae writin that doon, said Veronica.

– *to wipe my bum, the most lordly, the most excellent, and the most convenient that ever was seen full stop.*

– Is a full stop the same as a dot? said Tarry.

– Bigger, said Peem.

– Carry on, boys. *Once I did wipe me with a gentlewoman's velvet mask comma and found it to be good semi-colon for the softness of the silk was very vo-vo-voluptuous to my fundament full stop.*

– Slow doon! said Casey.

– *Then I wiped my tail in the sheet comma, in the coverlet comma in the curtains comma with a cushion comma with arras hangings—*

– Come again? said Tarry.

– *with arras hangings comma with a green carpet comma, with a table cloth—*

– I'm goin hame tae tell ma mither when I get hame, said Isobel. That's nae wey tae treat a tablecloth.

– Just filth, said Veronica.

– *with a napkin comma with a handkerchief comma with a combing cloth semi-colon in all which I found more pleasure than do mangy dogs when you give them a rub full stop.*

– That's me needin a new jotter, said Casey.

– Sorry, there are no new jotters. You'll just have to write on your sleeve. No. Just put your implements down, all of you, and listen. For Urquhart cannot wait for us; Urquhart, as always, sails on.

– *Afterwards, I wiped my tail with a hen, a cock, with a pullet, with a calf's skin, with a hare, with a pigeon, with a cormorant, with an attorney's bag—*

– We're gaain tae complain tae the headmaster, said Isobel and

Veronica, standing up in their double-desk. You said *cock*.

– Sit down on your sweet backsides, said Mannie Martin. *But to conclude, I say and maintain, that of all torcheculs, arsewisps, bumfodders, tail napkins, bung-hole cleansers, and wipe breeches, there is none comparable to the neck of a goose, that is well downed—*

– Please, said Iris.

– *if you hold her neck betwixt your legs full stop.*

– Please, Mr Martin, said Iris, who had been holding a hand up for quite a while. I don't know why you're reading this. We're too young.

– I don't know either, Iris. I'll stop now. Will you remember it?

– Yes.

– Then that's why I must have read it. And so you can smile, next time you see a goose.

– Puir goose. How would you like it, Mr Martin? said Veronica.

– Not a great deal, I imagine. Now I want you to ch-check your spelling before you hand in your dictation.

– How can we? said Isobel.

– Aye, good question. How—? said Veronica.

– Peem, your spelling's usually good. Pass your jotter to the girls there. And could you also take this note down for me. It's for one of the teachers.

– Ju— ju— just say, you don't mind waiting for a reply, please.

He didn't crumple it this time. But opened it in his sweaty palm and read it, sure enough.

BEATRICE BELLISSIMA

Spring Approaches

Ponte Unione

8pm

DANTE

He knocked.

– O. Better come in.

She wasn't in the mood.

The infants were rolling their plasticine into thin-fat-thin snakes, snakes like they'd gobbled pigs. Or infants.

Miss Florence with finger and thumb put a long lock of her blonde hair back over her shoulder.

She slid the letter into a drawer.

– Mr Martin said I could wait.

A slight shake, and the lock of her hair swung forward again.

Peem stopped on his way back up to his classroom and looked out of the top landing window. The haar was lifting. He didn't want to see Mannie Martin's face get worse, it was already red and blotchy.

She put it in the drawer.

She was in the middle of plasticine.

Over the school's back wall, the sycamore were swaying, poking the air with their hard sticky buds.

– Miss Florence said she'd reply later.

– O.

– Please can I have three sheets of paper? Sir?

– What?

– Please, sir. Paper?

– Paper's nearly finished.

– Two'll be fine, she said. My Mum, she's doing a petition.

april

rinso, oxydol or surf, usually persil

– Spring, eh, I'll gie ye spring!

Every spring, Peem's Mum started on about washing machines, and this spring was no exception. Well it was right enough, it was ridiculous the whole washday rigmarole, like out of the Middle Ages. You were allocated a day of the washhouse and the green, let's say Endries get Monday, Morrisons claim Tuesday, Paterson Wednesday, Hirds grab Thursday, McMorencys free run of Friday, and whatevertheirnames, black bun wallahs, Crichtons, on Saturday, Sunday a day of rest.

Woe betide, Peem kent fine, anybody who arrogated to themselves boiler, mangle, wash-rope or green when it wasn't their day.

Later he came to think that *Seize the day!* must have its origins in back green rights, because there would be girning aplenty if you pegged so much as an orphan sock outwith its occasion. With some kinds of folk, there seemed to be certain irreducible aspects. If that was human nature for you, communists maybe were wasting their time?

The boiler. Sconced in the far corner of the lean-to wash house, it was grey, a broken flakey plastery gray, like a burial mound seen through fog. Its grate was accessed by a cast iron door, and fire was fed to it at six in the morning: an *Evening Express*, split sticks, broken skirting, foosty doormats, fatty dripping. By their joint effect the boiler proper, slowly filled by a rubber hose, was brought just off the boil.

Clothes of an innumerable monotony, and of an equality of filth, ordure, barkitness, griminess, grubbiness and soil, were then set to seethe in rapidly murkied water, in which flakes of patent Lux, Daz, Persil, Rinso, Oxydol or Surf, usually Persil, perished in passes of bubbles.

From time to time it was prudent for the celebrant to fish with wooden tongs for a pair of what classically came up as long bloomers, formerly salmon, their gussets sodden, elastic lost, breaking the surface like rorquals and issuing with water down both legs. This, coupled with a half-hearted stir at the other denizens, was very much part of the monitoring programme.

Soon, or by the back of ten, a full-scale transfer of scalding fluidised linens could be attempted, using the tongs and an enamel basin, until cavernous porcelain sink No 1 had been part-filled. Then proceeded many splashy rinsings, as between cavernous sinks 1 and 2, while the spectrum of *affablack, stillaffablack, naeasblackasitwis*, and *stillnithinlikeclean* was steadily traversed.

Peem knew little was ever said during all this time, for it made Oscar Wilde's treadmill seem like a day at the swings.

Then there was the mangle. With that ancient inexorable iron mangle it was possible to throttle double blankets, moor tankers, and flense small whales, whereas the contemporary wringer, a white rubber-coated Acme, with adjustable gapping and demountable handle, shuddered at the touch of a lady's hankie.

Moving out to the green, this was a square of exemplarily shorn grass, cropped by a rota of conscriptee tenants or their proxies. Between the long winters, sheets could be bleached on it, in the baking sun. But for the quotidian washing, all that was required was to string a rope from the hollow pole to the Anderson raid-shelter, hang out your laundry with tinker-sourced pegs, prop to the winds with a V-notched stick, then dash out per half-hour pronto against squalls, eventually humphing a dripping basket upstairs to the *communal*, the word was too strong, loft.

Thus, above a farrago of retired crockery and hickory niblicks, a vermicelli of mouse-droppings, airless, eclipsed and dank, every last sheet might droop in the loft to a staleness.

Fancy wanting a washing machine!

foo's yir doos? aye peckin?

Mannie had looked pretty disappointed. They hadn't done anything good that afternoon, just nouns and adjectives. Spermy went out to the toilet three times, that was pushing it.

– Have ye got the skitters? Peem asked him after school.

– Skitters? Na.

They walked back together, kicking a stone for company, if a stone happened on their path, and then another.

Back along nondescript Nelson and out across non-thronged King Street. There was a soot-blackened kirk at the junction with Urquhart Parade. The stained glass windows were abstract and dusty, hampering light with wire-mesh stoneguards.

You remembered how dull it was when you went to Sunday School.

Twice. Really dull.

You wouldn't tell Spermy you'd been.

Opposite the Presby kirk was the barber, Toddy Naylor, who, over the last five years of sixpenny servitude, had forced a *shed*, a parting, into your hair. Who wanted a shed in their hair, it was daft.

– Dae ye go tae Toddy's?

– Grease does me—

Spermy's hair was darker and stickier these last few weeks. He quiffed it up with a plastic comb.

– Are ye a Teddy Boy? asked Peem.

– Better nor a Toddy boy.

– Right.

He was pretty gruff, auld Toddy, and used to greener – *gads!* – into a paper towel, crumple and bin it. He buzzed your neck with ill-set clippers that tweezed and plucked more than cut, and gave you boils oftenish, because of the general dirt. He kept a quarter of whisky, behind the taller lotions.

Every time you went forward to take your place in the chair he'd say exactly the same. *Foo's yir doos?*

He never made great long speeches, not like Chaplin's barber. *Foo's yir doos? Aye peckin—?*

the hale game for nithin

It was Saturday and he went round for Tarry.

– Fit's wrang wi Spermy the day? said Tarry.

– Nithin, why?

– Ye're aye hingin aroon wi him nowadays.

– No I'm nae. Well, you aye hing roon wi Raymie.

– He's awa wi his father's van.

– Far they playin?

– I dinna ken. Buckie or somewey—

– That's a big empty shell.

– Naw, a toon as well.

By this time they were up at the top of Rosin. There were a few extra cars parked.

– Fa's playin? A Glesga team?

– Hearts. Edinburgh.

– Are they good?

– Tap o the league.

They turned left then right past the cemetery, and got onto a wild-daffodiled path that went up a tiny hill.

– See, ye can see the hale game for nithin.

Peem looked right and saw the sea of gravestones and shrouded urns on the rolling cemetery. He was told to pay attention.

There was a huge roar. Some figures in red ran out.

– Is that the Dons?

– Naturally.

They could see a microquadrilateral of pitch, no goals, only the distant corner flag and the players' tunnel.

– Good, eh?

There was a smaller roar as figures in maroon ran out.

– Is that Hearts?

Then three figures in black walked out. Then the figures in maroon ran back in. Peem stamped his feet. After five minutes they were replaced by figures in white.

– Foo much langer is the game to go?

– It's nae started yet—

– Cos I've a book tae put back tae the Mobile Library.

– Wait, there'll be a goal in a minute.

the misers' billy

For the third time, he peeked at the assignation in Mannie's note, then stood and looked at the frosted glass of Miss Florence's door. They still hadn't done the putty.

Mannie had been funny that morning.

– What are you reading, Tarr?

– A programme.

– For what?

– Football programme, sir.

– Hold it up and show everybody.

Tarry must have picked it up off the ground after the Hearts game.

– Aberdeen versus Heart of Midlothian. Do you know what

Heart of Midlothian is, Tarr?

– Team, sir.

– A prison. The Heart of Midlothian is a prison, a tolbooth. All government is based on prisons and the fear of prisons. You might expect that the Heart of Midlothian might be a fountain or square, for couples to stroll in. Do you, Veronica?

– Do I what, sir?

– Think Heart of Midlothian might be a fountain.

– Sir—?

– With water glistening upwards and falling back into itself? Caressed into shapes by the breeze—

– Mebbe, sir. Can I leave the room?

– In a minute. Once again I warn you, all of you, never to read Scott. Do you know why?

– Burstin, sir.

– Drivel, that's why. Okay, go, Veronica. Monumental drivel. Better to put your head in a bag.

He knocked on the cold glass. She came immediately to the door and smiled.

– Come away in.

– It's a note.

– I see that.

My, she was bonny the day. It was difficult to take his eyes off her as she unfolded and read.

On her teacher's table she had pale yellow primroses, afloat in a shell, did somebody give them to her? Would she like daffodils? He could snap off tons on the Miser's Hilly—

– Well, now. It's nice to see you today. But Mr Martin keeps you far too busy. I'll have to tell him, sometime. She splayed the note open carelessly.

She would give him a kiss.

– Dae you like yellow flowers, Miss?

– Yes, I do, actually, Peem.

Peem!

– I could easily get some—

– Infants, gather your chairs in a circle.

On a special table sat a village of pink and green plasticine low cottages, with pencil-pierced chimneys and nail-nicks for tiles.

Nobody had made a two-storeyer, nor nobody a tenement.

– Aren't they pretty?

nae problemo, peem

Off King Street itself lay St Patrick's, where you went for football. They had green pitches with hollowed goalmouths. It was hardly good country for Catholics, Aberdeen, they got no haar in Italy, Spain. Along from St Pat's was Marchetti's. From March till Christmas his striped awning kept the worst of the weather off his threshold. For the other two months he didn't even open. He said he went back to Piedmont every January, but others said to his granny in Peterhead.

– Dirty boy, gone from my door! Mr Marchetti shouted. Spermy gave him the fingers, reversed Victory.

– Fool fuckin Eyetie—

– Eh, Peem, ne ye be sae timory, come inta ma parlour. Ye wanta big cartone, ye wanta tuppenny cap?

– No, nae money the day, sorry.

– Ne money, getta a job!

– Tell me somethin, Mr Marchetti. Fit does Ponte Unione mean?

– Ponte Unione—? It's easy. Union Bridge.

– O. Union Brig. Ta.

– Ne problemo, Peem. When ye hae the money?

Spermy was kicking the wall outside.

– Ma sister's comin for a week, Haze.

– Is that her name?

– Aye, Haze. I'll see if she wants tae dae anythin. Ye interested?

– I dinna play wi girls—

– She's only thruppence.

a sleepyround woman

Dinah said after tea, Can I ask ye something, Amande?

– Sure, you ask me all you like, Dinah.

– Ye say somebody special's comin on Wednesday. Is it a man again?

– Non, not a man, no. It's my daughter.

– I didna ken ye had a dochter!

– She is the eldmost. Also one son, he is Georges, more young than Jed. They stay with the grandmother. Georges is quite étincell- ant but my daughter, foolish.

– I'm pretty foolish, masel, sometimes.

– You are pretty, and foolish not at all. You are only my friend just now.

– Your only friend, dae ye mean?

– My only. After the boat sinks, the Torry people is not happy with me. They say I bring bad luck on the whole family, and kill three men. They say I am bad sleepy woman—

– Ach, come here, said Dinah. She reached past the last Strathdee's scone and over the rhubarb and ginger jam on the occasional table, and gave her an awkward cuddle. She held it as long as she could, in that position, while the Frenchwoman sobbed.

– A sleepyround woman—

– Ach, come on. I'm goin oot for a bottlie o somethin. Ye comin? Mutch's is licensed: he's open till 8.

– Red please, if you buy wine. I don't go.

ba game wioot a ba

Spermy was out and about. He knocked at Peem's door.

– O, is that you, loon? said Peem's mother. Wipe your feet an come in, he's through in the bedroom playin.

Peem looked up from the blue figured carpet, looked back and checked both dice. Cowdrey was batting. 1 on the red die, 2 on the blue die, therefore Cowdrey had had his chips. Cowdrey was 1, therefore out – 2, therefore bowled.

– Hi.

– Hi.

– Fit ye playin at?

– Cricket.

– Far's the ba? Did it roll aneath the bed?

– Dinna need a ba—

– A ba game wioot a ba?

– So?

– Onywey. Just wanted tae say. She's on for def.

– Shut the door! said Peem.

– Okay. Haze, ken? On for def. Settirday, lock-ups, 3 o'clock

– 3 o'clock's nae really ideal. I've tae help ma Da wi his *Daily Worker*s.

– Div ye, or div ye nae, want tae see her?

– I dinna ken, I havena seen her afore—

– Plenty has. Right, one o'clock, then. An ye micht as well ken, she's thirteen noo, she's up tae fourpence.

lobbyfuck, then run away

Dinah came back with a bottle of red, in its own basket.

– Wine of Spain? said Amande. This is serious.

– O, sorry. No but, it's quite good. Billy and me once had it. I spotted the basket.

– Billy and me, what is this Billy and me I sometimes hear?

– O he went away. Quite sudden like. He used tae work in antiques.

– You told him to go?

– No, aye. Well—

– I'm sure he is very sad.

– Aye, he was sad. A bit intense, a bit ower young.

– Where did he go? He loved you?

– He said he did.

– Come on.

– Aye, poor Billy. He loved me alright.

– And also?

– And also I liked – well he was a bit skinnymalinky – whit you caa mince.

– And—

– And so I didna really fancy him.

– Fancy?

– Want him.

– Is it that you don't fuck with him?

– Sort o.

– You should have fucked with him. And now he's dead, isn't he?

– No, no. I've tellt ye a lee. He wasna an antique collector. He was a bucket man.

– I don't know *bucket men*. You sit a long time here, Dinah, too long inside in the evening. You have to go out.

– Ye're the one tae speak.

– Ah, but all the world knows me here, ici, in Torry, Urquhart.

– So—?

– Aberdeen is nice sweeped town on surface, but big scared of reputation. Men just want to lobbyfuck, then run away.

Money. He could buy coke and fetch it round the doors for desperate neighbours. Coal was delivered by the coal mannie, but if you ran out, or when you had to eke the coal, then a sack of coke. Coke was coal with the gas out. *Hauds the heat,* his Dad aye said, *but buggers the glow.*

It was a Scots mile to the Gasworks, along Urquhart, down past the City Hospital to the windtugged Links, then skirt Constitution as the guff got grimmer. With southard-like or westish wind the whole Beach Boulevard was stinking with coal gas. They roasted fresh coal on a furnace grid till the gas flew out, then raced through piping to fill the grey Gasometer.

That made it rise. The Gasometer just about filled the view at the top of Rosin Road. Or was it sink?

Then smaller and smaller piping took it into everybody's house.

Because of perished rubber hosing, it always leaked—

Because a door draught snuffed the flame—

Because you were a tinky drunk and didn't turn the tap off right—

Coal-gas, you'd think the stink alone would wake you—

Before it killed you.

The Gasworks furnace, how on earth did they keep that going twenty four hours?

Peem imagined cotton rags, fatty pigs, and awkward twigs brought down off lime and sycamore in gales.

They let the great deadened nutters out of Cornhill at night. A long line of nutcases tucked fasces of broken twigs up the flapping arms of their trench coats, and each pushed a dead pig, in a wobble-wheel wheelbarrow, down through the mausoleum that was Aberdeen, down to the Gasworks. In return they got white mugs of Typhoo, which they took up solemnly, as though they were liberators.

The residue was nuts of denatured coke, to marry in your grate with splintery sticks, ripped Kelloggs packets with the coupons saved, and curd of lard out of the frypan.

Transport was still to choose. The most he could fetch was a sack at a time.

Out in the shed Dad had jointed and welded sledge, stilts, scooter and cairtie.

Peem's sledge's runners were rust.

Stilts all got when up to tottering.

The scooter gave many a spin these days to Annie and Megan.

He purloined Hughie's cairtie: Hughie'd definitely outgrown it.

It ran rubber-smooth. With aery coke a hundredweight sack would weigh half and feel much less.

Who decided what a weight was—?

Just off the end of Constitution he passed Jobby Numbers, wheeling his dented, coke-filled pram the other way. Jobby was a queer kinda jigger, lived in Jasmine. Chaplin without the hat, the countervailing bowler. Not all that ancient, he happed his head, summer and winter, in a navy balaclava.

Folk said he'd been on too many Russian convoys. Folk said he'd swallowed every last chapter and verse in the Bible, and could spew it back for the asking. Folk said kids shouldn't torment him, but kids being kids, always did. Peem too, sometimes, a bit.

– Aye, aye, Jobby, fit like?

– Cauld. Jesus wept.

– I ken—

And Jobby squeaked on his way.

Blast! Three ill-sorted dogs came prancing past him: shitty wee Scotty, plump devil-black Lab, and that huge Alsatian he hated seeing. Sniffed each other's arses, went on by. Cats were sinks for affection but dogs, what was the point in the city?

The German Shepherd detached itself from the triad and scudded across the Links, chasing a cloud of herring gulls into the air.

Against corporation privet Scotty propped a leg and jetted.

Black Lab suddenly spinning, it lunged at Peem, and toothed at him, slavvering his stocking in an attempted nip.

Abandoning Hughie's cairtie, he raced away, trying to get off the street but with nowhere to dodge to. Even the Gasworks gate was closed. He threw himself flatling at the big brick wall, one toe wedged in a weathered hole and fingers high in dislodgements. Gawked up – the cope was a Cuillinn of broken bottles, fangs of glass. Even could you scrabble over you'd slash all your palms. Keeked down – at the two big dogs.

RUFF!

With his loose foot blindly he kicked and kicked, that would please them. He heeled softness, a muzzle—?

RUUUFF!

Some bar or stick went RAT-TAT-TAT along the iron gate.

– GET! Get awa, ye dirty brutes!

The weighbridge man was good to him. He'd heard the barking, aye, sure. He gave him a sack to garner spilled coke, from where the lorries swerved at the gate. He made him a warm mug of sweet milky tea, an Abernethy with it, which he dunked.

– Why dae ye keep broken glass on top the wa? Is it burglars?

Such a relief to ask the man stuff.

– Na, just a precaution. Dae ye like the school?

– Aye, okay.

– Fa's yir best teacher?

– Miss Florence. An Mr Martin, of course—

– Fit does she gie ye?

– She gave us the Art Gallery.

– Fit, a hale Art Gallery?

– Na, she took us to see it. It's lovely an calm—

– Och, I prefer a bit o excitement. Masel, I've nivver gone in for that art caper.

– We were only six.

The fierce knot in his stomach loosened. It was ages ago.

He was trundling his cairtie back up to the junction when he saw Spermy and a lassie twenty yards off, strolling along Urquhart from the beach direction. God, some big lassie! He bent down, undid a lace, and tried to tie it again. Bumping in her pink cardigan, she had bouncing pigtails with scarlet bows. He redid his lace, hardly managing his fingers. She was carouseling a message bag, round and round her body from hand to hand. The unbuttoned wings of her cardigan flew out.

Then they passed and presumably went into the house.

At the fifth door, he sold his bag of Coke to Mr Dargo, Raymie's Dad. Mr Dargo had that dance band that went far and wide in a purple van through the North-East, Danny Dargo and the Dargosies.

– I'm nivver in when the coalman comes, so it's a help, said Mr Dargo. How much is it?

– One an thr—, one an six.

Nothing off for transport, nothing for supplies. Clear profit – 1/6!

Then he went to get washed and combed.

– I've never seen ye sae clean, said his mother. Ye'll want tae put on your helmet, on a cauld day like this.

– Nae a helmet, nae the day. Stupid—

– Nae sae stupid as catchin pneumonia.

Supposed to be from a Spitfire or Hurricane, who did it fool, it was just a thin soft leather helmet, fleecy inside, from the Co-opy draper, with a brown press stud.

– Fan's that laddie comin roon for ye, fit dae they cry him?

– Jed.

– Sounds mair like a cowboy than a schoolboy.

– Uh-huh. One o'clock.

– O no, ma lad. Ye canna go oot wioot your dennir.

– I'm nae hungry—

– Ye must eat something.

– Is it a pie?

– No, steak mince.

– Can I hae a mince sandwich in ma haun?

– I dinna ken fit the warld's comin till. Ye'll get an ulcer rinnin aboot fan ye're eatin.

– I'll chew it thirty two times.

– Once for each tooth, ye'd better.

– Gotten your gelt? said Spermy.

Peem took out a fat coin with a portcullis, brassy with presence. Plus a penny with the Queen's profile, and on the flip-side, in poncy chariot, Boadicea.

– Ach, I've made them sticky wi mince.

– Stickypricky. Cock luves fud.

– Eh? O, aye.

You saw that plenty on playground walls – COK LUVS FUD – inside a chalk-white heart, sometimes corroborated below – TRUE SINED COK.

Confidence and diffidence were soon on the cinder roadie leading into the lock-ups. Cinders from? Steam engines, the kind that came puffing into Joint Station, with their fancy wheel configurations, 0-4-2, 2-6-2, and 6-8-10-12-2, the Juggernaut that squashed him once in a dream, with great gashes of steam. He loved waiting for trains on bridges.

The lock-ups was just a name for clapboard or tarpaper garages with no cars in. Aberdeen was waiting an economic turn-up, the Yanks to release their post-war Lend Lease grip on the UK, or something, so said Frankie Groat.

Squint through old nail holes, the lock-ups had pieces of bicycles, exiled cabinets, half-lidded tins of putty and paint.

Peem drew his toe through the dust.

– Come on, min, said Spermy, quit muckin aboot. Penny for a look, tuppence for a poop, thruppence for the hale damn lot.

But there was no sign of his famous big sister.

Spermy drew three marbles from his drawstring pouch.

– Okay then, stick ye—

Peemie took out three clayers.

– Nae doddies, said Spermy.

Peemie replaced the clay doddies and took out three glassers with that whorl of cerulean blue, insipid buff or lemon curd yellow.

Spermy dug a kypie-hole with his heel. They took a ten-stride along the cinders, turned, and lobbed one apiece. Spermy landed nearest and got next go, bouncing his scarlet marble into the conical cinder hole.

– Nae rollies, nae drappies, said Peemie, then made to put his feet in a reversed V behind his marble.

– Nae Chinese feynies, said Spermy.

Peemie made the V the proper way, an easy harbour behind his marble for Spermy's should it miss.

Spermy took out a rusty ball-bearing.

– Nae steelers!

But he was late with his nix.

Spermy took aim with the giant steeler triggered on his thumb-nail.

Next thing Peemie knew his buff glasser exploded in bits, globe and chip, and the brute steeler dunted the tender bone inside his ankle.

– Ooya-oocha!

– An that's anither glasser ye owe me, I'm nae for a smashed ane.

They looked up. A strange loon was sklumpering out towards them from the labyrinth of the lockups. Probably Catholic.

– Nelson whiters! he shouted, once he was past and turned for the Beach.

– St Pat's shiter! yapped back Spermy.

– Fit's a whiter—? asked Peem.

– A hoofter.

Appearing from nowhere, Haze beckoned them slowly with cupped hand. Manky and sunless, between the lock-ups, dockens could scantly grow. They traipsed one tin alley, then squeezed round the back. Peemie kept tucked behind the negotiator.

– Far's his dosh, Elvis?

– Here it's.

– Fit? Ye'll nae get far for fourpence!

A flirt of cold wind blew in from the North Sea.

– Gie's a haud o it onywey.

– But Haze, said Spermy that's fit ye tellt me yesterday. Fourpence.

– Couldna gie a toss, it's up. Aathin's up in the shops. Ye dinna get nothin for nithin nooadays.

– Here's sixpence atween the two o us then, said Spermy. Haze, come on, see's a look, we winna touch ye.

– There shouldna usually be twa o ye.

– Well one o us is only your brither. That doesna count.

– Hmmph. Hauf-brither, ma auntie says. An fa's your pal wi the funny helmet?

She hauled doon her navy bloomers and lifted the jib of her skirt.

A tangle like brambles over a railway line.

– I'm nae daein nithin for young loons. Ye're aye useless. Ye can watch me pish.

She squatted down next to a faded Green Final, the headline *Hearts Dump Dons*, sensible sandals with white socks planted apart. Steaming out of some undisclosed tunnel, a yellow gush pulsed forward, a Ganges through ashes, then slowed to a delta.

Words dried.

Haze hiked up her drawers.

– Satisfied? Hae tae skedaddle, I've three smoked haddies tae get for our tea.

– Is that aa we're gettin? said Spermy.

– Fit's wrang wi a bit o yella fish?

She stepped across her recent river.

– Seize ye later, alligator.

And was away round the corner.

– An fit dae ye mean, *hauf-brither*? shouted Spermy. Fit's *hauf* aboot me?

– Hih, eh? said Spermy.

– Aye, she can fairly pish, said Peem.

They half-ran, half-slank over the Broad Hill, across the municipal salt-crazed cricket squares to the hazy beach.

– *Sisters and brother have I none—*

– Fit ye on aboot?

– *But that man's father is my father's son*.

– Hey min!

– It's just an auld joke, my Dad aye says it.

– Well it's nae that fuck o a funny.

They loose-hipped it down the concrete steps to the sands, then balanced their way along a wooden groyne.

the workers parted

Like the Gasworks, like Hall Russell's, Scottish Fertile worked on Saturday, half-day. The hooter went at 1 and the process workers and skilled men grabbed their piece-pokes, coats, bikes, or motor-bikes, and went for home. The foreman, Mr Mount, waited until the last had cleared the gate at thirty seconds past one, and then drove his Standard Vanguard through the throng.

There was a little grime on the boot, where somebody had capitalled *FILTHY RICH* and somebody else had scribed *The Working Class Can Kiss My Ass*. The workers parted as the bulbous car nosed through them at five miles per hour.

Andy arrived home by ten past.

Lunch was mince and tatties, prunes and custard.

– Far's Peem?

– O, he had tae go oot wi his pal.

– That Tarry nickum?

– Na, he's taen up wi the McClung laddie. Couldna get oot o the hoose quick enough.

– Hmmph. Andy placed the last of his five prune stones on the sloping rim of the pudding plate. Fit time's he comin back?

– He didna say.

– Well, I'll just hae tae tak the *Worker* masel, then?

– Watch an nae get indigestion, fleein aroon. It's nae as though the revolution's the morn.

– It certainly winna be if we dinna get the *Workers* oot.

– It's gey thin for a paper—

– Aye, better than a big wad o capitalist lies, ony day.

Andy fetched a sheaf of *Daily Workers* from on top of the box bedroom tallboy, went to the door and then went back to discard half. He walked into the kitchen living room.

– That's me.

– I'm goin tae hae a lie-doon while the bairn's sleepin, said Madge. Annie's fine pleased wi her heid in a book, an Hughie's oot in the shed I think.

– Aye well, Madge. That was richt good mince. I'll bet it wisna tinky Guffie's.

– Ye're nae far wrang.

He went down to the corner, and started along Urquhart Parade, the first house past the butcher.

a headwarmth

Watching the rollers slanteying in, white then rumbling over, sending swash to lick at his feet.

– Dreep, said Spermy.

Then the backwash, rattling a thousand pebbles to grit in the sea's maw.

– Fuckin borin here—

A speck darkening, on the horizon.

– Wauk up, ye dozy fuck! shouted Spermy, from high on the beach.

Peem could make out a long hull, black with a—

CLUNK

stunned &
dizzying over
he saw the half-brick
bounce from his head
& felt headwarmth
run – *christmahelmet*—
tumbling on
unstable cobbles
gabbing wild stuff
sblooood—

Salt cold came.

no answer

Andy started at the bottom and worked up. There was no answer from either of the ground floor flats. There was a wireless playing in one of them.

a jingle of shingle

Crocked, brainstunned, primeval, a croc swishing: reduced to irrelevant tail.

And Salty wanted to come out of all that, to feel dry under its belly, to comprehend firm land, not this slather of pebbles. And Salty flowed up the rough Beach and along the smooth Bellyvard, swish across Kong Street, swash up the Gollygate. Waddling past Muddle School, widdling in the door of the Kirkgyte Bar.

And Salty Croc met in with the other Diles, Miss Fluence holding their snout composed, Mr Martyr tweaking their tails to uproar, as they slithered on together – Starry, Rammy, Permy & Jezebel – loud & louder, roaring in endless round—

Roll up,
roll the log—
See the
coconut dog?
Awa ye
fuckin rogue—
See the
COCK
on that dog!

Until, just past the Orkhard and slowing their swish, they drifted past Graze Collage. Salty Croc and the Diles entered the hollow revolvy portal of the Heart Galley. Fountains stopped falling, copper went swiftly green, pink pillars thrust like piston rods, caught in the flash of the quarryman, the finisher's corundum. Children gnashed imaginary gum, uttering the little *o*'s of come. Hollowed, they felt revolvy. Up and down the wide white deep-veined stairs, the tenementary ones.

Bronzes, hangings, stains.

On broad canvas, a Landseer, *Highland Mud*.

Wedges, walls of mud burst down a glen of trees. They pulsed past a croft roof on which a sprawl of clansman, a startle of goats, a skitter of ewes, a heel of dogs, his peely daughter and her terrified brats, clung to thatching, happed in kilting—

Salt came swish in Croc's long nostril.

A jingle of shingle, something entered his pouch.

va, go, cochon

Andy knocked on the right-hand door on the middle landing. The brass plate said *Demaison*.

He heard slippers on lino, then the letter flap plucked from inside.

– Va, go, cochon-fucker. Go, get from me, FUCK OFF.

happy as a cut worm

Peem drained slow from the roughfluted hollow.

Shingle sludged away from him. He stumbled up and moved towards the no-one on the Prom. His shoes picked up bad flaffs of sand.

Hottish stuff coursed down his temple, chose its channels across his cheek, and mustered at his chin.

Pressing a hand to his helmet, he heroed across the Prom.

– Spitssalt, spitswater, spitsblood, spits—

Happy in a way, happy as a cut worm.

Pairs of legs in slack slacks and wasp-waist skirt were coming – he lapped a meander of blood from the crook of his lip so as not to disgust them.

Pairs of legs came closer: pairs of legs moved off across the road.

sold a worker

Andy Endrie sold a *Worker* to Jock Spaver at top left and made his way down past the middle landing.

The door flew open behind him, and a green bottle zoomed past his lug and smashed on the lavvy landing.

– It's only a scalp wound, said the nurse.

– But he's bled tons, said his mother.

Obviously.

– Och, I'll soon get him cleaned up.

– Good.

– The doc will be along in a minute tae stitch him.

O, great, fantastic.

– Will he need an X-ray, nurse, for his skull?

– No for me tae say, but the trouble is, it's no warkin.

His skull?

– We'd a broken airm this mornin set by guesswark.

A brain X-ray—? It could change your sums into algebra.

– Yon's a Fife accent. What did ye say your name was?

– I didna. Dinah. She started wetting his drying wound. Trainee Nurse Wylie.

– Go on. Was your Ma by any chance in the WRENS? A Gladys Wylie was she?

His best blood blossoming in the enamel bowl.

– O, that's right, she aye goes on aboot it. Weir nooadays, Gladys Weir.

– U-boat detection?

– Think so, yeah.

– Padstow?

Red amongst the cloudy Dettol.

– Aye bletherin aboot Padstow, that's my ma—

– O, super! The times we had! Gladys Weir. My, my. But of course, ye were born afore the start o the War. She was that proud o ye. Your granny, wasn't it, that brought ye up for a start?

– Ye ken mair aboot me than I do masel.

– Well, maybe ye'll come roon an hae a cuppie o tea wi us sometime, Dinah?

He felt for what was left of his marbles.

– That'd be braw, Mrs—

Gone.

– Endrie, Madge Endrie, 72 Rosin Road, ye canna miss it, bottom right.

– Gee, I'm just roon the corner frae ye.

He drew from his pocket, damp-pouched against his skin—

– Aye, I thocht I'd seen ye.

– Just above the butcher's there.

A pale blue stone—

– O, nae that terrible Guffie's!

With a round hole that fitted his eye, amazing!

– Peem, stop actin the bloomin goat! Let the nurse get on wi her job.

never happen in russia

Spermy wasn't in evidence next day. Peemie got a row from his father, not for the bloody head, the wet clothing, the trouble he'd been to his mother. He had been supposed to go out, as per every Saturday afternoon, with a tote of *Daily Worker*s under his oxter, but lust for the unkent had led him astray.

Dad got his quota from the Party every Saturday. Of course he had regulars, lots down in St Clements, far fewer in Torry. You just chapped at the door and Dad would say a word about the world situation, the Yanks, and folk would reply *Aye, it's awful* and Dad would say *Aye, that would never happen in Russia*, and the folk might give you tuppence, and the door would close again. And Dad would knock at the next door.

Some folk would retort *Nae the day, Andy*, as though revolution could wait till the tickman was squared.

Or else Dad would beam *Daily Worker, the only paper that*

tells the truth! And a mannie in braces-and-baffies would come back *Awa, ye ken I never read that dirt!*

In Torry last week a loon mumbled *Ma Da says he's nae in.*

And Dad replied *Run an tell him it's nae the Witnesses.*

The loon came back *Ma Da says he's nae in for naebody.*

And Dad laughed *Tell him he's won the pools.*

And last week a young wife in a glass-buttoned cardy in Victoria Road said *I dinna ken, fit is it onywey?*

And Dad said *Daily Worker, the only paper that supports the working class.*

And the lass replied *That's communists, intit? I've nae time for communists.*

Dad countered it was the only way to get council houses, world peace, and bigger pay. Peem was proud of that idea. He didn't want to have to move house though.

The wifie didn't believe him anyway. *Ma man's a fisher. Catches nithin, company gies him nithin. Communists can mak gowd rings oot o brass washers, can they, aa o a sudden?*

Well—

Dinna nane think it.

Maybe they sold ten *Workers* in the hour, maybe a dozen.

Never mind, he'd said. *Let's awa ower to Pittodrie and catch the supporters gaain in.*

Some supporters would buy gladly, thinking it was a special sports edition. But, blessed in Moscow, published in London, the thin page of *Daily Worker* soccer featured only Chelsea and Spurs.

Those with a cargo of beer would mill and heave.

Ish-shat-offishul – offishul programme?

In a wey— had said his Dad.

But Scottish revolutionaries drew a line. Hand to shoulder, Dad had propelled the drunken bauchle – across the streaming hordes in Merkland Road – to the proper vendor.

Opiate o the people, he'd said, on the road home.
    Fit is?
    Maist things. Beer, the Kirk, pictures, fitba.
    They had been passing under Marchetti's awning.
    Ice cream?
    Ice cream's okay in the summer.

It wasn't until the day after his accident, the Sunday, that Peem caught up with the new *Daily Worker. Soviets Save Poles* was the headline, and the subhead was *Rebels Defeated in Fierce Street Fighting*. And then about how reactionary forces in Wroclav had been trying to smash the people's revolution, acting as Trotskyist spies and agents provocateurs, whatever they were when they were at home.

His head was throbbing with the five stitch-holes, the palpable crevasse, the oozy dressing.

But now the desperate Wroclav folk had asked for help, and Khrushchev had sent a battalion of tanks to stand shoulder to shoulder with the Polish comrades and distribute bread. Tanks were good like that.

He needed an opiate, though.

Right enough, Khrushchev was an awful good man, a shining baldy like his Uncle Dick. Any headwound would be hard to hide in their two cases. But Uncle Dick was a capitalist tool and travelled for Sang's Aerated Waters, fizzy ale. Capitalists would water the workers' beer, puff air in your ice cream.

He took an Askit stirred in water.

Uncle Dick sold so much ale to roadside inns and country shoppies that he'd bought a bungalow out at Hazlehead. And Cousin Archie seemed to get a new Dinky per month, from Scammell bucket-lorries to Aston Martins, the fill of a square biscuit tin. And a panoply of cigarette cards to flutter. Aye, that was capitalists for you, aye with a great fancy hoard. Yellow-creamed meringues, melty chocolate éclairs and harlequin Battenberg squares. And you could have two, Aunt Betsy never minded—

The Askit wasn't working.

That Sunday night, he could have done without it, a good lot of the Party came round the house. Uncle Hugh with his squeezebox, Theo and Marcie, Tam Clunie, Billy Mill, Frankie Groat as well.

They laughed, full of laughs and confidence and decrying they were. The first song was Theo's favourite, *The Wild Colonial Boy*. Then they did the one with the embarrassing ending.

The waiter bellowed through the hall—
'You can't have bread with one meatball'.

These were Party songs, Peem kent fine, about world imperialism, or plain poverty. That night Uncle Hugh sang a Cornkister, *McGinty's Meal an Ale*, and though everybody knew it wasn't a proper Party song, it was still okay to sing it – it showed you that working folk could make fools of themselves if they drank owermuckle but have a good time doing it, after all their travail.

– Aye, drink's aye the curse o the working class, said Billy Groat.

– I mind when we were in Spain, said Tam Clunie. The Brigade ran oot o anaesthetic. Wine wouldna do the trick, it was a big slug o brandy.

– Did Lenin drink?

Uncle Hugh just liked singing, that was it. He'd probably already been to the Kirk that morning, to get some extra singing in.

– Gie us *The Volga Boatmen*.

That was the best, a real worksong, though you didn't hear it to advantage in the house. The room didn't have the acoustics, what with the soft double bed in the recess and the stone sink under the window.

And besides you needed the deepness for it, like Paul Robeson.

Peem had gone up Union Street to hear him the previous year, the time he came to Aberdeen, but he was too late, the Music Hall full-up, the place stowed out with white non-communists wanting to hear the great black Communist singer. So Peem just stood out in the entrance hall, ear pressed to the carved relief door, and vibrated as the bass came through.

Yo-$_o$ HEAVE-$_{oh}$, Yo-$_o$ HEAVE-$_{oh}$,

A

A

A

A

AAAH.

Yo-$_o$ HEAVE-$_{oh}$.

You believed every word Paul Robeson came out with, you would surely have marched to the ends of the earth with him.

I'm gonna lay down ma sword an shield
Down by the riverside,
Ain't gonna study war no more—

Better than *Onward Christian Soldiers* any day. He hoped his Uncle Hugh refused to sing that one.

may

a bit of may day melodrama

At first it seemed it was just one of Dad's stories, a bit of May Day melodrama to enliven the liver, bacon and tatties, the prunes and semolina, the bread and tea and jam.

– Fit's wrang, said Mum. Ye're affa quiet.

– I was up tae Woolmanhill the day.

– Ye hinna hurten yersel?

– Na, it wisna me. Ye ken Ludwig, fae the plots. Aye, well, he'd a bit o a do.

– A do? Ludwig? said Peem.

– Aye, a bit o a so-called accident. Bloody Time-an-Motion merchants.

oats, barley, ballads, potatoes

Royston and Cran spent the first week at the chemical works walking around. That was popular.

Scottish Fertile, snarled with corrosives, was its usual tuppeny carnival. Two labourers uphowking a foul sump, plumbers piecing replacement piping, the blacksmith forging a buckshee flange. And a terrible ammonia in the air.

– Chaos— said Royston.

– Just the standard chronic panic, said Cran.

– The tough call is identifying regular jobs.

– How regular does it hae tae be?

– Amenable to the stopwatch.

Scottish Fertile

Inputs: sulphur, guano, industrial chemistry

Outputs: superphosphate, hi-nitrogen, in hundredweight bags

Deeside, Donside, Banff and Buchan

Inputs: sweat, rain, sun, fertiliser, by the hundredweight bag

Outputs: oats, barley, ballads, potatoes

Royston (and Cran)

Inputs: timing, analysis, targets, hurry

Output: temper, short-cuts, a hand – in a hundredweight bag

if

It wasn't as though Dinah hadn't seen plenty.

Most accidents happened in the home, as the authorities rightly warned, apart from those that occurred on roads, on farms, in shops, on ships, on fishing boats, off railway bridges. But what is an accident? And can it be an accident if it is waiting to happen?

She kept rerunning Billy.

If she hadn't shouted.

If he hadn't turned.

If the wind hadn't lifted up and scudded.

If she wasn't a selfish cow. He fell.

If she hadn't said she liked him fine. He slipped.

If she hadn't been rampant, one weekend.

How could he have jumped? That's useless.

He should have eaten more, so thin, the wind just blew him—

It was an accident.

beethoven, are ye fuckin deif?

Andy Endrie was the safety rep. Shop steward for the sparkies, and overall safety rep. He sat on a committee of two with Mount, the works foreman, that met every three months.

– Safety? Safety can be overdone, said Mount. If you wrap production in cotton wool—

– Machine-guards, said Andy.

– It's easy seein you're no shareholder—

– Wire-mesh fastened tae steel rails, said Andy.

At their March meeting they'd at last agreed: on siting two new first-aid boxes.

Ludwig had been working with Scottish Fertile for eighteen months now.

At first they were happy enough to shove him on barrowing and bawl at him. Soon as he donked the barrow of blocks down, to change his grip on the hollow handles, it was take turns to shout.

– Hey, Jerry. Ye winna win wars squat on yir erse.

Or if he burst a bag of grey fertiliser to spew in the general dirt.

– Hey min, Kraut-features, that's sabotage. We could hing ye fae a girder for that.

Or if they explained to him what to do in impenetrable Doric, *Dinna clart that hopper reamin fu, ye Hun twat*, and he still continued doing it.

– Beethoven, are ye fuckin deif—?

After a year and half's rough apprenticeship, he was moved from barrowing to the bagging shed.

Superphosphate entered the bagging shed at roof height, bobbling along on a concave belt. The belt came to an end, or rather doubled back on itself, so the granules rained into a huge hopper through rising cumuli of dust.

Inside that hopper it was vital an electric auger rotated downwards, ever downwards, for steady discharge into the bags. Else, in a sudden whuff and abundance of phosphate, the bagmen could have choked, been whelmed.

Per shift there was one chargehand and six baggers – plus Ludwig, the baggers' mate.

At the start of the morning shift, the chargehand Roddy pressed a green button to start the auger.

It was *This little piggy went to market, this little piggy stayed at home—*

Abe and Ally held open bag 1 to let it fill, then moved it along to the stitcher, Bert and Bob stepped in to fill bag 2, and Chic and Conal stood ready with 3.

Then Abe and Ally placed 1 on to a pallet, Bert and Bob slid 2 away to the stitcher, and Chic and Conal held yawning bag 3 to let it fill.

Then Abe and Ally skipped back to fetch bag 4, Chic and Conal scuffed 3 along to the stitcher, and Bert and Bob plunked 2 on to the pallet.

It was a dampish day as Abe and Ally held gaping 4 to let it fill, and the granules took in moisture, as Bert and Bob sped to ready bag 5 and the auger clogged, as Chic and Conal humphed 3 on to the pallet, and though Abe and Ally held 4 well through the stitcher, bag 5 was left at the kirk door, so to speak, no more superphosphate could drop through—

Roddy pressed the red button. Cran stopped the watch at fifty one seconds. Royston wrote for a good ten minutes.

Theory alone raced on.

– Ludwig, ye bitch's twat, clear the tap o that fuckin hopper.

– Nein tap is here.

– Tap, top, tap—! Deif bastard!

– Nein problem.

Up on his platform Ludwig reamed away at the clogged auger with his ram-pole, as far as he could reach.

Abe and Ally took over bag 5.

– Dinna fuckin let that happen again, ye haunless Hun.

Roddy the chargehand pressed the green button to start the auger.

It was *Here we go round the mulberry bush, the mulberry bush, the mulberry bush*—

Abe and Ally held open bag 5 to let it fill, then moved it along to the stitcher, Bert and Bob stepped in to fill bag 6, and Chic and Conal stood ready with 7.

Then Abe and Ally placed 5 on to a pallet, Bert and Bob slid 6 away to the stitcher, and Chic and Conal held yawning bag 7 to let it fill.

Then Abe and Ally skipped back to fetch bag 8, Chic and Conal scuffed 7 along to the stitcher, and Bert and Bob plunked 6 on to the pallet.

It was a haary day as Abe and Ally held gaping 8 to let it fill, and the granules soaked up moisture, as Bert and Bob sped to ready bag 9, and the auger clogged, as Chic and Conal thumped 3 on to the pallet, and though Abe and Ally held 4 well through the stitcher, bag 9 was jilted, so to speak, no more superphosphate could fall through—

Roddy pressed the red button. Cran stopped the watch at fifty two seconds.

Royston wrote for twelve minutes.

Early analysis poured out.

– Ludwig, ye Boche bauchlin bastard, keep reamin that auger.

– I try. The pole isnae longer enough.

– It'll be langer enough if I shove it up yir fuckin erse!

– Make good Nazi.

– Fit did you say?

– Need the khazi—

He hung right over the rail and progged at the cloggings.

Abe and Ally took over bag 9.

– Once fuckin mair an we'll loss wir fuckin jobs.

– Keep ram-rammin.

Roddy was in charge and pressed a green button to start the auger.

It was *Mary had a little lamb,*

And it was always gruntin,

She took it round behind the shed—

And kicked its little —— in.

Abe and Ally held open bag 9 to let it fill, then moved it along to the stitcher, Bert and Bob stepped in to fill bag 10, and Chic and Conal stood ready with 11.

Then Abe and Ally placed 9 on to a pallet, Bert and Bob slid 10 away to the stitcher, and Chic and Conal held yawning bag 11 to let it fill.

Then Abe and Ally skipped back to fetch bag 12, Chic and Conal scuffed 11 along to the stitcher, and Bert and Bob plunked 10 on to the pallet.

It was a filthy day as Abe and Ally held gaping 12 to let it fill, and the granules soddened with moisture, as Bert and Bob sped to ready bag 13 and there was a little cry from above as Chic and Conal humphed 11 on to the pallet, and Abe and Ally held 12 well through the stitcher, and Bert and Bob stood at the altar, so to speak, as a hand dropped through, which Royston observed, and made no sense of, for about five seconds, then his shout mingled with the terrible skirling from above, Roddy woke from his hard-on, and pressed the red button—

– Better get up that leddir, somebody.

– Ye're the boss, Roddy.

that's nae your problem

Ludwig had his right wrist tucked into his left armpit, out of sight. His powdered face blanching, his overall reddening, grim chameleon.

– Ludwig, fit have ye gone an deen tae yirsel?

– Are ye aaricht?

– Wunderbar—

– That's the attitude.

Ludwig squeezed his oxter harder but the flow never stopped.

– That's richt, compression's the secret at this game. Far's that bastard first-aid?

– Foo should I ken, Roddy?

– Baggered now—

Ludwig began to shiver fierce as his blood ran out.

– C'mon we'll soon get ye doon this ladder. C'mon, boys, aabody grab him.

– Baggered now. Need my hand on back—

– Dinna ye worry, that's nae your problem. It canna have gone far.

the crocodile briefcase

To Woolmanhill they swung in the knackered works van, Ludwig stanching himself, Andy, the safety rep, driving like hell.

– Keep a grip o ees haun.

For Royston sat there too, on the bench seat, with his hastily-emptied case. It was Cran that had done it, on Andy's say-so, dumping Royston's records onto the factory floor.

Inside the crocodile briefcase was Ludwig's hand, thoroughly dusted with superphosphate.

you'll feel a little prick

– We'll not be needing that, said the duty surgeon.

– It's okay, I'll dispose of it, said Dinah quietly.

– Certainlich it is not your hand for disposal, said Ludwig.

– Sorry.

– Now I'm going to give you an anaesthetic. You'll feel a little prick.

If you're lucky, thought Dinah.

She turned to Andy.

– Who and where are his next of kin, mister?

– O, I dinna think he's ony o them, said Andy. He's never mentioned ony relatives in aa the time I've kent him. He's German.

– O, that's tough for him. But haud on, wha's that in the corner? I think I ken that ither gentleman—

– You know me, said Ern Royston.

it only brought them closer

The 11+ test was due in four or five weeks. Spermy hardly spoke to him now, maybe the beach thing, maybe he knew he could do nothing of note with a pencil.

But Mannie's teaching was falling away again. Peem was through with the day's sums and thought he would draw Tarry into a nonsense, along the back row. Half the ploy was in flicking papers behind Bapface's back, her arm curled round her jotter protective like, as though it was sooking her pap.

– *Dear Tarry, Am bored! Please send a swear by return.*

– *My dearest Peemie, I say, fack off, you Raj.*

– *Esteemed Tarriness, Begone, you kunt.*

It was basic Billy Bunter stuff, on bubblegum papers.

Mannie Martin glanced from cajoling the front row and saw the flitting of sweet nothings across the back.

– Take that bubblegum out here, Tarr.

– It's nae bubblegum, sir.

126

– Chewing gum then. Take it out.

– It's nae chewing gum, sir.

– I don't care what it is, Tarr. Take it out and you with it.

– It wasna me, sir. It was Peemie Endrie that deen it.

Peem gave Mannie Martin his due, he did falter. He'd know that once they were out, Tarr and his top boy, his go-between, they'd both have to be belted. You couldn't fetch boys down to the front just for a news.

– Belt them.

– Wallop them.

– Swots never get the scud, said Casey.

– You lot can stop ga-gawking and start pecking.

– Broon Hen has spoken— said Spermy.

When he got the length of reading the notes, Mannie Martin split his blotched face in a grin and what Peemie liked was he didn't try to hide it.

– So that's the way with you boys today. Well let's see if this gives you a few more ideas.

With that he unfurled the leather scud from the drawer where the blue mark book was stowed, and nodded for Tarry to hoist a hand up horizontal.

Thwack!

– Now you – em – Endrie? Again that dachle in his voice.

Peemie had never been belted, not even by the Meggezone Kid at her most crabbit. His heart beat like a time bomb against his cotton vest.

Thwick—

Christ, he'd taken his hand down too quick, Mannie Martin had leathered his own thigh, like the Pendulum slicing into Fitseesname.

– Again, boy.

– Lay it on'm, Broon Hen— said Spermy.

Thwack!

– Oo-ya, oo-ya! said Spermy, on Peem's behalf.

But the rest of the afternoon, Peem could have sworn it only brought them closer, maybe it was Mannie Martin sharing the soreness on his own leg.

not on the political menu

Ludwig disappeared on a trolley through to theatre, with Dinah at his side, tending the blood-bag.

– Ye'd better be coming back doon tae the works, said Andy.

– I prefer to locate in my hotel base to file reports, said Royston.

– Accident form first, said Andy

– I wasn't a direct witness, to be fair.

– Tae be fair! exploded Andy. Ye micht as well hae amputatit him yersel.

– I had no wish—

– Wi your supercapitalistic aix!

– Ex?

– Aye, I wish it was *ex*. If we owned Sandilands, ye'd never set foot in the works again, you nor your crony Cran, na nor nane o your Time-an-Motion.

– If you owned Sandilands?

– Aye, we dae aa the wark. Fit wey should we nae own the place—?

– Because ownership is already taken care of, by IPI, Imperial Phosphate Industries, through its local subsidiary. Are you to come as a thief in the night, Mr Endrie, I hardly think so.

– The real thievin's been gaain on a thousand year. Feudalism, capitalism, imperialism. It's restorin goods tae their richtfu owners I'm spikkin aboot.

– Communism is not on the political menu, Mr Endrie. Scotland is not Russia. If you want to play games in the street—

– Games in the street! There's a man lost a hand the day!

– If you have a problem, when this has cooled, I can arrange, I can have it discussed.

– Aye, that'll be the day—

– Till we meet again.

still under, sleepin

Dinah didn't know why she said yes. It was partly surprise, partly connection. He was standing inside the outside door, when she came off shift at 6 o'clock.

– Ah, Dinah, how is he, the man?

– Stitched, transfused, still under, sleepin—

– You look so weary now. May I escort you, a taxi, where would you like to go?

– You certainly can not.

Straight home. But Amande would have the place in a mess.

– A little refreshment, then? Our paths keep crossing.

She was hungry.

– That's mebbe called coincidence, Mr Royston.

– Ern, please. Dinah, I was thinking of a little place off Bridge Street.

concocting plays

Mannie had given Peemie, and Iris Gray as well, special homework that night. Concocting plays for a competition. They were hoping to hansel the new Children's Theatre up the top of King Street.

– First Children's Theatre in Britain, said Mannie Martin.

– Hardly, said Casey. Nivver seen this class—?

– And sae that was puir Ludwig connached. Useless b's.

 – Far is he fae, again? said Mum.

 – Hamburg.

 – O, Hamburg.

 – An fit was he daein afore?

 – O various jobbies. When he was a POW, they made him hyow neeps an stook corn, oot by Huntly he was tellin me. Eftir the War, well there wasna much tae go back for, was there? So he just bade on, he got the odd fee, and soon he startit in amang horses. Nae, of course, that that was sae very wise.

 – Why not, Daddy?

 – O, I didna ken ye were luggin in an aa, Annie!

 – Did a horse stand on his toe?

 – Na, it wisna horses that stood on his tae, it was tractors. Aince the tractors cam in, like in big numbers, the auld grey Fergies, an aa the Masseys, well there was whit ye micht call a big clear-oot. Hands werena needit aroon the fairm, if ye'll pardon me, ye ken fit I mean. Hands werena needit, unless they kent how tae wark a socket set, or howk the coke fae a cylinder heid. It was only natural.

 – Dad, I've tae write a play—

 – Have ye tidied your bedroom first?

the dented pewter measure

Royston and Dinah were sitting in the cocktail bar of the Royal Hotel, just off Bridge Street. They were the only ones in the dark-panelled bar. Royston perched on a stool, the barman footering around with the dented pewter measure, and spilling a couple or three drops each time he canted into a tumbler or thistle-graved glass.

 It was port and lemon for Dinah: for Royston a Whisky Mac.

 – Thanking you, Fred. No, make them doubles. And have one

yourself. I'm just going over to sit with my lady friend there.

– Aye, thank ye kindly, Mr Royston. A nice young lassie by the look o her. A far-out relation of yours, is she, pardon me for askin? A niece or something?

– Yes, far out about puts it, Fred. We've been pretty far out and now, well we'll just have to see.

– Aye, vera good, sir. I'll just be through in the front bar if you want to give me a shout. Here's health. Slàinte.

– Bottoms, as we say, up.

a haze of wine fumes

Amande heard a knock on the door through a haze of wine fumes.

– Va, go now, she said to the man with the hairy forearms who stood there.

The man waited a minute outside the closed door, then knocked again.

make it singles

– Port-and-lemon your usual poison?

– I havena drunk for ages, said Dinah.

– Well you've had a trying day.

– And now it's your day to try, is that it?

– I don't get you.

– Trying your hand.

There was a bit of a silence, a bit of swilling. Freddie hirpled over with the second round.

At half past eight, the door swung open and in strode Harry the lecturer. He looked at Dinah, and saw she was pretty flushed, saw Royston and gave him a wink.

Royston went up for another two drinks and stood next to

where Harry had perched on his corner stool.

    – How are the groves?

    – Again—? said the lecturer.

    – The groves – the ivory tower.

    – My ivory tower's still in good shape. Yours?

    – A piece of inside gen, maybe?

    – Sure, said Harry.

    – What you were saying, last time, remember. But a nurse, of course, would be pretty safe?

    – A nurse—? said Harry. A nurse!

    – Keep the decibels down.

    – Same again? said Freddie.

    – Make it singles, said Royston. And one for my friend.

feel school

– Richt, have ye done your share o the dishes?

    – No, Dad.

    – Well there's nae plays the nicht, then. Stories, sangs, plays, nithin.

    – It's for school.

    – I dinna care whether it's for primary school, Feel School or Harvard College. C'mon, your mother's tired, ye can surely see that. Far is she onywey?

    – Oot.

    – Oot? Was she dressed like?

    – She had her coat on.

    – She never said she was gaain oot.

    – *I'll just be a whilie* she said.

When she came back there was no sign of Andy, and Tammy was greetin in Hughie's arms. The Panther was gone from round the back of the house. *The Party, the Party* – she could see it far enough. Hughie could no more change a bairn's nappie than flee in the air. She spoke to Peem a bit about his play and sent him bedwards. Annie was coming down with a coupla spots – could be impetigo, might be nothing. It was half-past ten before Andy was in.

– Far on earth have ye been?

– I could ask the same, I thocht ye were awa wi that damned petition.

– Mrs Hird's taen that on.

– Well she's time on her hauns.

– I took the bus up tae see Ludwig. Ward 8.

– O, that was good o ye. Ye hardly ken him.

– I've met him afore. He was gey dozent wi the anaesthetic. I left him a pound o fudge.

– Fit like was he, did the doctor say?

– Better than maist folk that's just lost a haun. Aye, an far were you then?

– We were just plannin the *Worker* Bazaar.

– Plan as muckle as ye like, ye ken I winna join.

– Why nae?

– Ony country that has nuclear weapons is just a bunch o dopes, run by savages. That's Britain, America – Russia an aa—

– The Soviet Union needs tae defend itsel fae incomin missiles. It's a deterrent—

– O aye, nae doot France'll be needin it next. Madame Cami-knickers roon the corner is facin an unco set o missiles these days.

– Madge, this is nae like ye. Ye must be tired.

– Ach, leave me alane.

– Come here now—

They both won scrolled certificates, Iris and Peem, and Bapface got her play actually put on. *Lady Emily's Emeralds* was his title, set at a country dinner party where most folk were so awfully, awfully clever they could hold forth despite a large marble seemingly lodged in the cheek.

Everybody was hee-hawing and admiring her ladyship's emerald necklace and drowning out *Danse Macabre* on the gramophone. But, as the skeletons began to rattle, her handyman had rigged the gramophone arm to trip a circuit to douse the electroliers, so's he could nip in, nick the fantoosherie off her neck, and nobody none the wiser.

It was a complex piece, a bit light on character maybe. Green for greed, of course. Peem had squeezed all the electrical ins-and-outs of it from his Dad. But it had too many ab-dabs for amateurs the Children's Theatre thought.

Iris's was brilliant, it was about a spinster who went to France thirty years after the War to lay flowers on her dead fiancé's grave, only to find a Frenchwoman there too. They were angry at first, and then walked and walked. The two girls who played it on stage were a bit shy, but in the final scene in the café with the boy waiter and the boy accordionist, they began to enjoy themselves.

– Very well done, I'm so impressed, said Dame Flora Robson, stooping, whatna films she'd been in! Iris had to go and curtsey. Peem went up next, with his short breeks pressed and stockings straight-gartered. He just shook her hand. She had tired kind eyes.

When he came back to their front row seats, Mum on his left squeezed his arm. Mannie Martin tapped him on the shoulder, happy and red.

Andy had to rush off to the *Daily Worker* Bazaar.

– Nae bad, he said. Have tae dash.

He was running their money-spinner, the Wheel of Fortune.

Peem half-turned towards Iris on his right.

– Good. It was good! he whispered.

– Thanks, Peem.

liberty is the best of all things

So then the whole jingbang of them had a week snipping a theatre out of cartridge paper and cardboard, to take their minds off the 11+.

– This is borin, sir.

– Look we can put a real trap-door in there.

– It's only catboard, said Casey.

– I've got glue on my curtains, said Isobel.

– You girls, I want you to find the name of Flora Robson's play, if you're passing His Majesty's.

– We're never that far up the toon, said Isobel.

– Ask Miss Florence if ye want tae ken aboot fancy theatre— said Veronica. We just ging tae the pictures.

– Can I get money tae go to the theatre?

– I dinna think there's ony need for that. We've tryin tae save for the holidays.

He went up past anyway, on his bike.

He scanned the theatre billboard, *The Mousetrap*, Agatha Christie, and copied the cast. Future attraction *A Song for Scotland*, Robert Wilson and the White Heather Dancers.

– Peem!

He looked across the road at the massive statue. Below it, Bridget.

– O, hiya.

He wheeled his bike across the road and joined her.

– Ciamar a tha, mo dachaidh?

– I'm fine, Bridget. I won a certificate.

– I was hearing that.

The statue had its own traffic triangle, part-laid to grass, with conker trees. All on its own, its plinth pink granite. Above stood William Wallace stern and black, right hand covering his claymore hilt, left hand wide, outstretched and open. A yo-yo hung from his ring finger.

– It's fine to see you out on your own. You're a big boy getting.

– Why does he have a yellow yo-yo?

– What colour would you rather?

– Why a yo-yo?

– Students—

– Do they mean he'll come back?

– Charities Week.

– A yo-yo comes back.

– There is always hope.

The yo-yo blew gently at the end of its string.

– We never see you.

– Well your Uncle Hugh – ach, you know.

– Look at that inscription!

– It's fine too. Copy it, I would.

– Are you waiting for someone?

– O, surely – guess! Tell him I'm cold with waiting, and I'm off for a wee suspicion. Just tea. Can I get you something?

He knew it was far too cold to ask for ice cream.

– No, I'm okay, just eaten.

He began writing, using the back page.

> *When I was a youth, and under the care of my uncle, all*
> *that I could carry away from him was a single proverb,*
> *but it seemed to me above all price, and I never forgot it.*

It was this: 'I tell you a truth, Liberty is the best of all things. My son, never live under any slavish bond.'

Over his eyes from behind, he felt strong hands.

– Uncle Hugh—! Bridget was here.

– Aye, she's a one for the national heroes, Bridget. Though I'm feart I'm nae ane o them at the moment. Bum's oot the winda—

– Well ye're late—

– A bit. I was oot West, deliverin fags.

– The way they've put him, Wallace is facin about south-east, isn't he?

– The doonfa o many, Bridget would say.

– It says *Liberty is the best of all things.* Is that true?

– Could be— Aye, I fairly think so.

A student with enormous tits and a red wig came rattling towards them.

– Pitapennyinmatinny!

Bob Clunie was crossing the road to meet them.

– Aye, aye, Hughie, good tae see ye.

– Students, eh? said Uncle Hugh.

– Bloody students, said Bob. Drove the trams in Aiberdeen tae brak the General Strike.

– That wisna very bright, said Uncle Hugh.

– Neither bright nor helpful, said Bob. Ma faither threw cassies through the tram windas, till the cops baton-charged them doon Correction Wynd.

– Good for him, said Uncle Hugh. Far's that Bridget o mine flitted, Peem?

– The Fountain.

– Bad mood?

– Said she's havin a wee suspicion.

– I'll awa then and leave ye till't, said Bob Clunie. It was good seein ye.

june

titles were always open

The 11+ test was coming up fast. It was back to the grind, back to Intelligence Tests. Like when Peem chanced a note to Tarry.

Dear Tarry, Twat, dick, fanny, fud, which is the Odd Man Out?
Dear Stupid, Dick.

Sums, too, till they were coming out their ears. And composition till it became rote.

Composition titles were always open – *The Outing, A Day in the Life of a Grey Stocking, Lost in the Hills*, or some such. So open you could shuffle along from year to year with the same basic plot.

Say an outing with Dad on high Lochnagar, getting dismayed by driving cloud, all sorts of starts and stumbles, deer appearing – and sudden grouse. Then mist to lift and sun to set in time for the *Tired but happy* – school stockings changed to a rich peaty brown.

Nine out of ten.

under isobel's desk

The big day dawned. The 11+ was held in their own classroom.

Spermy left home but didn't arrive at school.

A puddle gathered under Isobel's desk.

The required title was *My Toybox* or *Someone Less Fortunate*.

Then they had Parents Night and Mannie Martin spoke to his Dad, Mum having stayed behind for an early bed.

– Where are you thinking of putting him when he leaves here?

– Gordon's College, if he passes his 11+.

– He'll pass alright. I was wondering if Eton, maybe, he could try for a place down there?

– He'll work away fine in Aberdeen. We couldna be daein wi that sort o thing.

– No, no, a scholarship—

What consummation to send a pupil there, confirm his boozing mere genius scorned.

Andy Endrie just looked at him.

florence of arabia

Everything just fell into place, the 11+ came and went, although the results were kept stewing in some office for weeks on end. And while everybody waited to be branded, though most wanted no further than Frederick Street School that looked like Colditz with extra wire, still Mannie Martin got everybody to work together for the last time.

– What shall we make?

– Spaceship, sir.

– Buckingham Palace.

– A boat.

A real smarter of a boat, a steam trawler made out of strips of paper and floury paste, layer upon layer, then painted, Spermy insisted, the round bottom with a kind of red lead, the rest of her some colours, some livery they just made up. It took the best part of a couple of days.

– And what will we call her?

– *Titanic.*

– *The Lady Urquhart.*

– Miss Florence, sir.

And in she came, bringing some note from Mr Bain, the Infants always went home early.

Then everybody chorused *Queen Florence, Florentina,* Sir, sir, *Florence of Arabia*.

She laughed, a tinkly pleased-enough laugh. And poor Mannie Martin got a beamer, Peem knew he'd have sailed away with her any day, and never come back.

So they fixed a plan between them, the next day being Saturday, they'd all get up to the Westburn Park and sail *Queen Florence* round the pond, round and round to let everybody have a shot of their handiwork. But only if Miss Florence would come and give her a proper launch, like at Hall Russell's.

And she laughed again, said she had an appointment, but just might be passing on her scooter. So Mannie said he'd buy fizzy ale for everybody, and they all clamoured.

– I'm comin, sir, what time?

Going home that night, Peem scuffed a chuckie along the pavement, he wasn't himself. He had wanted to say *Fleur-de-lys* after the fancy spikeheads on the big green railings round the school. But he didn't often shout and was jealous now, he wanted Mannie all to himself, or, better, Miss Florence all to himself, that was the way of this 11+ test, you got on and did things fine on your own, he found it ill to share after all the sweat he'd putten in.

Well he wasn't himself right enough, and next morning he was up with a fever, O maybe not so bad as the scarlet one lang syne, yet *het enough tae fry eggs on*, his Mum said.

He lay there in a lather all Saturday. At one point his mother put her head round the door and said, Guess? We've a nurse in the hoose!

– So—?

—It's that Dinah, mind, her that saw tae yir broken heid?

– I dinna want tae see ony Dinahs. Keep her awa.

– It's okay, she's nae workin. Me an your Dad are just havin a

140

blether wi her, ower a cuppa tea.

– How mony *Workers* did he land up sellin?

– Her mither was in the WRENS wi me in Cornwall, fifteen years ago, just fancy.

– Ony juice—?

– Amazin.

When his mother closed the door for the second time, leaving him a cool glass of barley water, he felt under his pillow. He pulled out the sea-smoothed stone, small and blue as a wheatear's empty egg. And peered through it.

Wheatear was posh for *whitearse*, Tarry had told him.

He saw faded wallpaper, then unsteady images – something yawing wreathed in smoke.

auld loveletters

It wasn't till the Monday, and him still not back at school, that Mannie Martin sent round a deputation. Spermy wasn't among them, there was still that stand-off.

– Here's twa o them to see ye, said Mum, chapping on the bedroom door. And before he could think who, in came Tarry and Iris bearing between them none other than *Queen Florence*, O a bittie damp sure enough, and her funnel raked all to the one side, but a bit of school right here in his own bedroom.

– What happened tae her?

Iris spoke.

– Mr Martin didn't know if ye'd be back, Peemie, and it's our last week comin on. We all got ice cream from Miss Florence and everybody got Iron Brew from Mr Martin.

– Ye should have been there, ye missed yersel, said Tarry.

– But that black hole in the bottom o her—?

Tarry creased, then repositioned his glasses with a strong twitch of his nose.

– Well, we soon got fed-up puddlin, so we put her in the burn, but there wasna enough water this time o year. So back to the pondie we trailed an Mannie Martin says *Has onybuddy got ony paper handy, bubblegum paper, or auld·loveletters?*

– He looked right at Miss Florence when he said that, said Iris.

– And we ryped our pooches for paper and dirt, an Mannie Martin built a pyre he caad it, deep in the hold o the boat. Syne struck a spunk till her and poked her oot in the mids o the pond wi a great lang stick—

– Miss Florence had to go then. She had an appointment.

– Smokin like billie-o—

– Then fit?

– Fit dae ye think ye glaikit gommeril? Just lay on her side an sizzlit an sank, fit a fuckin laugh, sorry Iris. We wadit for her.

Peem held the charred soggy vessel in two hands.

– And dae ye ken what Mannie Martin said then? said Iris. She was a bit raised, by her standards. Dae ye ken what he said?

– Nuh—

– *Story o ma life, story o ma life. Fire was oot afore it could get a richt haud.*

maybe a blockage that time will free

Madge woke at night, most nights, every night. She checked that Andy still lay beside her, or got up for a cup of water, walked the lino, curled in the rexine chair, or dozed. There was something there. She minded what the doctor had said.

– It could be constipation, Mrs Endrie. No? Maybe a blockage that time will free. Have you tried a hot water bottle? Yes? That's good. A hot water bottle will help to free it, give it every chance. And an Anadin, of course, a couple of Anadin even, before retiring. Come back and see me in a couple of months if it shows no better.

plenty scope

Mr Martin walked up King Street after school. He walked past the Saltoun Arms and The Gordon Bar. He hesitated at the Royal Oak, but he had been in just last week. He turned right along Union Street, there was plenty scope there.

Peem saw him and waved. But Mr Martin was scanning the near horizon, and didn't see him.

Mum and he were on their way to the Loch Street Co-op to spend their twice-yearly dividend at the three-storey draper.

The Co-opy draper had a pneumatic brass pipe-system for sending cash and receipts in slim brass cylinders with felt collars. The assistant popped your stuff in the cylinder, rotated it shut, popped the cylinder in the up-tube, closed the brass latch, *Whop,* and off it whoomed—

All the money was handled in a higher office, with clothes being expensive. A decent interval for calculation, then you heard it whooming back, tumbling into a basket on its fat felt ends.

The Co-opy had a customer lift with telescopic mesh-gates that closed behind you. Up you went at the press of a button, as smooth as anything.

He was needing a summer shirt from downstairs and – good – his mother a new white blouse from the top floor.

the new opium

It was Mum that spotted the mamba first, one night, a black mamba under her bed. A mamba!

It made its living, probably, from the mice that skittered across the lino, like refugees on an ice rink. There must have been a hole in the skirting, or maybe in below the sink where Singy Bridge scrubbed and flannelled Annie bare-naked before the window.

Annie would cover herself if Paterson hove in view from the backie, trauchlin in with a bleached sheet in her basket, or sticks and Shilbottle in her pail.

But she was worried now.

– Is it safe, Bridget?

– What, Annie—?

– Safe up here from The Mamba?

– Horo, you'll not be catching a mamba in soap and water.

– Else they wouldna be sae black! said Peem.

But it was no wonder, the whole thing, the family was scared stiff about snakes. When they went near the hills, they went expecting to be bitten, with a rowan staff in one hand like a Druid, and a vial of permanganate of potash in the other, to purpify the puncture and counter the poison.

Because there were a lot of adders. Peem had pointed to a scrub of bracken once and asked Cousin Archie *How mony eddirs would be in there?*

A dizzen, easy.

That previous Sunday, the *Sunday Post* had news of an eagle fighting with an adder. Peem saw the eagle picking up the black snake by its middle. It was like lodging a liquorice lace over your upper lip to say *Hoo Flung Dung*, taking the mick out of the Chinkies. Not that there were any Chinese in Aberdeen. Only for the black viper to twist and insert its fangs in mid-air, so that both crashed to the heather.

That was the *Post's* story. A stag couldn't prong salmon at Inverpolly, nor albino stoat kill lamb on Sgurr of Eigg, but the *Post* would get chapter and verse from one of the stringers they kept across the Highlands.

– It's the new gospel, the *Sunday Post*, said Dad to Jehovah Morrison they shared the lavvy with.

144

– What?

– Aye, the new opium, it has to be. More than seventy per cent of Scottish folk are absorbing it every Sunday.

There were a lot of opiates, right enough.

Jehovah Morrison raged at that. They were out in the brown lobby. Peem lugged in behind the banister, there were furious words he'd have to look up. *Unutterable* and *balderdash* were easy, he'd heard them plenty. But *apocalyptic*? *Catechism*? Or was it *cataclysm* he'd heard Jehovah say?

A *cataclysm* could be an accident that happened to your pussy. Maybe a sea otter malagaroused it, round the back of the fish shop in Ullapool.

Thus it was no wonder Mum dreamed about mambas, she'd have dreamed about anacondas if there had been space in the bed-recess in the kitchen living room. Because after Peemie and Annie were packed off to the bedroom parlour, and Hughie to the box bedroom, that was where she and Dad had to bed down, at least they'd the last of the coal fire as they undressed to cheer them. And maybe they were right loving, Peem guessed, after he found Durex, an unopened packet of three, in Dad's old trousers when he was raking for a hankie.

– What's Durex? It's nae in the dictionary.
– Teeps, said Tarry.
– Oh. Okay.

– What's teeps?
– Ask ma mither, said Spermy. She's got a jumbo box.

Iris would know he imagined, she knew some about love. He couldn't imagine asking her though.

Peem minded when they camped about three years earlier. They were up past Braemar on the wrong side of the river, with Annie in the canvas rucsac on Dad's back. It was a bonny day of sun, when they came on a skinnymalinky adder warming its blood on the path. Dad raised his rowan rod and belaboured it, as Annie went *boing-boing-boing* up and down in the rucsac till she was nigh-on sick. But Peemie saw the adder slink away.

Another time, they were blaeberrying up the Quoich, and an adder amongst the small fruit was sent fleeting by Hughie with the beginnings of a sore head.

And he read aboot kraits and cottonmouths and was right glad he didn't dwell in a hot country. Plus sea snakes.

– Peemie, what's a black mamba, I thought there was only green mambas?

And Peemie had answered faithfully.

– Na, Mum, there's baith kinds, only the green mambas live up in the jungle, but the black mambas live on the grund and they chase ye—

– O no, that's ma same dream, there's a mamba under ma bed!

– Well dinna put your hand under if ye lose your slippers because it'll bite ye, it will Mum!

It was good doing vocabulary with Mum, they had to make up myths and stories to vivify the lists. Like when he was seven his homework had words accidentally next to each other like *rude pudding* and *terror plunged*.

Only this time she was taken with the Mamba, and it bade in the house for weeks.

a hole in the base

They were out with the *Workers* again, trying to keep the half-quire dry between the showers.

– Watch this hoose, there's a feel wifie. *Feel* didn't just mean foolish, it was stronger than that.

When they got up to the middle landing, there was a row of about nine green and clear bottles, beside her prickly mat.

When they were coming down again, she opened the door.

– Keep going, said his Dad.

She smiled at them, she was in her dressing gown.

– What can a person do with so much empty bottle?

They stopped and tried not to look at the swoop of her wrapper.

– Ye could aye mak lamps, said his Dad. Bedside lamps are aa the rage.

– La rage, rabies, you make fun of me.

– Na, na, fit's the first o your name again—?

– Amande.

– Na, na, Amande. I mean they're affa popular. A hand-painted bedside lamp goes doon a bomb.

– Down a bomb, pouf! For me, I know no electrique.

– Och, come roon tae the shed sometime – I'll show ye how tae safe-drill a hole in the base o a bottle, tae tak a flex.

– Dad, are ye really goin tae help her? That's Mandy, that's Spermy's Ma—

– Well, sure, if she comes roon, like. But I canna really see her botherin her erse.

It was lashing again when they got outside.

It came the last days of Primary and he had strengthened a bit since the sudden fever.

Dad said to him one Friday, Let's awa tae the hills the morn.

It was the peak of the hoeing season. Besides which they'd taken on Ludwig's allotment, a bit of a pest, to bring on his peas and brassicas till he recovered. But with that much rain, the plots were too sodden to work.

– Let's hae a look and see if we canna climb Mount Keen.

Annie was fey for climbing hills, she'd as soon colour her lips with cloudberries, or sit and talk cross-legged to a puddock, till it hopped away.

Mum couldn't come either, not with Tammy so young, and not feeling so great these days, though she liked the hills fine and Dad told at breakfast how she'd once hiked bravely, down off Braeriach in a sudden storm.

But first she'd sat for ages in the soft air at the top, the roof of Scotland, she minded, soothing her bunion in the cold source of the Dee. Her commando boots unbending, thrown to the side. And as she'd gazed across to Angel's Peak, with its corrie lochan green like a northern eye, she'd sensed wee dotterels run in about her, with their warm chestnut breasts. *Wit-e-wee, wit-e-wee, wit-e-wee.*

An t-amadan montich Bridget called them, *mountain fools*, there were worse things to be.

But Mum was in distress now, there had been a red unnameable thing at the bottom of the toilet, and she seemed glad to bide.

– One thing though, will ye look oot for *wit-e-wees* for me? she asked Peem. *Wit-e-wee, wit-e-wee*—

– Aye, Mum.

They got a fair way up, puffing and peching in the heat, and Dad said, Peemie, fit dae ye ken aboot the birds an the bees?

And Peem kent mair aboot golf balls an snakes.

– Fit, Dad?

– Well, ye're eleven noo.

– Nearly twelve.

– Okay. Well, ye've seen Annie in her bath, haven't ye, an ye ken ye're baith different?

Bath. It was hardly the fine bath-with-soapy-bubbles Cousin Archie got.

– Aye, Dad.

– And dae ye ken why ye're different?

– Sort o. Having hired Haze for her lock-ups display he was none the wiser.

– Well, it's aa aboot babies, isn't it? When they get married the mannie puts his *mannie* into the wifie's *wifie*, and that's how they hae a bairn, because his seed meets up wi her egg and, as soon as they get on, the baby starts tae grow, just like rhubarb at the plot.

Peem kept looking at the bare heather.

– And nine months later oot comes a fine wee baba, just like you and Annie when ye were wee, and that's aa there is till it.

Peem digested this.

– A sandwich—?

It was hot and close, even though they'd open shirts and khakis on, bare legs and dubbiny boots. They topped out on Mount Keen, gazed at their old pal, Lochnagar, and dropped on the other side.

A bittie tired, the first walk of the season, but swinging downhill quite swack-like to the loch below, when Peem glanced across.

Dad's boot was passing above a fat black coil. A shout now could kill—

It was still dozened, only out for the bonny day like themselves. But Peem gathered stones *like David's apprentice*, Dad said, and they battered the adder, three foot three when you poked at it cannily and streiked it all out.

– Let's tak it hame to show Mum, said Peem, when the dust settled. They used the V on the rowan stick to flip it zigzag into a billy-can. Last of all its black diamond head. Dad clanked on the lid. Peem wiped Dad's staff on the short heather.

Hunkered beside each other, they looked around, with the strange stupefaction of killers. Over Lochnagar rose an anvil of cloud.

– Better be gettin a wiggle on, said Dad, and Peem looked across at him and laughed.

– *Wiggle on*—

Five minutes later, a fang of rain came plash on his open neck.

They huddled under the camouflage gas cape, and let it spatter off.

– How long will it last, Dad?

– A whilie.

– This gascape's affa smelly. Has it still got gas?

– Uh-huh—

– Has it though?

– Sorry, I was thinkin o somethin else.

– Dae ye ken Ludwig's gettin fitted up for a hook?

– Is he? How will he haud a spoon?

– Jist hae tae howk an aipple up for his puddin.

– Dad, thunder's a lot nearer.

The echo blundered through the soft walls of the Mounth.

– Aye, well. Sit in aboot.

150

It was good, his Dad almost giving him a cuddle. The adder's billy-can outside their cape, pinging in the rain.

– I tellt ye aboot the *Scharnhorst*?

– Nuh.

– Shelterin in aboot Brest—

– Breast?

– Hitler wanted them back to the Baltic: we were happy pennin her up. And the *Gneisenau* of course. We used Beaufighters, Bristol Beaufighters, I was groundcrew, lookin eftir the new radar—

A garish flash came through the gascape.

ye're nae a mother

Even near the coast the heat was gathering. Amande was muttering.

– Carry me in a couple of bottles, it's so hot weather, she asked Dinah.

Then Dinah went out to work the weekend shift, and Amande locked herself in.

Spermy had been out a stravaig round the docks and came up the stair to find the door locked against him. He knocked and knocked. She'd be zonked out snoring across the bed.

The Council had spread fresh chuckies on Rosin Road. The old tar bubbled like black putty, impressed by traffic and thumb. Spermy picked up a handful of loose, and went back into Urquhart Parade.

His first fling didn't work, but then reinforcements, Tarry and Raymie, arrived. A flak of chuckies from three hands was soon splattering at Amande's window.

The sash jerked up.

– Dinna frappe when I'm fuck and sleeping, petit bastard!

– I'm nae a bastard.

– O, you are bastard, Jed. Pure bastard—

And she slung out a bottle, a green bottle – then another – to explode on the cobbles. Glass sheared at their ankles. They danced clear.

– I'm gettin the police tae ye, ya cunt! shouted Spermy. Ye're nae a mother.

aa I can see is a thoosand dots

– Well ae day—

– It's gettin heavier—

– Well ae nicht actually, one of oor Beaufighters was arrivin on station abeen Brest, when the navigator got a richt shock. *Radar's on the blink*, he says to the pilot. *The blink?* says the pilot. *On the blink*, says the navigator. *Aa I can see is a thoosand dots*.

– Were they fae Aiberdeen? said Peem.

– No, they were Canadians, it was a lot o Canadians this squadron. *Waal*, says the navigator. *All Ah can see on ma screen, baby, is a thousand dots*.

– *Dots*! says the pilot. *Waal dog my cats*.

– Dad, just tell it ordinary.

– *Well*, says the pilot, *that's a scunner an a hauf. We'd better flee hyne awa back tae England, we're as much use here as a brass banana*.

– Dad, ye're spoilin it. Is it just another ghoster?

– So they flew straicht back, and Sergeant Andrew Endrie came oot ontae the runway tae check their radar.

– That was you—

– Me, indeed, an nithin wrang wi it. Just like the Hieland mannie fan the Yankee wifie asked him *Hector, can you reveal – is there anything worn under the kilt?* And the Hielan mannie said *Very kind of you to be asking, Dolores. It's aal in perfect working order*.

– Dad, tell me true.

By the time the Beaufighter had got back, *Scharnhorst* and *Gneisenau* had broken out, unspotted, unannounced, and were halfway up the English Channel.

To be fair, the thousand dots had been an exaggeration. Four hundred though, four hundred Messerschmitt 109s and 110s, a dark umbrella.

Pursued by lumbering Swordfish far too late, the big ships made it north to Kiel.

– Wow. Is that in the history books?

  – Some o it.

  – Why just some?

  – There was a cover-up, there aye is—

  – Did Churchill cover it?

  – Churchill? No, he would have liked tae court-martial the Canadians as cowardy custards, *for desertion in the face of the enemy*. But fan they came tae double an treble-check the radar, O it was faulty richt enough—

  – How?

  – Somebody wi a wee screwdriver made damn sure o that!

  – Did the high heid-yins ever find ye oot, Dad?

  – Nae chance o that! See top brass? Wouldna ken a cross-wired rheostat fae a poke in the een wi a wire poppy.

They had to break from cover, and pleiter down the brae, the glens still smothered.

What would Spermy think now – an adder? Some game. Probably say *Nae a patch on the Loch Ness monster* or *Fit ye goin tae dae, sell it for sausages?*

What a skirl Mum gave out. The snake was jiggling on a flattened *Worker*.

– Tak it awa, it's gonna bite me! Coorse devils ye, tak it awa, it's stinkin. Fling it in the boddom o the bucket, this minute!

The billycan clanked as he stepped out into the lobby, nearly ramming into Miss McMorency, as she came back from the evening service, with her long face.

Behind him the storm continued.

– Andy, that's sheer vratchery, I'm surprised at ye—

But Peem wasn't putting his good adder out in the bucket, not till he'd flegged Raymie, Tarry and a fair few more. Haze! He'd soon pay her back for peeing and running off. Say he'd a big secret and charge her a shilling.

He gave a loud rap at Spermy's door.

– Is Haze in jist noo?

– Doesna bide here.

– Is your Ma in?

– Nuh.

– Naebody?

– Nuh. Dinah's at the hospital, and ma mither's in the jail.

july

with their respective tools in hand

Before school ended Mannie Martin was redder in the face than ever, and off oftener than a pint of old milk. Spermy said he'd heard a clunk from the drawer when Mannie'd reached into his desk for the scud for him, and Iris said she heard glug from his prickly brown jacket when he was enthusing over a new play that was out, *Look Back in Anger* or something. But it was Peemie that got the worst proof, that first night in July.

After weeks of pleading he was allowed into the night pavement brigade, Frankie Groat being on holiday to Banff. Preparations began before dark.

Out in the shed, Dad and Tam Clunie were adjusting the consistency of whitewash, and reducing the *Daily Worker* to a set of slogans. These they capitalled onto foolscap which was placed, rolled, in Tam Clunie's pocket. Tam had fought the fascists and their comforters, in Spain. Dad, being younger, portered the whitewash and brush, inside a soft-handled plumber's sack.

The two men wore check bonnets, a kind of Lowland tartan, pulled to the left, and low. Peem, in his soft leather flying helmet, was to keep watch.

– Pull yir flaps doon.

– Why?

– Naebody'll recognise ye.

The helmet was still a bit stiff where his blood had dried.

They walked Urquhart, King Street, Mealmarket and Littlejohn Street, down then up Schoolhill, and curved into Union Terrace, past massive Wallace and doucer Burns, with their respective tools in hand, claymore and daisy.

Pubs had bellowed *Last Orders* ages ago. The last frizzlers had been rousted out of the fishfryers. All tall trams had swayed to their terminus.

They emerged onto Union Bridge, dark and wrought. It was a broad affair, straddling high above the sets of rails that flowed through Aberdeen from north, west and south. It had a dozen metal lions about the size of half-starved cats perched on the top of the bridge railings. He wondered what Theo would make of them. Did Theo and Marcie ever come out whitewashing?

– What way do they call it Union Bridge? said Peem.

– Ye have tae be in a trade union, tae cross it, like, said Tam.

Black Edward VII was sitting on an broad throne: he had a cannonball cupped in his left hand, a cannonball with a Cross.

Tam took the tin of whitewash out of his sack.

– What did Edward VII do? said Peem.

– As little as possible, like aa the rest o them, said Tam. He took a penny out and unlidded the whitewash.

To the left of black Edward there was a black woman planting her foot on a sword, curving it against her sandal. A black boy angel was attending, with wings like a swan from the Duthie Park. It probably must mean something.

– Will they mak a statue for you ever, Dad?

Dad was suppling the bristles of the three-inch brush against his thigh.

– Mmm-hih.

– Will they?

– Na.

He was concentrating, to block a one foot letter—

H

To block a second white letter, then another—

HANDS

Slogan, Bridget had said. From the Gaelic.

– Hands off Sue—?

– Peem, we ken ye can read, keep yir een peeled—

HANDS OFF SUEZ

– Look tae the wastard!

He did for a while. Nothing out west—

END MAU-MAU

His Dad was bent over, daubing, standing back, approving, bending again. He was gradually sidestepping towards Jamieson the Jeweller at the eastern end of the Brig—

MURDER SUPPORT UK SEA

They felt a wee gust. Tam Clunie was looking eastward, towards the police station at Lodge Walk.

– Hae ye muckle eneuch whitewash, Andy?

– Think so. Dinna want tae cut the slogans doon.

– Good.

For they knew in their heart their slogans, if the rain held off through the night, could clarify things for weary geezers trundling home from the night shift, or taking the early tram.

Peem zipped his jerkin to the collar. Watch, you always got to watch, it was boring.

– Dae ye want a haun? said Tam.

– Na, ye're okay. Tak a dander an keep your circulation going.

HANDS OFF SUEZ END MAU-MAU MURDER SUPPORT UK SEAMEN GET TORIES OUT GET HOUSES UP DEFE—

Suddenly Tam gave a low whistle.

Lidding the whitewash, Dad packed up, and set off two steps down at a time down into the Gardens, to stash their kit under a bush. Tam hirpled off towards the docks. Peem scampered west as decoy, then doubled hard back through Golden Square.

Huffing round into Diamond Place, he bumped into a guy.

– O!

– Schcuse me—

– Hey, sorry, is that you Mr Martin? Are ye okay?

– Schalright. He tilted a bottle of Red Ruby. He hadn't recognised Peem, not with collar high and the lug-flaps down.

– Sir, have tae dash, I'm in an affa— awful hurry.

– Schir? O, choo, Endrie.

– Sir, it's okay, have to dash, they're after me.

– Yesh, think they're after me too.

– We've been sloganing the streets, Union Brig.

He wasn't sure why he was telling this.

– Schloganing the streets, eh?

– I'm a Communist.

He was sure.

– Schplendid! The moving finger—

– Sorry, sir?

– The moving finger, Endrie, having writ, moved on. *Rubytwat of Omar Khayyam* – schould read it.

The laugh staggered him back against the wall, left leg folding, smashing his wine.

– You're not – are you cut, sir?

– Only half. Bloody cheap winesh.

– He unfolded a white, ironed square and offered it to his mentor.

– Sir, got to— See you.

You didn't say *See you* to a usual teacher.

As Peem ran towards His Majesty's, he heard a police whistle go from down in the Gardens. Another whistle ahead, along by the Art Gallery.

So he ducked between the chestnut tree and the granite base

of the Wallace statue. Not that much shelter. It might be possible to climb the plinth, find nicks and bosses, though a fool could spot the crux would come five blocks up.

He heard a whistle close at hand, and set off, stepping up the easy bits till he stood tight under the great man's shadow. He was lithe enough, *swack enough,* as his Dad would say, till he reached the crux. He edged to the right, but found himself under an overhang. His fingers were no way strong enough to hook himself up. He retreated and edged to the left, but was stymied there by an awkward gap. He minded the commando advice from Uncle Hugh. *Aye hae at least twa points o contact, but best hae three.*

A crack above gave little hope. But he reached up and inserted his right palm endways and clenched it into a jammed fist. He raised his left leg up, and hauling down on that fist, raised his left hand too. But his left hand waved like a vane. He had to retreat again, left hand and foot, his right fist beginning to burn as though in molten lead.

Two bobbies came at a bobbing run along Union Terrace.

He inserted the left palm this time, to make the fist, found a temporary niche for the left foot and, committing everything, swung his right foot high, till it soled against the rough sloped mass. Depending on these two points, left hand, right foot, he braced, he tautened – became girderish for a moment – and threw his right hand high to clinch a ledge.

He wanted to yell, he wanted Wallace to notice, to head-pat him. One more heave. He was up.

The bobbies were on their own. He wondered if they'd caught his Dad and shoved him in the Black Maria.

He moved round in behind Wallace's plaid and pressed himself tight there, behind his bossed shield.

They stopped for a breather right below him.

– Commies, eh, slippery kind o lads.

– Ach well. The Shirra would only gie them a £5 fine, fourteen days as an option.

– Aye, but if we canna catch twa men an a hauflin loon, fit would we dae if the Russkies came?

So his Dad was still free.

– Is there word o that?

– A million men wi snaa on their boots.

– Nae muckle snaa if Khrushchev sends ower his bombers first.

– True. Sooner we get that big radar clapped on Mormond Hill, sooner folk'll sleep easy in their beds.

– Are ye nae sleepin just noo, like? Is Jeannie aye pittan her haun across?

– Aye, likely. William Wallace, eh, I wonder fit he's thinkin aboot it aa.

– Well he'll be thinkin aboot it in fower different places—

– Fit wey?

– Cause eftir they pit him on the rack, an howkit ees guts oot in front o his een, they quartered him.

Peem cradled his bruised right hand.

– That's the story, eh, I never kent that. I hope we got wir quarter in Aiberdeen—?

– Couldna say, I'm sure—

– Wait an I'll see. *On 23rd August 1305. this GREAT HERO*, in capitals mind you, *was led to Smithfield and, with Edward as an Eye-Witness was there put to death, solely for his love of liberty, his effectual resistance of aggression, and his fidelity to his native land.* There ye go, nae a word aboot whaur they divvied his body tae.

– Suppose Edinburgh got their quarter – ye ken them.

– He must hae deen something else.

– Fit dae ye mean?

– Apairt fae lovin liberty.

– We aa love liberty.

– That's why ye mairried Jeannie, eftir aa.

– O, nae that pishin rain on again!

– Aye, let's beat it. The Commies'll aa be hame noo suppin cocoa.

If he tried to climb down, his gymmies would have no purchase on wet stone. If he fell, his skull would crack, or worse. They would probably stoop over him on the pavement and make wondering noises. *Nae mair chance fae that heicht than a doo's egg.*

And, if he waited till dawn, they'd spot him, point, and send the Fire Brigade. He'd be all over the papers.

So he checked the leafy bough – below and a decent spring away – of the big conker.

drunk and fairly orderly

In that night's paper Alex Martin (42), 38 Donfield Place, primary teacher, was lifted. Drunk and disorderly. He was actually drunk and fairly orderly, thought Peem. Apart from the smashed Red Ruby, and that was an accident.

They had Inkster again for the last couple of days, and that was Primary over.

the fall of france

Spermy had disappeared, *Off to the Broch* somebody said. *Run awa to sea* scoffed others. *Run awa fae himsel, mairlike*, was another opinion. *Fancy gettin the police tae yir ain mither.*

She'd come up in court on breach of the peace, but the whole thing got out of hand.

Amande refused to speak a word of English.

– She's French— said the defence to the sheriff. She'll need an interpreter.

– How long has she been domiciled in Scotland?

– Sixteen years. She came over at the Fall of France, with her brother, a fighter pilot. She was 14 then.

– And you tell me she speaks no word of English, pas un mot?

– Sorry?

– Not one word?

– She's in shock, depressed, a lot has happened.

– Very well. Since the Court has no immediate recourse to translators, I give you leave to instruct a teacher from some local school or college to attend. The fee will be a matter for yourself, but they are available. Our pedagogues are ever on vacation.

holiday

snaffle that trojan

Mum naturally wasn't going to come on their annual holiday. She was still pretty grim at times, and Peem had seen her hold herself plenty, and once found her greeting in Dad's arms.

– It's high time ye went tae the doctor, Madge dear.

– O, I've been tae the doctor.

– Weil – mebbe time ye went back again, then.

Most years usually they went camping by bus. It was simply a matter of fetching the impedimenta down from the loft, the ridge tent in its burlap hammock, the socketed ridge, the screwtogether poles, the alkathene groundsheet, pegbag, guybag and mallet—*far's that mallet?* – the latrine tent and the trenching tool; the REME bivvy, an olive-green army store tent where Uncle Hugh could drop by and sleep; three full-size and two half-size inflatable LiLos, one double and four sizes of single sleeping bag, an axe, a saw, a basin, a pail, the Primus, the little Primus, paraffin, meths – *see if there's a suppie meths fae last year* – plus the kettle, three saucepans, the frying pan; walking boots, gymmies, wellingtons, anoraks – *maps!* – toothbrushes, toothpaste, Steradent, soap, flannels, midge cream, TCP, scissors, Elastoplast; cricket bat, tennis rackets, the red rubber quoit, trout rod; oatmeal, jerseys and Creamola Foam.

You got the best water in the world up Deeside, it made Creamola Foam taste great.

They would ferry it down to Urquhart Parade bus stop and onto the Number 21 doubledecker, and stick it under the stair behind the chromium rail, the conductor grumphing or giving a hand. Or rather on three buses. For the space under bus stairs, designed for a collapsible pram or half-set of golf clubs, found it ill to accommodate three tents, four rucsacs, eight (8) lumpy kitbags, plus one string bag of final essentials.

Thus the expeditionary force, debouching on to Union Street in waves, the vanguard would have to cover their kit by the expedient of sitting on it, while waiting reinforcements to arrive. They would gaze across the street at the Majestic, where Phileas Fogg ballooned around the globe twice nightly, with a matinée on Saturday afternoon.

At last would come the rearguard. Taunts about armchairs. Reminders about sinks.

The total boot of the red Braemar coach would be commandeered – and off to the highlands they would go. *Far we gaain this year?* Dad would say. *Are we Deesided?*

Strange – hardly any families went camping, what with B&B in Rothesay, what with Blackpool.

It would be too much for Mother, though, this year, the pleadings had subsided, a sort of glumness had set in. Without Mum it wouldn't be so good and a lot more jobs, though you wouldn't have to shoosh for Tammy all evening.

– I've had a brainwave.

– Aye, Andy, an fit'll that be?

– No, listen Madge. I'll get the auld works van, the Trojan.

– They'll charge ye the earth.

– Just for the twa weekends, the various fitters only use it through the week, tae cairt their stuff.

– Twa sevenths o the earth, then.

– Na, na, dinna worry. Mountie was caught on a homer last week, a big homer, a set o lathe-turned banisters for his Bieldside villa.

Mr Mount was the Scottish Fertile foreman, bully and creep rolled into one.

When homer nods, he'd never worked that one out till now, when Mannie Martin said that, what it meant.

– And on tap o that, Mr Hall's been tryin to hing in wi the workers this last while. Tryin tae wheedle the Time-and-Motion boys back in, sook up tae his Scottish Fertile bosses in Leith, please their IPI bosses in London. We'll easy snaffle that Trojan if we pey the diesel.

– Surely Time-and-Motion widna show face, nae eftir Ludwig—

– Ye'd like tae think so.

The Trojan was a basic upright van with a snub nose and a wooden floor, top speed about 39, off the side of a cliff maybe. Mum could sit in state up front, the kids could jam in the loaded belly.

a bag of cherry lips

They even managed to wedge in four bikes. They headed away from the sea.

Broom and ling soon sweet in their nostrils, they lay cramped on their sides and watched the low country unreel behind them through two square windows: *corn, hay, hawthorn, pine*, and at some open bends saw a twinkle of Dee. Higher ground rose on both sides the strath.

They shouted hard for ice cream at Ballater, but the driver took the by-pass, the Pass of Ballater, he was all for pressing on to the camp.

So they tumbled out, *stiff but happy,* at Coilacreich just past three o'clock.

Mum sat on a canvas stool and changed wee Tammy, who'd lulled and shat – *the wee mite* – while menfolk pitched the heavy tent, smelling of last year, green with Kanvo. Annie went off with a bag of Cherry Lips to trade blue flowers from the fairies. When the last peg was malleted in, Peem dived into the silver birch, looking for cricket stumps.

– C'mon, shouted father. We're needin the flysheet fixed first.
Annie came back with three bold purple orchids.
– Bonny, aye, said mother. Bonny. I hope they'll live—
– Grub up! shouted Dad.
Tea was bangers and mash, and plasticy tea.

On Sunday Dad drove the Trojan back to Aberdeen, then Panthered the fifty miles back out.

what's a subject?

On Monday they knew the Royals would pass by the top of the camp-site. Brother Hughie went to a hefty Scots Pine by the roadside, its reddish bark all tacky with resin. He swarmed up a knotted rope to a horizontal bough.

Peem tried to clamber up after, but his hands still felt raw from the Wallace affair, right shoulder half-unsocketed from swooping onto the conker. He fell back on the awkward roots of the pine.

– Useless, said Hughie.
– Can ye see some—? skirled Annie.
– Fit, Royals? said Hughie.
– No, my squirrels.

Peem was laying criss-cross twigs on the hot road tar, like a lion trap, when at quarter past two, fully ten minutes late, the Rolls Royce swished up from the railhead at Ballater. She must have given excess of her time doling out crests.

She could never humph a month's lobster in a hamper from Sandringham, so she had to live off the land, the Queen. Ballater's gun-and-tackle shop got her first crest. Then the baker and licensed grocer each got a bright coat-of-arms, to plonk on their outside wall.

Thus she could aye put a bullet in a passing stag – though a bit out of season – or try her worm on the king of fish. Then a slice of roast flesh in a flooery bap, and wash it down with a pint of Pimms.

Maybe she'd been doling one out to the filmshop-cum-chemist:

By Royal Appointment
To Her Majesty Queen Elizabeth II
Purveyor of
Snaps and Teeps

The lilac glove waved, as the Rolls crushed the lion trap with no swerving. Hughie, from his overhanging bough, dropped a pearl of spit.

– Pathetic, said Peem.

– The wind got it.

– It's nae windy, said Peem.

– I see Maggie's in wi them this year— said Mum.

– Aye, the face that lunched on a thousand chips.

– Andy!

Peem looked at the fleeting car through his blue stone.

– What's a subject? he asked, and his mother smiled.

a service of dedication

They went for a spin on Wednesday. Dad lodged Tammy in behind Mum, in a Dexion cradle, with cushions and straps. Tammy had his white cotton sun hat on, a fine summer smile, and a streak of chocolate. Annie got her seat on a crossbar, sandals braced on a bolt-on perch, with Dad hunched over her. Hughie sped off on his racer and had to be cried back and given the role of rearguard. Peemie trundled in the middle, tolerating his old bike's lack of colour, its loosely-cottered crank.

Then down they freewheeled, down into Ballater in single file, hair streaming, everybody laughing. Brakes squealing and releasing as they swung into the level town.

Leith the Baker had that brilliant warm smell, the fresh bread smell. But the Ballater ice cream was poor, *By Disappointment* more like, watery water-ice.

– Have ye nae proper creamy stuff under the counter? said Dad.

The girl just looked at him.

– Cream, he said, ice cream. Dinna tell me Queenie dribbles that weet muck doon her chin.

– C'mon, Andy, said Mum. It's oor holidays.

They crossed to the South Deeside road and headed west through the pleasant land. They stopped instead at a roadside well, with a dull bronze cup chained to a slab, the water pure and cold. There was a scrub of fireweed and foxglove around.

– Annie, come awa fae that flooers!

– Want a purple hat for Megan.

– Fit's she needin a purple hat for?

– Sunny.

– Well tell her the foxglove's poisony.

– Megan says she doesna care.

A hive of bees sent ambassadors round their shorts, so they mounted and rode on.

They had got near the length of Balmoral Brig when Mum slowed, put a foot down skidding on either side, and let her head droop on the handlebars. They'd been a bit too ambitious.

– We'll be back inside twenty minutes and ye can hae a lie-doon.

But when they arrived at the Brig, there were red-and-white sparred hurdles linked across the road.

They had unlinked two of these, when the inevitable constable came out from the gatehouse with a raised hand.

– Aye, sir. Afraid it's turn round now, sir.

– Ye're kiddin. An accident?

– Bridge closed to the public for at least the next hour.

– Onybody killed?

– Hardly, sir. Orders, sir.

– But ma wife has taen nae weel.

– Her Majesty's at a service of dedication in Crathie Kirk.

– I'll gie her dedication—

The other bikes were gathering round Dad in a phalanx.

– Back by Ballater, sir?

– What, extra miles an thon muckle brae? Look, once and for aa, the point is—

– Your breath's wasted on me, sir.

– The hale point is there's naebody needin Balmoral Brig till Queen Bessie's finished her sermon, whatever it is, her cairry-on—

– Restricted access, sir.

– We winna wear her Brig oot, for pity's sake!

– Security.

– It's a stick-loaf I've got in this rucsac, nae a stick o gelignite—

– That's as may be, sir.

Hughie was still angry five minutes later.

– Why did we nae just barge past? Only odd bits o wid.

– Och, a mannie like that's just a dupe. C'mon, we'll show them.

– I hope she gets what she's prayin for, said Mum.

– We're nae goin back the length o Ballater are we, Dad, are we—?

The Dee was maybe possible hereabouts – but with potholes, swift and swirly.

– Daddy, Megan can't swim.

Dad tied his shoes around his neck.

With Mum first, pressed to his back, he began wading. Shrugged her higher. Unshipped her on the far shingle, waded back for wee Tammy. Slipped – nearly – twice, then popped the bairn in Mum's arms. Pushed through the swirl again to fetch Mum's green bike. Saddle digging into his shoulder, so as she and Tammy could ride off early.

They all waved, but she didn't wave back.

Annie now.

– Okay, lovie?

His own bike.

– Bluidy Moses, eh?

Peem's bike.

– Democracy—

Hughie's bike.

– In a pig's lug!

Peem and Hughie risked it side-by-side, through the rushiness on the rounded boulders.

skimmers

Hugh and Bridget came up the middle weekend. Hugh had his mongrel collie Dick Herr or something, *Fat Man* it meant, though everybody called him *Digger* and Uncle Hugh gave in. When Uncle Hugh had been a Marine mopping up through Nazi Germany, he had come back from Hamburg with a bonny inlaid travelling chess set.

– Thocht ye micht need this if it rained, he said.

– Guid o ye, said Dad.

– Ach, hardly mair than a blackened shell, he said. We must've fire-bombed these poor folk tae hell.

Annie liked tiddling with the two slightly jammed drawers of light and dark brown pieces.

– When can I get a chest set, Daddy—?

Hugh was a tennis champion, and played a fierce left-half for Rosemount. He had blue eyes. His fair hair parted in the middle, like the opposition. Bridget was up with him for the day, but there was nowhere for her to sleep.

– *Coilacreich*— she said, the end of the wood.

They played quoits and rounders and French cricket and shootie-in. They keepie-upped, hide-and-sought in the woods, raced flowers and logs in the river and cast for trout. They built dams, bridges, lades, harbours, dish racks and wigwams, fetched food, fetched water, fetched firewood, and sand for the latrine. They said *Cheerio* to Bridget.

– Why won't ye bide? Peem had said.

– *Mar gum biodh cearc air tor nid. Like a hen in search of a nest*, she wrote in his notebook.

That same afternoon, who should drop by but Ludwig, on his Triumph Speed Twin.

– Ludwig, ye're amazin.

– They got me a justable hook. Look I grip, no bothers. Throttle is on the left now, switches around.

– Madge is sleepin. Are ye hungry? We were just awa doon tae play at the Dee.

They went to play skimmers.

Ludwig watched as they selected stones from the tiny strand. They bent their torsos low to the river and, with flick of wrist and finger-spin, sent over the curdling pool each skimmering, stalling, slowly sinking stone. Uncle Hugh preferred roundish, Andy took angular if flat, Peem searched for bevelled slate. Hughie chose a heavy one that could half-hop and subside, a whale's flurry.

– Ludwig? said Andy

– Ach, I'm nae left-handed enough—

They fetched pure water out of the spring, and drank still-circling Creamola Foam in turns from a mug.

– Round wi the sun, said Uncle Hugh.

– Did you hear about the Arab wi the camel? said Andy.

– A story now, eh—? said Ludwig.

– Well, ye see there was this Arab that lived in Libya, and he had tae cross tae the next oasis. But it was five hundred mile, and his camel could only haud wattir enough for fower hundred, it was a real problem.

At that moment Andy saw, like an approaching headlight in a dark tunnel, that this was hardly the joke to tell, not with Ludwig.

– And—? asked Peem.

But it would be daft to pull out. Soften him up.

– And the camel was loaded already, so it couldna cairry jerry cans.

– Named from Rommel, said Ludwig.

– Named fae Rommel, said Dad, I didna ken that. Onywey—

– We Germans carry a can for everything.

– Aye, very good, said Dad. Onywey, the Arab had tae get his camel tae drink a lot, lot mair.

– But it took the hump? said Uncle Hugh.

– Na, it'll be me that taks that. Far was I—?

172

– In the middle o the desert, said young Hughie. Thank god for Creamola Foam, otherwise we'd be deid o thirst waitin.

– Onywey, the camel, he taks the camel tae the pool, it's a male camel, did I mention that—?

– Ye've mentioned it noo, said Uncle Hugh.

– An the male camel begins tae drink its fill, sookin up the wattir like naebody's business.

– Naebody should be daein their business in an oasis pool onywey, said Hughie. That's dirty—

– An just as the camel was aboot tae be full-up, doon bent the Arab an pickit up twa flat stanes. Sae he crept up ahint the camel, an lifted the twa flat stanes way oot tae baith sides—

– Skimmers! said Peem.

– I'm nae sure I should tell this story— Onywey, on he creeps till he's atween the camel's hinder legs. The camel's fat lips were still jist playin wi the wattir, when aa o a suddent the Arab clashes baith STANES hard roon its KNACKERS, an SOOCH it SOOKS up anither ten gallon—

– Ooya, is that nae sair? said Peem.

– *Not if he keeps his both thumbs out the road,* said Ludwig. Nein worry your heid, Andy, I heard it twice aready.

– Far aboot in Germany dae ye come fae again? said Uncle Hugh.

– City of Hamburg. I come from it. I don't go back again.

– Aye, said Andy.

– Andy, I came out this road to tell you something.

– Your compensation come through?

– Nein. I want to join the Party.

– Crivvens, I'd just aboot put the Party fae ma mind oot here.

– Even in Paradise you need the Party.

– Well, that's great, Ludwig. Great news.

On the Thursday the much-awaited Test started against Australia. England would have a much better chance at Old Trafford than at Lords. Peemie drew up the batting order for both teams.

Peem was Cowdrey, May, Laker and Evans, though he found it a bit difficult to wicket-keep to his own bowling.

Uncle Hugh had decided to stay a couple of days, and was ideal as Richardson, Washbrook, the speedster Statham and the Reverend David Sheppard.

Mum was not likely to score very fast in her condition, so she was the stonewall Trevor Bailey, the anonymous Oakman and the slow left-armer Lock. Dad lined up as Lindwall, Burke, the captain Johnson and the Australian sensation Benaud, he really fancied his spinners.

Annie was pressed into service as McDonald Archer Mackay. Brother Hughie was clubbed together as Craig Harvey Miller Maddocks. He inserted the screwy sign in his forehead.

At the end of the first innings England were all out for 23, with Lock left Not Out - Nought, she had once trod on her stumps in an allowable mistake and had refused all the quick singles.

Benaud was pretty pleased with his 6 wickets, the tennis ball turning square out of the ruts, but Peemie May was quite downcast when adjudged caught out by Annie Archer on a manifest first bounce. Was that cricket, an excess of being fair?

Between innings the teams trooped in for Lemon or Orange Creamola Foam, in the alkathene pavilion. The Australians all took Lemon.

Then they duly smashed off the runs in two overs, their big player Burke being particularly severe on Laker's full toss, lamming it for six to the outer bracken.

Craig Harvey Miller Maddocks mumped it was a fix – not one of him got a bat in his hand. He turned to refining his bush telegraph with two bean tins and a length of sisal.

Annie went off chasing Orange Underwings and Silvery Arches that flew on the fringe of the birches, using the shuttering catching-jar of her hands.

– Did ye catch ane?

– Got away, Mummy.

– O, nivver mind.

– Got dust on my hand. Mebbe comes back for its dust—?

Peem went away too, down past the shy spring under the riverside pines.

At his feet the Dee chattered. He fired a long thin branch like a harpoon. It came up short in a riffle, waiting for spate.

old trafford was awash

It was still sunny next morning when he cycled in to Ballater, on a pretext of milk. He went up to the newspaper shack first, where the silver-haired widow in the black dress was still alive from last year, calm, amused by his eagerness. England had amassed 307 runs for 3 wickets. May had indeed been caught, not on the bounce, by Archer off Benaud.

So it was a bit premature, and difficult, promoting a second innings when Bailey Oakman Lock needed a long lie-down, and Lindwall Burke Johnson Benaud had to prick about with a misfiring Primus.

Reverend Sheppard Richardson Washbrook Statham was due for a last walk up the hill with Digger, but when air and sky grew oppressive, they stepped on the Aberdeen bus before the storm broke.

It was just as well the alkathene flysheet had been welded with strong sleeves, else the whole thing would have flapped off over

Balmoral. It was good hearing weather when you were snugged, the six sleeping bags laid out side-by-side. About midnight the drumming began. Dad went out to slack the manilla guys, which tautened when soaked.

Shortly after, Peem felt a cold serpent rippling across the groundsheet. He wriggled out of his bag, and was starting to undo the loops of the door-lace when his father woke and gripped his arm.

– Needin the lavvy?

– There's wattir gettin in.

– Canna be—

Dark chocolate-headed gulls were spinning on the pitch.

– Quick. Trenchin-tool.

Dad hacked a diversion while Peem built dams with the sods. Annie murmured something – *underlings* – in her dream. Others snuggled deeper and slept on.

submerging all the green banks

Next morning Peemie went to the river with the bucket but came back greeting, so Hughie himself marched down and nearly had his arm wrenched off.

– Dinna be sae saft— said Dad. We need wattir for the dishes.

Aghast at the brown river, they watched it gulf at green banks, barge uprooted pine into exile.

Their sleeping bag feathers got clotted and clammy. Dad flagged down a bus coming from Braemar and put Mum, Annie and Tammy aboard.

– Noo, if ye get stuck, Madge, go roon an ask that Dinah lass for a hand. Or send Annie.

– Aye, we'll see— said his Mum.

That put the kibosh on a Test resumption, and when Peem stravaiged to Ballater for news, he wasn't surprised to find Manchester also washed-out. The lady in black watched him steadfastly, and let him refold the bulky paper without purchase.

In two wet days Australia had squeezed only 30 runs, and lost 1 wicket.

files of fierce, paternal ants

Sun aslant through dripping leaves shone silver on the trunks. Dad had to Panther back now to refetch the Trojan.

– Tell your works ye didna get proper holidays wi aa the rain, said Peem.

Dad ruffled his hair, and gave a silver florin to Hughie.

– It's better here— said Peem.

– Ach, ye'll manage—

– Nae on twa shillin, said Hughie.

Dad gave him a pink ten bob note.

– Hughie made a useless tea.

– Ye've even burned the wattir—

Hughie aimed a swipe at him.

Wandering out in the dampness of evening, Peemie drove kicks at the masses of mushrooms. He struck brackets of fungus off the dead birch at the mouth of the wood. Why on earth herd so many into the city? Just so they could slave away faking fertiliser to flog to country folk in bags?

Moving the springy branches with swish aside, he poked deeper in. He minded Marvell's poem that Mannie had given them, just minded the two lines really.

He moves in shades the Orange bright,
Like golden Lamps in a green Night.

Poets created the real laws, Mannie Martin had said. You had to take the laws into your hands.

He came, in a small clearing, on a writhe of red stoats. Peem dropped and bellied in, over a Wetness of Grasses.

A myxie rabbit was tremoring on a knoll in the middle, its eyes bulging with pus. Needly stoats, snow-bellied, reeled around it, taunting.

Bloody midges soon found him at that level, clouding his wrists, a clot at one eyelid. He stumbled away, hit something loose—

An anthill showered out twigs and eggs – and files of fierce, paternal ants.

mesmerised

They slept late. The returning sun beat down on the tent, cooking a fug.

From the seat of the Trojan on the way back in, Peem picked up a *Manchester Guardian*. Amazing news, the whole of Australia bowled out twice on the final day – the stylish Harvey got a pair of ducks. Lock had little luck on the rain-softened surface, but Jim Laker had spun through 19 batsmen, he'd mesmerised them.

– Spinners, eh? said his Dad.

Tomorrow would be Mum's day of the green, so things could get properly dry.

august

it's the future

– Mum dae you ever dream when ye're awake?

   – Aye. I dream plenty.

   – Dae ye ever see strange things.

   – O, aathing seems strange, the aulder ye get.

   – Dae ye ever see intae the past?

   – Aye, the past can bother me, but it's the future I sometimes dreid.

   – I see the War in a daydream sometimes

   – Well that's probably the best wey tae see it, right enough.

   – And Jobby—

   – Puir Jobby. Well, I think I'll awa tae ma bed.

   – Are ye wabbit?

   – A bit.

book of job

Spermy had just come back from the Broch. They didn't let him run away to the herring after all, but set him to primp ashore with needle and twine. Mending torn nets. A night's graft on a drifter, under an occluded moon, was far too tough for a lad of eleven.

   – Dae ye ken fit a hole is?

Peem thocht they were back tae Haze, the sixpenny pee-show.

   – Suppose—

   – A hole's just nithin wi string roon.

They walked the docks first, Spermy liked that. He'd certainly caught the sea.

Dressed granite was loading in a coaster for London, for banks and palaces.

– Rubislaw Quarry, eh, biggest hole o the lot, said Spermy.

– It maks ye wonder, have they nae stane in England?

– Na, it's aa clay.

Esparto grass came on one freighter for the papermills up Donside, the bales swung lightly ashore.

– Fit on earth dae we need grass for?

– Makkin paper, said Peem.

– Jist use rags—

– Better for books, they say, mair fibre.

Guano was best, though. Guano was being howked out with a grab, white fragments of feather and bone flying off. And a hot stench, a stench that *stuck like shite tae a blanket*, his Dad's summation of rusted brakes, or clingy romance.

Leaving the docks in the shadow of the giant sheerlegs, they bumped into Jobby himself – Peemie hadn't seen him since that weird day humphing coke, the tryst with Haze, the sudden brick, his sea-washed coma.

– Aye, aye, Jobby, he said. He was shoving his pram. Have ye gotten a good load the day?

Jobby didn't even look up.

– *It is finished*.

– Aye, that back wheel sure is. Spermy mocked his outrageous buckle.

– Leave him alane.

– Awa an bile yir heid, said Spermy, he's nae sae poor he couldna chore a wheel fae a bairn's pram.

– Dinna pester him.

– Jobby, Jobby, peed in the lobby—

Straight back came Jobby.

– *Yea young children despised me;*
I arose, and they spake against me.

– Spik sense, said Spermy.

– *Suffer me that I may speak;*
and after that I have spoken, mock on.

– Jesus, said Spermy.—

– *Even when I remember I am afraid,*
and trembling taketh hold of my flesh.
Wherefore do the wicked live, become old,
yea, are mighty in power?

– Dae ye actually ken the hale Bible, really— ? said Peem.

– *And Israel abode in Shittim,*
and the people began to commit whoredom
with the daughters of Moab—

– Crap, said Spermy, and disappeared into a shop for five Woodbine and a book of matches.

Jobby shoved off along the quayside road towards Commerce Street. Peem sat on a rusty bollard to wait for Spermy. He could easy have given him a push with it. He should have. The day was clouding.

Raymie and Tarry appeared on the far wharf for some reason, probably taking in the new St Clements Bridge, or HMS *Charybdis*, minesweeper. Were there still mines?

He swung away, and drew out the blue stone. He looked through the sea-smoothed hole and spied a very small man, retreating to the distance.

– Hey, dozy fucker, want a fag?

– Na. Come doon the pier?

– Nuh.

It was too late to catch up with Jobby. He walked instead to the end of the great North Breakwater. There were three dead gulls in a pile, half way along. He gave them a wide berth. He got to the end, and leaned against the dumpy light.

He looked out north, across Aberdeen Bay, as the waves rose like circles under old eyes.

He imagined himself washing out in the surf, after the half-brick struck his head. How far would he have got in four months? Wouldn't have floated, probably, with no fat. Small crabs would have taken him to their hundred lairs, then dogfish or beardy cod would have eaten the crabs. Somebody would have then eaten the cod, eaten him, walking along, out of a newspaper. Somebody who was allowed chips—

But not his father – he didn't eat fish – at least he wouldn't have been eaten by his father.

He lifted the blue stone again, and peered north, through the cobalt hole. Things began to heave high, disappear – heave high, disappear – grey rolling shapes. Began to feel queasy and closed his eyes—

A convoy for Russia.

Aa the wey up to Archangel he was shitin himsel for U-boats. They would be hackin ice aff the steel railins when somebody would drap an aix, *clang*.

CLAANG! Jobby would flee into that wee deck-lavvy wi his hert gaain *clapclapclap* like a feartie, feart o the mine-clunk, the torpedo's dirl.

Eftir, when he was inower the liferaft wi the padre, the muckle swall hissin past them in the dark, the raft lollopin up an doon like an auld deen hure, they cuddlit thegither for the affa cauld.

He thocht the padre had a hard-on, and was faain in luve wi him. But when the mannie gave up the ghaist, and his face congealed, Jobby Numbers put his haun doon to see fit was fit.

Huddlit deep in the padre's greatcoat pooch was a buik.

Oilclaith covers. Jobby gruppit it oot. A *Holy Bible!* Aa o a sudden, under the full o the mune there were snaa-hills rearin aa roon, but the raft's flat erse was for whooshin them doon, doon tae the boddom in bree an grue.

A sair sooch to climb anither, but Jobby, wi ae hoof, got rid o the padre.

The raft bobbit fine, gled o the less wecht.

Jobby Numbers read like mad. His een were glued to the Bible but the pages got spumy, sipin.

Genesis soon floodit, and *Exodus* got the chuck, ower the side in a sotter, just as twa waves partit to the reid sword o dawnin. And he saw a pink-gray corvette curvin towards him, some chariot, on coggly wheels.

Aa the wey back in the sick-bay hammock he nivver let go o his *Bible* avaa, he pillowed it, oxtered it, ate his piece aff it.

Fanivver he opened it, it was like seein a slush-swall comin to brak ower his heid, once again. Een flasht like a Leica, and would nivver forget.

Some other survivors, Bleck Jock, ravin McTavish, Mealy Jerker and Ae Ba, chored their pages in turn aff Jobby for rollin a smoke. *Just the ticket* said Ae Ba, settin a spunk till it.

Nae muckle sacrifice. Jobby, though he spoke nithin tae nae-body, mindit ivvery word he saw. As they came in the length o Leith, wi shrapnel in the Captain's chest, and a bomb-hole through their deckin, Jobby had just wipit his dock on the last page o *Revelation*.

Years eftir, in the East End o toon, Jobby would come hurlin roon wi a hackit pram, pittin his haun doon in buckets for auld fox-furs, het-wattir pigs or duntit kettles, to hawk for a tanner tae Cocky Hunter. O the raft, the padre and the frozen mune, Jobby nivver let dab.

But come a summer's day ye'd aften find him sittin oot on his mither's granite steps in Jasmine Terrace. Must've been saft granite, it was worn bum-hollow.

Black duffler, balaclava, an rubber gas-boots wi reid-ribbit taes, the hale regalia. Kids sat roon'm, and daunsit up an doon wi tugs on the railins.

Ye hadna a job. Ye were saft in the heid, wi an affa fool smell. Ye went back in the hoose fan the sun went awa.

across the tram lines

Then Peem was walking along King Street, a different day, it was one day before the new school started, he couldn't think why he was walking, not hunting in bookmongers, not gawping in at Craigmyle's Sports, not lusting after fresh air nor fancy biscuits from some handy aunt. It seemed he was drawn to it, a pure walk of which he could give no account. If the Police had come roaring out of Lodge Walk with their sirens blaring, and dragged him handcuffed back to a cell, and shone a torch into his eyes real hard, and let a cold tap drip on his skull past nightfall, he still couldn't have confessed what the walk was about—

– Hello again, Peem.

Her scooter purred at the kerb, the sun on her goggles as she slid them up. His heart danced across the street, kicked its heels on the wall opposite, and rang the bell on the Brig o Dee tram.

– Aren't you pleased to see me?

His face so poor at translating.

– If you're busy, but there's something I thought would be dandy.

The Dandy?

– It's the competition, art appreciation. Hop on and we'll go in past and pick up the forms. It's Botticelli or Constable this year.

Hop on!

– You look all red. The wind will cool you.

It was a purple Vespa, bulbous at the rear where they kept the engine. A single-seater, with a chrome luggage-rack that curved backwards by design. Miss Florence had on a pink V-sweater, suede jacket, white slacks.

Moulding thin calves over bulbous wings, he perched on the rack.

He caught her scent.

– Move up till you're comfy.

Staying raked back, he tautened tum and thighs. For her he'd polish cobbles with his arse.

– Hold on, we're off.

He was clasping the merest hem of her jacket. But – bounced across the tramlines – he grabbed her hip bones.

september

bismarck terrace infants

Aberdeen maybe helped Russia win the War, but Aberdeen was a lot closer to Prussia.

Peemie, Spermy, Iris and company had gone on to Frederick Street Junior Secondary, some as a five month holding camp, some till final release. There was a BOYS' ENTRANCE and a GIRLS' ENTRANCE, their impeccable apostrophes granite-carved above the heavy doors.

Every Tuesday they were led, girls first, across to Hanover Primary for a hot shower with red carbolic and, after interval, the boys. Boys, being clartier, would stain the tiles and clog the drains. For the news on the wind was that none had seen bath or shower since the previous Tuesday. And who could dook in that sea?

Spermy would stain a wall at the best of times. He'd work a boner into his reddening cock, standing in the showers, then work it hard till it suddenly spunked against the porcelain wall. He aspired higher each week, and marked the grouting of the attained tile with a finger nail. It was weird to watch.

– Fit div ye think, eh, wee Peem?

Was thinking required—?

– Nae bad. Aren't ye supposed tae let the tool dae the work?

– Fa says?

– Ma Da.

– Well I dinna ken fa ma Da wis, an ma Ma's a muckle hure, so I jist please masel, okay?

– Up tae you.

186

Along the road, to make the set, was Bismarck Terrace Infants.

could have been the oval

They had two main teachers at Fredericker, Tinners and Pinners. Mr McIron, Tinners, taught Maths. Such personal insights as he had obtained from Messrs Euclid and Napier had been dulled by a succession of dolts. From time to time there was a little arithmetical progression.

Pinners' head was long and thin, like Hen Broon in the *Sunday Post*.

– Forceps, said Iris.

He had narrow views.

– McClung, don't let me ever catch you again going in the GIRLS' ENTRANCE.

Against the advance of winter, Pinners took boys for cricket on Friday Period 7 to the Links. It took 9 minutes to walk there, 11 minutes back. That left 20 minutes to set up stumps, buckle on the odd pad, and conduct two innings.

The Acid Plant at Sandilands was reeking brown. The Gasworks was guffing hard by. It could have been the Oval, and when Peem got in to bat, his team having second innings, he wasn't going to throw away his wicket like the rest of the loons. He settled down to play himself in.

Pinners was umpire, in a borrowed white labcoat. Craigser was bowling. He ran up from behind Pinners, and convulsed his arms and legs so that a hard red blob flew towards Peemie.

Peem stonewalled, playing 1, 2, 3, 4, 5 balls straight back or slightly squint. Trevor Bailey would be proud of him.

– Hit out or get out, Endrie.

Pinners had spoken. *Hit out or get out.*

Craigser rolled the next ball underhand along the ground. It had the decency to bobble. Peemie tried to bop it for 6, and was bowled.

a nightdress folded

When he came home that day his mother was packing the fibreboard case, with the checked paper lining.

– Mum—

– Hello, Peemie. How did ye get on the day?

– Fine.

Her white blouse, no, it was a nightdress folded. There was a flannel and a drawstring bag. A rectangular mirror, with a pink plastic frame, and a leg to stand it.

– What book are ye going to take?

– O, it's just a few days.

She tucked in her red slippers and folded a towel. Peem ran off and came back with *David Copperfield*.

– Thanks, I'll maybe just take ma *New Testament*. And dream aboot ma dotterels.

Wit-e-wee, wit-e-wee, wit-e-wee.

luve an hate

Next day the boys had to traipse to Causewayend for Woody. They walked up without escort, fighting and cavorting. Peem had already made the Pipe Rack, though Dad didn't smoke anymore. You had to imagine different pipes, let's say Indian, Sherlock, soapy bubble and meerschaum, measure and carefully chisel.

Today they were on to the Cigarette Case, with green baize for the fags to lie comfy, and a bit of bevelling.

– Please sir, is it okay if I call mine a Jewel Case, it's for my Mum—

– She'll get her Dovetailed Toast Rack later on.

What on earth was dovetailed toast, for pity's sake.

– But she's going into hospital the day.

The best of going to Causewayend wasn't the screw-gauge, hacksaw or chisel. It was the pies. Rock the Baker's back-window gave out onto the playground. Tuppence for a mince pie, penny for a fruit pie, it was like something out of Aladdin. All you did was tap on the window, and out came this feast at cost, wreathed in steam and baker's fug.

– Pies are great, eh, he said to Spermy.

– Better than a slap across the face wi a piece o yella fish.

Craigser came up to him. Peem was his rabbit now.

– Fit wey the schoolbag the day, Wee Peem? Ye dinna need yir schoolbag fan ye've got Woody, even us dopes ken that.

– Shut up, Craigser, it's for ma books fae the big Library if ye must ken.

– Dinna tell me to shut up, swanker. I'll bet ye dinna even ken one sentence wi *luve* an *hate* in it.

– Eh?

– *I luv het pies!* And with that he stole Peem's pie and stapped it into his leather schoolbag, so that it dreeped greasy mince over his Dickens.

– Hey, min, fit's that for? Fit would your Da say if he kent ye'd gone and spiled a Library book?

– Ma Da widna care a preen. The only thing ma Da reads is his paypacket, he wouldna let a book in ower the door.

He had his bunny now, so he deaved and tormented.

– Hit oot or get oot, Endrie. Or maybe just get oot, snob, get oot and never come back, eh, acause naebody likes ye. *Dreamy Peemie pees ees breeks, Dreamy Peemie pees ees breeks.*

– Shut up, Craigser.

– Mak me!

– Ye're jist a bully.

– Pruve it—!

– Well—

– Eftir school the morn then—

a wee operation

He went to the hospital that evening, with Dad. Brother Hughie stayed with Annie and Tammy, Hughie saying he would see Mum after the operation.

– Dad, fit is Mum really in for?

– Jist a wee operation.

– What for, though?

– O, Mum will easily tell ye, when she's better.

– Will she get gas?

She was sitting up with a smile ready, her left hand with the gold and diamond rings spread on the turned-down sheet. Peem gave her flowers from the front garden. The season was getting late, so it was gladioli: lemon, violet, dark blue, scarlet, white, a flower from each of them. The young nurse ran for a vase.

Somebody had donated from their will a TV to the ward, in a walnut cabinet. Mum was watching the endless *Potter's Wheel*. It kept them looking away from each other.

Peem liked *Bilko* and *Lucy* at Cousin Archie's. There were 400 lines of dancing electrons and, for football, 400 balls.

They kept glancing back and away.

– Fancy a grape? said Dad.

The wheel kept turning.

– In a minute.

A programme came on about Cornwall, a general travelogue, clay and tin.

Mum placed her hand over Dad's.

– O no, nae that— surely!

For the film had cut to a fairground by Padstow, the usual swings, shies, chutes and roundabouts, but then panned away to trees and bushes over rolling ground. Peem watched them share a grin.

– What is it, though?

– Nithin, Cornwall.

– And— ? Why ye grinnin?

– An that's far Mum worked, Signals, Coastal Command.

– Did ye, Mum?

– Och, just a bittie o decodin and encodin messages aboot U-boats.

– U-boats!

– Uh-huh. Their codes were cracked, so we kent far the wolfpack would surface next. I used tae tap signals oot tae oor corvettes an destroyers.

– Really, Mum?

– Really. And Dad came doon tae see me wi his pass.

a ragged ring

It was nice to be *thought o*. That's what his Dad had said last night. *That's far ye were first thought o*. Padstow. Outside a fairground in a distant country, at the back of a bush. He looked round the class. Bet not a one knew where they were first thought of—

Craigser sat two desks away, smirking, waiting to kill him.

Pinners had abandoned parsing and was attempting *The Lady of Shalott*. He was trying to get some answers out of Peem, Tarry or Iris that would be in the right territory, amendable. All Peem could think was how the Lady of Shalott didn't know how lucky she was. At least she had a tower to hide in, no risk of Craigser nailing her and belting her round the chops. He wished Spermy would scrap for him.

But the Middle Ages were past now.

When the bell went, down the stairs he went, a zombie. A ragged ring in the centre of Frederick Street parted to admit the duellers.

– Ye'd better chuck me your jerkin, said Spermy. Nae point spoilin it wi gallons o bleed.

Craigser danced sideways in and jabbed the air.

– Go on, then, mak me. Clear connection to the *Shut up, Craigser* of yesterday.

Peemie put his jouks half-up.

Craigser jerked his tie out of his pullover.

Peemie tucked it back in.

Craigser jabbed again, closer.

The stoats were restless, gathered for a death, and not about to be cheated. Peem reached a limp paw out. But Heidcase Casey dunted him in the back, and shoved him forward so that he palpably aggressed.

Head down, right, left, right, left – Craigser, anonymously, to the guts. Then he jabbed Peem square on the mouth.

– Ye've splut his lip! shouted Tarry.

He let go a fierce uppercut that papped the tip of his nose.

– Go for'm Craigser. Kick ees erse! they skirled.

– Bleed him. Fuckin mak him bleed—!

Heidcase Casey stamped from foot to foot, as though he was chief buyer for a black pudding factory.

I am tired

That night Singy Bridge was doing the babysitting. When Hughie came back before Dad from the hospital, he tapped at the window above the sink.

– Secret.

He summonsed Peem to the washhouse. When Peem got there, he was playing with the wooden clothes tongs, and dived them at Peem's breeks. Some secret.

– Think it's hycterestomy.

– Fit—?

– Hysterectomy. They tak it oot o her belly, ken?

Bridget made tea and Dad said it was a very good hospital, it had been built by public subscription before the War, with everybody, the railwaymen, the shop assistants, allowing a penny a week to be deducted their wages, till a whole half-million was raised.

– That's fit we fought the War for.

Peemie felt lost at that, and a little chilly.

Some hairs escaped from Bridget's bun and came swinging across as she dried Annie vigorously.

It was simpler for Dad and Hughie to go away out to the shed.

Peem fetched the household brass, the shovel and brush, the awkward coal tongs and easy poker. He spread an *Evening Express*. The Brasso tin had like a black rising sun.

– Bridget, dae ye ken I'm really Cornish? Truly really—

– Whatever next. Och, that's what'll be helping your Gaelic. Come over here. Your lip, my brave hunter, is needing a dab of the Dettol.

– Chan eil—

It is not. *Ha Nyeel* you had to say. *Ha Nyeel* – aided considerably by the scab blocking his nose.

He buffed and buffed away at a bonny slipper ashtray, that nobody now used.

– Bridget—

– What?

– It's nothing—

– What is it though?

– *Tha mi sgith*, Bridget.

can babies eat wood?

Tammy was playing up. He stood in his crib and bit at the paint and grat.

– He's teethin pretty bad, said Hughie.

– Pretty bad? said Dad, I'll say. He's through twa coats o gloss, an undercoat and a primer.

– Can babies eat wood, Daddy?

Peem got to go and see his Mum on the second night, she was awful pale, and didn't want to say much at first, just a faint smile, lying back on her pillow.

Tammy didn't cry for nothing. He had a stuffed dog with floppy ears, some kind of hound that Auntie Betsy brought round. He craned the dog up by the ear, dumped it outside his crib, then roared and grat.

– Get his bloody retriever for him.

– I jist got it.

– Well get it again!

On the fourth night, Peem took in a special game for Mum, Spill 'n' Spell and they played it. It was a dice game with letters, and she solemnly rolled her five dice on the hospital tray, propped on three pillows. But with *Q, Z, E, A, S* or *K, P, N, O, U* what could you do? Sometimes they got a bad run of no-worders.

Tammy was growing up, he could swing his hound halfway across the room.

194

– Tie that stinkin dug tae his leg, said Hughie.

– C'mon, said Dad. C'mon, wee Tammikins.

And he lifted Tammy for the tenth time that day, and crooned to him.

O sleep till yir mammy,

My bonnie lammie,

Sleep till yir mammy,

My bonnie doo—

Ye'll get a bosie

Ye'll be sae cosy,

Ye'll get a bosie

Fan yir Mam comes hame.

october

punched in their columns

Mum came out of the hospital at the start of the month, and then it was into the harvest. Dad levered the fork, his left hand grasping a scalp-knot of shaw, and the tatties broke clean through the surface, Kerr's Pink and King Edwards. Peem followed, gleaning them into a paper sack. Despite Dad's best efforts, some were pronged and gored.

He knew Mum's word. He'd looked it up in the dictionary.

Hughie didn't have to come to the plot, it wasn't fair, he got to stay and make some motorised buggy out of strips of perforated steel. Annie had come to hunt the last of the rasps, in between the tall staked rows, which she did with two helpers, and found seven. Then Dad went into a terrible rage over his carrots. The plumes bent, feathery, in the breeze. The tops seemed green and red, intact. But once he loosened them with the graip, festering great holes were revealed, punched in their columns. The insidious fly had been at work.

Peem felt sick. Maybe it was the compost heap.

pulp off the pith

The *Worker* fell a bit by the wayside. They had the brambles to consider. There were only so many hours in a weekend. So off they set, the lot of them, on their bikes. Mum was very gingery at first and did a lap of the block.

– Where will we try?

– Auchinyell, Bieldside. Blairs if we draw a blank.

At Auchinyell they leaned their bikes on a three-wire fence and scrambled down to the railway line. Peem got down on the ballast and laid his ear on the line, harkening vibration. The sleepers were massive, rich with creosote, the steel itself had a slight bloom of rust.

– Mum, look at the brambles.

  – Aye, lovely and plump.

He watched how his Mum's stained fingers eased the pulp off the pith.

nae time for atomics

Through that week they felt the first stirrings. There'd been a couple of notes folded through the door, when they'd been away. On Tuesday Frankie came round. Peem thought it would be Dad getting a telling-off for not keeping his *Workers* up to the mark.

There was a broad alloy pan on top of the stove, with brambles afloat in their purple liquor. Slow-circling foam showed the sugar at work.

At first it was about China. The great Mao had swum the Yangtse. *Chinese Leader's Epic Shows Way Forward* said the paper. On his back. Amongst the treacherous swirling waters at Wuhan. They all pored over the paper on the kitchen table. Wuhan was where the railway workers had pushed forward Sun Yat Sen's rebellion in 1911. Now, seven years into the glorious Communist era, it was fitting that the great warrior-leader Mao should show his power and confidence in harnessing the natural forces of China for the good of his people. Peem thought it was great. At last the *Worker* was getting a bit of sport on its front page.

– Aye, said Frankie, what a turnaround. His brother had been on HMS *Amethyst* when it was under perpetual bombardment as it strove to exit the Yangtse in 1949. A shell splinter had lodged in his skull.

– Think this'll put pressure on Khrushchev? said Dad.

– Na, dinna think it would be in the *Worker* if Moscow didna approve.

– I mean tae front-crawl the Volga.

– Aye, right, said Frankie. O, I suppose ye heard Queen Lizzie on the wireless, openin Calder Hall.

– Openin fit was that—? said Mum.

– Calder Hall. Harnessing the atom, for peaceful purposes.

– I've nae time for atomics, said Mum, and picked up the paper.

– Thocht it was fancy racehorses she liked tae harness, said Dad.

– Aye, but this horsepower's cheap, said Frankie. Atomic electricity, rinnin like milk and honey in the land.

– Aye, she's aa hert, oor Lizzie. Doon tae Rosin Street she'll be in a flash, tae haul oot aa oor meters.

Mum had taken the inside sheet, the *Worker*'s background article. Apparently there had been many objective difficulties for Mao to overcome, whirlpools and upwellings, *chow chow* and 'flower water'.

– And river snakes— she said to Peem.

– Nae river snakes!

– Hey, ony chance o a cuppa tea? said Dad.

– O, my God! The purple liquor, all boiled up, was on the point of lipping over.

to test the speakers

Peemie was playing on his own these days. Against a great blank gable he threw his sponge ball, and skipped to collect it before it bounced twice. The gable was at the bottom of Rosin, at the junction with Urquhart, at the only corner without a wee shop. Usually you shouted *Leave-i-o!* at the very instant of throwing, a double expulsion. But on your own it was daft to exclaim. It was also pretty difficult to surprise yourself.

A black Austin glid down from the cemetery. You stopped. A Standard Vanguard throbbed up from the town. You started again, a high fling. There was a smooth rumble on the lower road as a flat-nose Morris came by with a load of fags.

A hand lunged for the ball, just past the side of your lug.

– Hey, min! Dad—?

– Dinna be late in your bed, loonikin.

He was off to the Market Stance, to test the speakers for the Hungary rally.

beauty was made from the seed of time

Pinners gave them a camera, that was some shock. *The Lady of Shalott* was coming near the end of her innings. He'd scraped together funds for a Box Brownie, and the three bright sparks were sent off on a recce, while the rest got the last of the first verse off by heart.

There were twelve snaps in the spool.

– Cocky Hunter's first, said Tarry. He got a shot of chipped ewers, golf bags and a tartan shawl, hung up in the doorway.

– What's the point in that? said Iris.

They went round by Hanover Street, and Peem leaned the Brownie on the retaining dyke to catch the older girls exiting, with rats' tails dripping and glistening combs.

– Closer maybe—? said Iris.

– Fucker, awa an play wi yersel, said a showeree.

Tarry wanted to snap the welders as they sparked and arced at Hall Russell's shipyard. They went to the aperture in the big sliding door.

– It's too dark, said Iris. It's only a box.

So they had 9 shots left.

Peem wanted to get the guano. All these gull-droppings being brought from the bottom of the globe amused him.

– As though we didna hae our ain sea maas!

– Probably got deeper shite in Chile, said Tarry.

– Probably—

He used two, because on the first he missed the swing of the jib.

Iris was getting irate now. They traversed till they got to the Timmer Market. The stallkeepers were setting up and she moved amongst them. She recorded an old woman testing a monkey-on-a-stick. She was squeezing two spars that tautened, propelling a two-dimensional chimp into loose-jointed somersaults. Iris chose to blur the chimp to get the occupied face.

Everything was supposed to be of wood. Hughie hardly went to the Timmer Market now, but Annie of course liked to get something. There were wooden spurtles, tattie-mashers, lopsided yoyos. There was a great deal you could do with wood, and a great deal you couldn't. Scrubbing brushes, chopping boards. Iris took about six portraits.

– Let's get a view o the hale toon, said Peemie.

They crossed Castle Street and went to the door of the Salvation Army Citadel. It had a mediaeval kind of turretty top to it. They explained to one of the dark blue Salvationers what they were up to. You saw them playing their brass all over the town, in their red-banded caps. Soon they would be getting in tune for Christmas, trying to siphon coppers for orphans. If history was anything to go by, tonight they would be down at the Market Stance, brazen circle on the rounded cobbles, trying to drown the Party's megaphone.

– Aye, ye can go up, if ye like. None of the sashes open, ye should be safe enough.

They set off up the curl of the stairs.

– Ye're just eftir the Lady o Shalott, said Tarry.

– Wouldna ken fit tae say tae her—

– Ye have tae be polite. Ye're supposed to say *See's a rugg o yir mammies, darlin.*

Iris was a bit behind them, a bit puffed by the top.

The turret window gave along the granite mile of Union Street – from the blackened crown of the Castlegate below them – past Sheriff Court, Town House, Athenaeum, Esslemont and Mackintoshes, towards Union Bridge, then narrowing to the West End's vanishing point.

It was the trams impressed Peem. Swaying under their cables, they swung in retained tangents from King Street, and held their line up Union Street, right in the middle of the road. Folk had to bravely issue like tall ants in the teeth of the traffic.

– Look, the Provost's Rolls Royce, said Iris.

– Daimler, said Tarry.

– Look, fa's that on the Vespa—?

He hadn't really known what to do. They'd scootered back to Miss Florence's place, he thought it was going to be the school they were off to. O nothing grand, an upstairs flat, but lovely too, and she gave him a cup of coffee which he'd never had. They'd sat opposite at a cane table by the window and she'd brought out a box of arty postcards.

– So, how do you like this one, *The Birth of Venus*?

He rattled his cup down—

– To write about, what might you like?

– The scallop, it's not just the shell, the sea's all scalloped too.

– So it is. Scolloped indeed.

– And I like the bays, all the pink roses, tumbling down.

– Do you like the way Venus is presented?

– Do you mean—?

– Well, Venus was conceived from two things, you know *conceived*—? The warm Mediterranean, but the seed of a bad god.

– O— His coffee was far too hot. He placed it down again.

– And in that moment— Chronos, you know, the Time God, castrated his dominating father, with a sickle—

– Uh—

– And his seed fell in the foam and became Aphrodite, Venus. So we must always remember, Beauty was occasioned by the sickle of Time.

– Uh-huh.

– Or Beauty arrested Time, whichever you prefer.

Now she was losing him. She was soaking a broken perkin in her cup.

– O, selfish me.

– Uh, thanks, Miss.

– You don't need to call me Miss. Call me Alice.

– Miss Florence, I don't—

– What don't you? Won't you write your thoughts about *The Birth of Venus* for me, for the competition?

– I'll try *Primavera* this time. Is that—?

At least she kept her goonie on.

– Yes, that's good too, *Primavera*, very rich. I saw them both in the Uffizi.

– Or Turner I could, I did him before with Mr Martin. *The Fighting Téméraire*.

– A bit inchoate, Turner.

He tried a third sip, still hot, and replaced his cup unstably, in the ring of brown.

– Would you like to go to Italy?

– Don't know. Don't like macaroni.

– The ice cream though?

– Do you come from Italy?

– O, no. My grandfather no, my great-grandfather had a stone yard. He discovered a new way of polishing granite, using corundum. Well the Egyptians had done it four thousand years ago. So I suppose he rediscovered it.

– Great—

– Then he pioneered granite statues, with a pneumatic chisel. Otherwise, as you can imagine, granite statues take far too long. But then, why use granite at all when you can have marble?

– I know.

The Vespa had gone.

Peem placed the lens flat against the Salvation Army glass. But then it pointed too high, where a Union Jack was flapping near the Britannia statue perched on her high lintel. So he angled it down at the folk in the street, and pressed the button.

It didn't go in.

november

the full picture

All through October there had been difficult news coming out of Hungary. There were workers out on the street.

Counter-revolution, according to Tam Clunie, according to the *Worker*.

Tank crews had rolled in from Russia to explain to the workers the full benefits of communism. Some of the workers were misguided, some had given ear to bourgeois forces out to destroy the revolution in Hungary, Poland, Czechoslovakia and East Germany, for there was no doubt bad ideas could quickly spread. It was good the tank crews were there.

Khrushchev Stands Shoulder to Shoulder with Magyars, the paper said.

Then on 1st November came the news.

All Russian tanks had been withdrawn beyond the Hungarian frontier. This also was cause for rejoicing. It proved that the crews had done their work in countering the propaganda of the narrowly nationalist middle classes.

Then on 5th November came the news.

Soviet tanks had gone back in. It was difficult for a few tank crews to have spoken to everybody. The tanks were carefully selecting bourgeois targets. Several facades collapsed, including the radio station and the chamber of deputies, the post office, the army barracks, several shops and many houses associated with anti-

Leninist-Stalinist fronts. These quickly crumbled.

Matters came to a head in Aberdeen when a few of the stalwarts refused to sell the paper, Uncle Hugh for one. Dad went round to see Uncle Hugh.

> – Aye, it's difficult times.
> – Vera difficult—
> – We're probably no seein the full picture.
> – That's what I was feart for.

spikkin pish aboot fish

Peemie never saw Spermy much these days. They met at school, exchanged a word, or had a quick run-around. The teachers were showing resentment now, against Peemie, Iris and Tarry, who were due to stream off to the senior secondaries after Christmas.

– Longest river in Africa, Endrie?

> – Eh, Volga, sir. Fool, he'd meant to say Volta.

> – Nile. They'll expect you to know that you know, and all the tributaries.

– Bismarck Terrace Infants, but who was Bismarck?

> Silence.

> – So none of our bright departing sparks know the name of the German Chancellor who united his country. Nor that the Germans were so grateful they named a kind of herring after him. *Bismarck Herring, Bismarck Herring*, never forget that.

> – Khrushchev Kipper, said Peem, behind his hand to Tarry. Stalin Smokie.

> – What was that, Endrie—?

> – Jist spikkin pish aboot fish, said Spermy.

> – McClung! Out here!

He played Leave-i-o!, occasionally with Raymie, but Raymie couldn't catch a spongeball in a month of Sundays, so what on earth was the point?

And half of Saturday he couldn't anyway. The street was double-lined with cars for Pittodrie. It was ten minutes walk to the football ground, or five to the Miser's Hilly. From the Miser's Hilly you could look always down and imagine the ebb and flow of the match, from the volume and tone of the roars, and the single visible corner flag.

It was wet this Saturday too. None of the Rangers supporters liked to see an eczema of stot-marks on the bonnets or boots of their cars.

Then, about five the rain cleared up and a wan sun gleamed on departing bumpers.

Uncle Hugh had come for his tea but the tea was soon past.

Peemie had to hack sticks for tomorrow's fire, but then he edged free.

He chewed a Penny Whopper, a sort of cardboardy chocolatey thing, and, hunched over a high dyke, let it drop down on a neighbour's green to simulate dogturd.

He began pitching the ball against the great grey gable with the sloping eaves that sloped like Stalin's shoulders or moustache.

He threw spinners, he threw dislocating steeplers, he threw vicious flatballs that ricocheted the width of the street.

Frankie Groat came up from Urquharter.

– Aye, aye, Peemie.

Then Ludwig came roaring up on his Triumph Speed Twin, unlocked his hook from the handlebar, and looked across.

– What likes the day?

Lastly Tam Clunie and Billy Mill got dropped off in a taxi, that was unusual. They possibly didn't see him, and said never a word.

The verve went out of his game and it was no great shock when a terrier leapt in and intercepted an easy one. It ran off unmolested up Rosin with the bald ball, all slavvered with teethmarks. So he trooped back in.

Never seen it like this before. Six of them were sitting tight in a broken circle, four at the kitchen table, Frankie and Billy in the easy chairs. Mum was hovering in and out, though Tammy was safely corraled in his cot. There wasn't a spare chair at the table for her. Ludwig sat nearest the door.

What an argie-bargie. It wasn't hammer-and-sickle, it was hammer-and-tongs. Just as well Uncle Hugh was there to take Dad's side.

– Aye, well, I'm mair a man for the squeezebox than a dialectician.

– Look, Frankie, I ken fine what ye're saying, that Russia had to move in to protect the Revolution, and maybe that's richt, but I some doubt it. That's nae the point—

Dad always knew the point. He would always argue the point, and never be deflected from the point.

– The point is that the Party's been pretendin, an the *Worker*'s been pretendin, that the tanks came in at the invitation o the Hungarian people. It's a flat lee, Peter Fryer tellt us it was a lee, an—

– Andy, surely ye dinna believe what a capitalist paper like the *Manchester Guardian* tells ye. You o aa folk. Dinna tell me ye would stand at the Market Stance or Pittodrie sellin muck like the *Guardian* tae the workin class? Come on, Andy, come aff it!

– That's nae the point, Frankie, an fine ye ken it. The truth's the truth, an the *Worker*'s been hidin it fae us.

Peem had gone through to the box bedroom, listening, squeeze-squeezing his spare tennis ball. He didn't like raised voices. There was half a quire sitting on the tallboy. *Magyars Thank Moscow* was the headline, with *Rebel Ringleaders to Face Trial* further down the page.

– Andy, Andy, dae ye nae see ye're playin into the hauns o the reactionaries. That's what they want! If they can get true communists fechtin amangst oursels, then their job's easy, we'll be helpin tae destroy our ain revolution.

Back stotted his Dad.

– Na. Na, it's nae that simple, I wish it bloomin well was. How can we defend the Russian Government rollin tanks against the Hungarian people: they're Communists an aa, ye ken, just like the six o us here.

Seven— thought Peem.

– Nane o us command tanks, but we ken whit's right and wrang. If the Hungarian Communist Party wisna meetin the needs o the people, then the people were right to demonstrate. We'd have done that. Fan aa's done, ye're nae a lump o wid—

Peem flicked through the thin sheets of the disputed rag. With a week to go Barbara Niven's Fighting Fund was just £4,700 short of her monthly target of £6,000. And a dopey wee pooch called Pif was still all there was in the cartoon section, he wasn't a patch on Biffo the Bear.

– Come now, comrade. It was getting serious if they'd stopped calling Dad by his own name, Peem could sense that. It sounded like Billy Mill speaking now.

– The Party line is what will see us through, and the Party line is that Russia has saved Hungary from counter-revolution. That's what's important. The Revolution is mair important than ony individual, even Peter Fryer. Peter Fryer has been ower close to the guff o gunsmoke and it's connached him. Na, I'm nae sayin he's a coward as such, but he's forgotten his basic duty tae the Party.

– Piffle! Dad never swore amongst the Party. That showed lack of discipline. *Piffle* was one of his strongest. Piffle! Just piffle! I'm sorry, Billy, to have to say that to ye, but bein in the Party doesna mean ye put your brains oot wi the empty milkbottles in the mornin. Somebody said, was it Ruskin or Mill maybe, *Truth is indivisible*.

– Nae relation o mine, said Billy.

– Never had occasion to ken what that meant afore, but I think I ken now. Peter Fryer kens it as well. The Party had better face up, I'm tellin ye.

– Remember Trotsky, Andy, remember Trotsky.

Peem minded he got an ice-pick in his head in Mexico, supposed to be so sunny.

– Ye're mixed-up now. I thocht ye'd mair sense, continued Billy. Preachin tae the Party, that's nae dialectic that's diabolical. Ye're chuckin awa everything ye've worked for this last seven year. Seven year, Andy, think o that. What use is it chuckin your hand in noo—?

– Aye, an look at Suez, joined in Tam Clunie, who'd seen Spain. British an French paratroopers! The West's nae one whit better. Nasser will just throttle the oil aff and serve us right. Wi petrol runnin oot, the West will soon be on its knees.

– Ah, Tam, Suez is neither here nor there.

Peem could hear Mum come trauchlin in with more coal.

– Fa's for a cuppa tea?

– Na—

– Naebody?

– No it's aaricht, Madge.

Peem could hear Dad still keeping his end up.

– Billy, I ken ye'll think I'm big-headit, but it's nae me chuckin the Party, the Party chuckin me mairlike, that's what it comes doon till. It's enough tae gar a body greet.

– Me and aa, said Uncle Hugh, who'd left his red button accordion buttoned in its box.

– Ludwig? Ye're sittin gey quiet there—

– Good roads isna easy.

Then began a shuffling of chairs and feet. Peem heard them all go out, out past the blown roses, down past the great grey wall.

And nobody sang in the house again or, or if they did, they never really meant it.

december

probably dae a lot less damage

Father got down to the washing machine after that. The days o the wooden bilers are past, he said to Mum.

– Aye— she said and just looked at him, a bit drawn.

Being misdoubted only spurred him on, and soon he was fetching or sending home different parts on a weekly basis, some from cheap scrappies, most liberated from the bowels of Scottish Fertile.

Mr Hall, the boss at Scottish Fertile, was frantic to get Measured Day Working in so that they could raise productivity. Mainly because Imperial Phosphate Industries had swallowed the Scottish firm up, and IPI were not in the business for the good of their health. Nor anybody else's.

Royston and Cran had done a neat disappearing act after the affair of Ludwig's hand. In fact Cran had disappeared altogether, no one knew where.

Then a postcard came, addressed to Herr Ludwig, c/o Scottish Fertile, Sandilands, Aberdeen. The c/o was a bit unfortunate, said Gordon Burns, Dad's former apprentice. But apart from that it was best wishes, like, *terribly sorry about—*

Cran himself was heading back to the Territorial Army at Rannoch, as a close combat instructor: *I'll probably dae a lot less damage there—*

Royston, it turned out, had been working close by on a short-term contract at the Aberdeen Combworks. But with Mr Hall desperate, he'd summoned Royston and back he had come with a new sidekick. They set out to go round every last workshop, hopper and planthouse with wooden clipboard and silvered stopwatch.

Andy was waiting for them.

– Aye, here they come again, the boss's nancies.

– Says you. We meet again, said Royston.

– I heard ye drove them bald at the Combworks—

– Not so. They presented me with a silver comb when we left. A special for Scottish Fertile: very fine tooth.

– That's you all over, eh – aye eftir ither folk's siller.

– Beg pardon— ?

The Sulphuric Acid Plant was the usual foul congregation of vapours, and what with escapes and leaks, its acids soon *burned to buggery,* as Andy said, anything exposed. One day, late on – the hooter had already gone – Andy was buzzed in the sparkies' workshop to mend a piece of wiring. It was a total scunner because he was just making arrangements for a galvanised drum, earmarked for Mum's washing machine, to get brazed up with a brass drainvalve. At least the wiring was overtime pay, time-and-a-half.

But when he marched out with his toolbox, along to the acrid corrugated shed, and once he'd clattered up the steel ladder and onto the external gantry – there were Royston and his sidekick waiting. For Time-and-Motion had to be on overtime too – to clamp down on overtime.

Andy ignored them, took one look at the melted insulation, and turned on his heel.

They spoke at his back.

– Zooming off why, mister, we're already timing you, said the novice.

– Time yir granny, said Andy, and clattered down the next few rungs.

– Need to work out a unit time for this job, said the guy.

– Unit? Ye're mebbe a unit, I'm nae a bloody unit—! said Andy.

– Is it possible to be more constructive here? said Royston.

Andy swivelled and stamped back up.

– I need tae isolate her, said Andy. *I—so—late*. Have ye nae clue?

– Why can't you isolate her from here, on the gantry—? said the sidekick.

– I didna design this flamin works, said his Dad, and kicked a live wire to hiss on the railing beside them. The air was blue.

It was Ludwig told Peem this, a good laugh, when he came round with more bits for the washing machine in the box on his bike. His hook came in right handy for lugging sacks round to the shed. Mum wasn't to see the constituent parts, the welded angle-frame, the galvanised tub, the cannibalised AC motor with the recycled fibre belt. In case she put two and two together.

Brother Hughie was up to high doh because of this invasion of his shed.

– Watch oot where I'm makin ma rocket, he said to Peem, when Ludwig had gone for a second load.

Rocket! A glorified dart for percussing caps.

jesus is gaain tae be busy

Anyway, what need could there be of Time-and-Motion, or even of new-fangled washing machines: there was a bad time coming, and the Morrisons knew.

They kept pushing copies of *The Watchtower* through the letterbox, part of their seasonal drive. In one copy the world was compared to a train speeding downhill towards a bridge, over a ravine. Only the Witnesses knew that the bridge was down. Only the Witnesses knew the brakes had failed and the engine driver was tearing his cap off in despair.

The wise were advised to throw themselves out of the train now, while there was time.

– Aye, Jesus is gaain tae be busy, said Dad.

– What?

– Runnin up and doon the side o that line, catchin folk.

– O—

– Jesus is still alive, said Annie.

– He winna be much langer if he rins aboot like that, said Dad. I suppose God's got him on Time-and-Motion.

– Andy—! said Mum.

It was time to start looking for paper too. The wind had been blowing soot down the lum a lot in the last two months, and the yellow walls in hall, living room and boxroom were starting to look real grimy. The trio of plaster geese was needing a wipe with a damp rag on a regular basis.

Choosing paper was a long-drawn process, involving colours, patterns, textures, weight, suppliers, discounts and ends of run. The end rolls of a run were usually cheaper.

Large wallpaper scissors, a broad battering brush, an adhesive but forgiving floury paste, an extended table, a steady stepladder, a stable division of labour between batterer and layer-on, and a couple or three evenings were all that was required.

Another copy of *The Watchtower* came through the door. For those who had made it off the train into Jesus's scurrying arms, a paradise of peace beckoned, thickly illustrated with dyspictic drawings. The lion would lie down with the lamb for starters. Camel would snuggle with kangaroo; tiger with terrapin; zebra, cobra and wolf make up past differences. In the background lairs were opening, and coffin lids were coming unscrewed.

No more than overslept, God's fortunate self-chosen were rising fresh in their grave-clothes to mingle with Nature's novel throng.

– Shite. Jist shite, said Hughie.

– Not— said Annie.

– So fit's the lion gaain tae eat?

– Lions like sunflowers, said Annie.

– O, right—

– And tigers like toffee.

– Cobras—? said Peemie.

– Cobras drink lotsa milk.

The Morrisons attempted further propaganda, not face to face, but by means of a large apocalyptic tome, left in the shared Lavatory on the window shelf.

As far as being saved, the constipated would be off to a flier.

They started in the hall, to get their eye in. As soon as the paper was all cut, battered, and slid into position, it was obvious the doors and the skirting needed a good seeing-to also.

– It's nae the best wey, tae dae them second, but wi a bittie o care we can still gie them a lick.

All the windows, and the lobby door, were standing open when Mr Morrison passed. Dad was giving a last touch to the skirting. All was glistening, fresh and white.

– Aye, aye, said Dad.

– Hmphm— said Mr Morrison.

– Ye dinna sound affa suited wi yersel the day?

– Hmphm, I see you're working on the material side – again.

– Material side, Mr Morrison?

– Externals, the superficial. *Beware the whited sepulchre*, as Jehovah behoves us.

– Beware the dirty fool orra sepulchre, mairlike. Sae ye winna hae heard the story o the mannie that was paintin the ootside o Huntly Kirk—?

– The Kirk has nothing to do with true witness to Jehovah.

– O but it surely has, Mr Morrison, just you listen— Ye see there was this painter chiel, hoose-painter, ye ken, nae like Michaelangelo, mair like Hitler. Onywey, there was this hoose-painter, an he won the contract tae whiten the ootside o Huntly Kirk. Well the mannie was an affa hunger, aye tryin tae get twa bob for sixpence, an he thocht he'd double ees profit by thinnin doon the paint. Sae he put a gallon o water in for every gallon o paint, and steered it richt roon. It still looked pretty white, well it wid, widn't it, it's nae gaain tae turn green just acause o a suppie water—

– I am fully busy— said Mr Morrison.

– Wait. Sae up on ees ladder he went, the mannie, an started clartin the Kirk wi a big dose o whitenin. Roon an roon the waas he went, at aa the different heichts – the warst was high up, but lucky it was a Free Kirk, sae it wisna a big steeple.

– A prayer meeting is due to commence at six in my house—

– Dinna fret, nearly done. Well the mannie was nearly done an aa, when suddenly the lift grew dark, black clood rolled in, and wi a great clap o thunder, the rain came absolutely lashin doon. Well fit dae ye think happened next—?

– I really have no idea—

– O, I widna say that, Mr Morrison, folk micht believe ye. Onywey, as sure as fate, the rain took a haud o the whitenin an diluted it even mair, sae that the hale lot came runnin aff the waas an was soon lyin – in a peely-wally moat – aa roon the boddom o the kirk. Noo the mannie was lookin in great sorrow at the ruin o his handiwork, fan suddenly the black clood parted and God looked doon on him wi a big angry face. The mannie got such a shock he fell backwards aff the ladder an fell on his dowp in the pool o paint. And God's voice was heard oot o the black clood. An div ye ken fit he said? Div ye ken fit he said—?

– I expect I am about to discover—

– Ye are indeed, Mr Morrison. And let this be a lesson tae ye.

For God said: *Repaint! Repaint! And thin no more!*

school is missed

Then Uncle Hugh came round with news from London. Aunty Ros, they'd almost forgotten about her, had died of lung cancer and the funeral was in a couple of days. The north core of the family would need to send emissaries on the sleeper, would Mum or Dad like to go?

– It's affa sad, said Mother.

– What was she, forty a day?

– No, she'd stopped completely in the last twa weeks.

– Ah, well— said Father.

– Tell Uncle Wilf that Grizel can come up and bide for Christmas if she's needin tae tak her mind aff things.

Grizel was fourteen.

So the urgency over the paper grew and, in a burst from Friday night to Sunday, the living room, then boxroom, were done.

The beautility sideboard was commandeered. Mother battered, Hughie proffered the lengths to Dad up the stepladder. Dad had a 2B pencil behind his right ear, Annie played with Tammy, who bit, and Peemie was starting *The Weir of Hermiston.* On a rexine chair – curled on the floor – in the lav – wherever he could get peace for improvement.

The book had arrived in the post two mornings earlier, parcelled in brown paper with lopsided sisal. Inside was *The Weir*, and a weird note.

Dear Peem,

Hope you enjoy ~~the~~ this – school is missed.

Look out for yourself ~~and~~

Best wishes,

Mr (Alex) Martin

It was good of him, quite troubling, he hadn't seen him since the incident in July.

He tried the first chapters. Here was hardly *Kidnapped* or *Treasure Island*, there was a shortage of nut-brown men.

She was never interesting in life, in death she was not impressive— he read.

– Give us a hand, Peemie, get your heid oot o a book for once.

Weel, there's some of them gey an' ill to please, said his lordship.

– Sae did onybuddy hear what happened tae the Morrisons' cat?

– No, Dad, is it alright?

– Just keep workin and I'll tell ye.

– Nae thon smelly ginger thing?

– Listen an ye'll find oot. Ye see the Morrisons had aa gone awa one day—

– Aabody? Fan?

– Last week. They'd aa gone oot tae deliver *The Watchtower* roon the doors, Mr Morrison, Mrs Morrison, Melvin and wee Melba. And of course aabody wanted ane.

– Why? It's rubbish.

– Because it's free. Because ye can stuff yir boots wi it, stick it in the jamb o a warped door. And if it lands up in the back o the fire, it's nae the end o the warld—

– Nice one, Dad—

– Onywey, that's nae the point. The Morrisons were awa, and they'd locked their cat in the hoose, but they'd forgotten to fill up its saucerfu o milk. Aa that was oot on the linoleum was a saucerfu o petrol, because Mr Morrison had been doin a wee jobby.

– What kinda jobby?

– Well, tryin to slack twa roosty nuts at the back o their atomic cooker. And he'd left the petrol oot by pure mistake. Well Smelly Benji was affa thirsty wi nae milk, sae eftir a while he comes sniffin at the saucer o petrol. An first he dips a white whisker, *sniff*, an then he dips a wee black snoot, *sniffsniff*, an last he dunks his lang pink tongue, an laps up aa the petrol—

– Gad's!

– And in twa shakes o a deid lamb's tail, he's aff roon the room. Roon by the sideboard an roon by the sofa – careerin through the legs o aa the chairs – roon an roon, fester an fester, tichter an tichter – skraikin an cluikin at the lino – till aa o a sudden—

– He blaws up— said Hughie.

– He collapses, faas doon. Nae even the tip o ees tail stirrin—

– He musta been tired, Daddy.

– Deid, I suppose.

– Wis he deid—? said Peem.

– Na. Ran oot o petrol.

The batter was getting lumpy, Peem had to make up fresh paste. All surfaces were occupied. He spread the *Evening Express* lunchtime edition on the lino, and was just beginning to stir, when he saw in a single column of snippets—

Ex-teacher found
In a two-room flat in
Donfield Place.
Uncollected milk.
Police said
there were no suspicious
circumstances.
Next-of-kin have been informed.

He really should have gone round.

a wilful convulsion

Grizel was delayed, they were down at the station for about four hours, something about frozen points. She came up most years, usually in the summer. She was a lovely lass, with grey eyes and a bit of a tear. Mum made her a special three-course tea with split pea broth, boiled beef and tatties, soft shreds of cabbage, whole boiled peas. The custard was through the boil and thickening on the hob.

Hughie sat opposite her.

She picked away at the stringy beef with her fork the prongy way round, but used it reversed as a shovel to win her peas. It wasn't fair to expect her to play Doctors and Nurses yet, not with her mother dead. The last pea rolled off her fork, bounced on the table, and into her lap. She looked up and blushed into Hughie's eyes.

– Peem, nip up to Marchetti's.

Marchetti's! Peem ran up and crossed in front of a tram, and raced back so that the seven scoops in the carton wouldn't melt.

Ice cream!

Tammy was banging with a plastic spoon in his high chair, and Annie was squirming.

– Serve Grizel first, said Hughie.

Grizel got the box bedroom, which made Hughie have to come into the front room and share. He was all legs and didn't tie his pyjamas properly, he was like a horse.

Dad was out on a call-out, while Mum had nipped upstairs to the Hirds. She said Annie and Tammy were *soundo*.

– Jingsypings, I've left ma thingummyjig under the other bed, said Hughie.

– What thingummyjig—?

– Ma yo-yo!

When did brother Hughie last play wi a yo-yo? He was away ages.

Peem fetched out his Stevenson from under the green quilt. He liked *The Weir* a bit better, now he was nearing the end.

> *He felt her whole body shaken by the throes of distress, and had pity upon her beyond speech. Pity, and at the same time a bewildered fear of this explosive engine in his arms, whose works he did not understand, and yet had been tampering with. There arose from before him the curtains of boyhood, and he saw for the first time the ambiguous face of woman as she is. In vain he looked back over the interview; he saw not where he had offended. It seemed unprovoked, a wilful convulsion of brute nature—*

Mannie Martin could have warned him the thing was unfinished.

So Peem sneaked through in his bare feet, for his slippers would surely squeak. The box bedroom door was open a crack, he dare not open it more, he inched it—

Grizel's heid was sunk back in the softness, Hughie's hands flat at each side. They were half-under the bedclothes.

The headboard began rocking, scuff-scuffing the wallpaper.

The headboard started to shoogle, puffs of fine dust arising.

The headboard rattled hard, and thence to a stop.

It had left a niche in the plaster—

Peem ran back in his bare feet before anybody opened their eyes.

Five minutes later Hughie the Horse jumped back in with Peemie, bashing him, whistling, tugging the pillow comfy. He felt something underneath.

– Hey, fit's this daein here?

– Nithin—

– Looks it—

Peem snatched the blue stone back from his hot hand.

He lay there and thought and thought.

He wanted to fit it on Grizel's nipple.

sanative

It was always on the cards that Spermy would run away.

He visited his mother once, behind the enormous dykes, the palissade of so-called sanative trees. On the drive he met a patient in long thick coat and slippers, with his head wrenched skywards, trying to utter—

Compared to that his mother in her room seemed normal. But she said nothing, empty and pale.

She had red marks on her temples.

– Did ye faa, then?

– Non.

– I'm awa tae the Broch the morn.

– Jed—

the good ice

He had to get out of the house.

Brief sun, a flurry of snow, in which he bumped into Spermy. Old puddles were solid with frost.

They walked sort of together up to the top of Rosin, and crossed. Peem poked his nose through the cemetery railing.

– A cemetery's supposed tae hae yews—?

– Fit use are they? said Spermy.

There were plenty granite memorial stones, though, the writing graved in gold or black. A few plinths with urns, some shrouded angels, not too many. Off in the scabby new part, with patches of discoloured grass and windblown posies, was a hill of soil and clods. A black tarp half-covered it, cracking in the breeze. Sun picked out a pickaxe, dropped like an amateur anchor on an edge.

– Sae div ye want tae be a grave-digger fan ye're bigger, is that it?

– Why, foo big dae ye hae tae be—? said Peem.

– Sax feet, they say.

– Ye're in good bone—

They walked up briskly, towards the neat baronial cemetery keeper's house.

– See, ye get a nice hoose an aa, thrown in.

– Aye.

– An folk are dyin tae meet ye.

– Can I ask ye somethin—? said Peem. Eftir last Christmas, ken, did they ever—

– Fit—? said Spermy.

– Find them?

– *Them*—?

– Ye're nae makkin it easy.

– Fit's supposed tae be easy aboot it?

– Yir Da, yir twa uncles?

– Ma *three Das* an ma *three uncles*, ye mean? Sure, the divers haled them oot, fan the wind stopped ragin.

– Fit like were they?

– They never said.

– It's aaricht, ye dinna hae tae tell me.

– Twa o them had hauns roon the third ane's throat.

– Eh, fit? Really—? said Peem.

– Foo wid I ken? I ran awa fan I heard they'd found them. Nivver went near the funeral. Mither near fuckin killed me.

– Fit like is she?

– Skivin awa in the madhoose. She sends me gelt.

– Look at this, said Peem.

He read out the *Trinity Cemetery Regulations and By-Laws*.

> 6.5 *The lairholder shall maintain headstones on a monument in a neat, safe and proper condition.*

Ye widna want tae be killed by a loose heidstane, eh? said Peem.

> 6.6 *Nothing shall be planted on a lair by a*
> *lairholder or a lairholder's proxy, without the*
> *consent of the Registrar.*

– I ken fit I'd plant on their three graves— said Spermy.

– Fit?

– Big fuckin cactus.

They heard the slow purr of an engine. Peem felt a cold prickle and turned round. Drawing up Seaforth came a long black hearse, a black Ford Popular, a pink idling Vespa. Miss Florence must have refused Mannie Bain's offer.

The loons slank off, zigzag down the cemetery lanes.

They walked and walked and didn't say much.

– Aye, funny mannie—

– Couldna belt, fuckin useless—

– Wish he hadna drank.

– Sent me a book— said Spermy.

– Sent you a book—?

– Aye, I can read, ye ken.

They kicked at a chip-paper for about half a mile to warm their toes. They went round by the Bumps.

– Foo did he die, again?

– Tarry heard Mannie Harrow spikkin aboot it in the street. Got ees usual doon ees neck ae nicht – a skinful – clambered up on a kitchen chair, an hung eesel fae the gas-pipe, which went and broke—

– Sae they dinna ken fit killed him—? said Spermy.

On the way back they started skiving onto buses. A 4 from the brick

Beach Baths to Castle Street. They sat on the green bench near the door, where they could spy the conductor upstairs in the fish-eye mirror. As soon as the conductor set foot to descend, the loons swung onto the open platform and off via the rail, braking on their heels, near-stumbling.

– Ye'll get the jail, ye'll get prison—! shouted the conductor.

They scudded off into the Market Stance, the Friday food market. No Commies or Salvationers today, nor chimps-on-a-stick. Just happy-faced apples, hands of bananas, crates and crates of fine stuff underneath.

– Apples, pears, bananas each, twelve plums for sixpence—

Then a 23 from the Regal to Union Terrace. It was packed to the gunnels, and they just pressed on and unpressed off, next stop, like slices of beef.

– Look doon inside ma jerkin, said Spermy. A jerkin wasn't really enough in winter, you needed Eskimo kit.

What did he have? A string bag of oranges, no, tangerines. Most were bare, some were tissued, three in silver paper, crinkle-wrapped.

– An I never peyed.

– Why no?

– Cos fit need have they? They've got plenty.

There was only one whitewash slogan as they crossed Union Bridge, the police must have been smart last night, or maybe the comrades were down in numbers.

HANDS OFF EOKA

– Fa's *Eoka*? said Spermy.

– Greek.

– Fa writes that shite?

– Communists.

– An—?

– They believe that things should be shared oot equal.

– That's why I tooken the tangerines.

– Well aye but—

– Well na but— An I dinna want nane o yir Communists comin roond ma door writin *Hands Aff Tangerines*, okay—?

– Okay.

They walked a good length, past the Majestic, right into Holburn. Then they took an open-ended No.1 tram down past the West End, speeding towards the Brig o Dee.

– Sae fit book did Mannie send ye?

– Book, ye still on aboot that? Jealous or somethin?

– Well—?

– I'm nae tellin ye. Aabody got some bastardin book, I'll bet ye. Thon Bapface got ane, for sure.

– Fa, Iris—?

– Aye, Izzy and Veronica pinched her bag, an it fell oot in the gutter. *O, look what ye've done to my set o Russian plays*, she says, ye ken fit like she is.

– Probably Mayakovsky—

– Aye, some shite or ither. I picked it up for her. I ask ye. *The Three Seagulls*.

When the conductor came round, they claimed they'd lost their tickets, so he demanded names and addresses.

– John Knox Halibut, 123 Raggy Row, Torry.

– Spell it. *Halibut* as in *fish*, is it? said the mannie.

– Nup. *Halibut* as in *neep*.

– That's nae an anagram— said Peem.

– Watch it! said Spermy. He raxed Peem up by his anorak hood, then led him a speed waltz doorwards, tramping on odd folks' sticking-out feet. Peem wasn't sure of his game at first. But they'd gone as far as they needed to go.

As they arrived at the roadworks on Riverside Drive they knew they'd never seen the like. The Dee was amazing, a mass of ice floes.

– Like great dinner plates, said Peem. Whales' dinner plates.

– Cracked— said Spermy. He stood on the north embankment and started flinging cold available cobbles onto the surface.

It must be absolute brass up-country, on the Cairngorms, past Coilacreich.

At first they threw their cobbles high and these pitted, but once you threw them flat they curled and butted. Their hands soon nipped.

– Are ye on—? said Spermy.

– Daft.

– Yella.

Spermy chucked a muckle cobble.

– Hey, though— said Peem.

– Fit?

– Well thon time, mind. When ma heid got splutten at the Beach. Ye never, wis it, did ye see ony—

– Wis it me? Trust you tae think o that, ye cheeky poop.

– Wis it an accident, though—?

– Search me.

– Well, fa else could it have been?

– Some fuckin rogue, likely. He'll catch it some day.

And Spermy slipped him the tangerine bag and skipped aboard the river in the wan sun. He skidded, then stuck in places. He skited out to the first pontoon, like the upturned hull of a granite ship.

– Come back!

But Spermy carried on. A bobby came dandering onto the brig in his dark cape and was looking over. He yarked the *Property of Aberdeen Corporation* thing off its hook, with its hank of rope. The red-and-white cork belt spun down to Spermy, who laughed back up.

– Fit's that for?

Spermy skated off under the brig. The policeman blocked the traffic with one hand and lolloped across the carriageway. He tossed the belt again for the emerging Spermy.

– Watch ma heid, copper!

Peem spied the middle channel had hunched and was moving.

– Spermy—!

Then he realised he'd theft on his hands.

His first miss mushed on the ice, as Spermy dodged and sang back up: *You ain't nuthin' but a Hound Dog / Cryin' all the time*. Peem bowled a tangerine bouncer, *Well you ain't caught a rabbit*, then steepled a silver-foil, *And you ain't no friend of mine*.

Spermy turned away, his legs spattered with juice and pith. He was heading downriver now. Trying to keep to the good ice.

Peem threw in arcs and higher arcs to the distance, to burst tiny orange differences on the ice.

The bobby blew on his long silver whistle.

Peem took the bus back into town. He dropped off in Union Street. A mile away, a pale new moon sickled over the Citadel.

Helen of Troy was on at the Majestic, *The Man Who Knew Too Much* was next, then *Moby Dick*. He'd never been to the cinema on his own, but it was far too cauld to be saving for bikes, so he joined the stamping queue.

As he shivered on the steps he read the display. A cast of thousands, simultaneous premiere in 56 countries and 23 tongues. *To citizens of the world's great free nations in their own languages: Canada, Thailand, Japan, Scotland, Greece*. The largest film prop ever made. A thousand pounds of nails. Eight foot wheels and forty foot high. Some horse. With air-conditioning in its belly, fine for conspirators.

There were no kid's prices, and only Back Stalls.

no doubt to kid the parakeets

As soon as Spermy got round the bend in the river, the ice was brashy, variable, he hopped ashore from floe to floe. The afternoon was nigh on night, it was a good bit yet to the harbour. He got in the bottom gate of the Duthie Park, and trekked his way up past the ghastly square yacht pond, the long dull slide, the chained-up swings, and onto the white veldt of the Park proper. The place to be would be the Palm House.

He nicked in a side-door and hid behind a clump of palms. The dark-clad keeper finished his round and banged his door shut from the outside. Whether the wood was bad-swollen, or the hinge ajee, he had to bang it twice, then lock it.

It was good and warm, and all manner of lights had been left on, no doubt to kid the parakeets and budgies they'd hardly strayed from their parallel.

Spermy strolled through the Palm House, humid and warm, raking for food. There was no kiosk to kick in, the wire bins had little rubbish, the palms were nothing but leaf. There should have been roastable lizards, soft bananas, boar trampling through yams—

All he heard was the sound of water.

He came on a rustic bridge, and leant his elbows comfy to look down on the indoor burn that glid over cobbles and looped into a guitar-shaped pool of fat and golden fish.

They bloated or swam idly, coasting each others' flanks, burping bubbles that spun and burst. One was lemon, some feverish red, others blotched – black on orange – like camouflage for a black-and-orange world.

Spermy minded the book *Fishing Methods of the World* that Mannie Martin had sent him. Trawl, seine, pot, trap, hooks, harpoon, dynamite, poison – he'd none of these.

– Come tae Daddy, ye fuckers.

they couldna gie a fuck for helen

The theatre was stifling smoky, yet he'd not a brass farthing left for a Kia-Ora. Peem plunked into a seat at the right-hand end of a row. He'd missed the cockerel crow of the Pathé News and the car adverts. So what. He'd arrived smack in the big film, just as they rolled the credits. It was CinemaScope, curvy panoramas plus big head close-ups.

The long Greek galleys hove into view, bellying their white sails. The slaves bent, their pained brows beaded, and their backs just rivered with sweat. They drove the galleys up the beach, confronting Troy's towers. The slaves slumped, the warriors leapt out.

Absorbed in the shifting scene of siege and repulse, he became Hector, became Achilles.

He heard a man behind him.

– Pure war, eh? They couldna gie a fuck for Helen.

me tarzan, you lianne

Spermy kicked out at one of the wire bins. It fell on its side. He puzzled a moment. Then he unclasped his knife from his back pouch, and haggered through a couple of long lianas, that trailed a bit on the ground. Lianne, there was a girl in his old Torry class called Lianne. He used to grab her hair and swing her round shouting *Me Tarzan, you Lianne*. That was one of the reasons they had to move.

A couple of ten foot lengths would do the job.

Spermy took a pair of ends and laid them out ready. He tied the other ends round the empty maw of an Aberdeen Corporation Parks Department wire litter basket. Liana turned out to be tough to knot, but he bent on a couple of large hitches. Then he lay on his belly by the pond edge, and lowered in the basket. The bright carp scattered. It would take time, were it trap or trawl. He took up the reins of his device.

He wriggled a little back from the water, so as to cast no shadow, no alien image on the Koi. One or two lipped at the basket, then swerved away. None dared in. Perhaps they could hear his belly rumble. The lemon was the one he fancied, but she was shy, and hung in the wake of a blotched orange-and-black.

At last he could wait no more.

Blotch was making a pass across the basket mouth. Lemon was on his tail. He stood up violently and yanked on the two lianas, running back on his heels, hauling the basket up through the water, tripping on a jungly root and falling back down. The parakeets screeched like crazy.

– Bugger o hell!

The basket stood in the shallows of the guitar-shaped pond. It was upright, maw in the air. Stepping across the paving, he could hardly look in.

But there it was—

His Lemon.

There was nothing like a cooking pot about. He couldn't wait for a bed of red embers. For Lemon was over 4 pounds, certainly over 3, and if he just plonked her on an ordinary fire, the fire would quench and go out. It would have to be some kind of spit.

He raced through the Palm House, looking for something that would serve. There were notices. *Do not disturb the fish. Do not feed the budgerigars. Beware of cactus.* They were wired to pillars. None erect on a rod that could make a strong spit.

He kicked two lugs off a lowdown cactus, and ferried them through on his jerkin. He sandwiched Lemon lightly between the lugs, their spikes entering her flanks.

Now what?

He put his last Woodbine on his lug and tore the fag packet into the bottom of the wire basket. He tweaked dry twigs from a bush. He laid the basket on its side, and then his Lemon sandwich about half-way up. He jumped on the basket till it caved in around the spiky sandwich! Then he flipped the buckled basket back on its base and poked, at the third attempt, a lighted cardboard match through the grid.

Flame sniffed then seared at the lemon one's scales. Her flesh began to steam.

gypit

Back and fore the battle raged for an hour, for ten years, till the last throw of Fortune's dice. The Wooden Horse was shoved and planted stark against night sky, an unwrapped gift. The galleys disappeared, raking off the beach.

Enemy gone, the Trojans creaked open the city gate.

– Canny noo— said the man in the row behind Peem.

They laid their shoulders to the eight foot wheels.

– Dinna be sae gypit, said the commentator. Put that horse back—

But soon the folk of Troy were wrapped in red and bloody flames – while Helen in some burly arms was snatched.

Two rows forward, some geezer squeezed himself up from his slouch. A sway of soft bronze ringlets, away from him and back again, small lips shadowed against flame. . .

kissing

his

him

quiff

o

with elbows out

232

he drew

a bone

comb through,

smoothing his

Tony Curtis

and

leaning

into his chest

Miss Florence

the bathos of his bonny lemon

From the bathos of his bonny Lemon, he managed to salvage four singed and half-raw mouthfuls. Still, he had caught her. He had his last fag, and tore lots of leaves from a handy tree, a mattress for his night's repose. It would be a warm night in the Palm House.

Suddenly at six the lights went out, and the parakeets' chattering too.

Were they on the blink?

He bated his breathing, but no footsteps came.

good for ye in winter

Nobody watched Spermy walking at dawn to the Brig o Don, at the north exit from town. He pouched a pair of rolls while a baker's van was loaded. Then the driver came out and recognised him *Aye, aye, ye're at it early?* and gave him two more. They were called buttery rowies, fine and salty. Full of fat, *good for ye in winter* Dinah aye said.

He stopped on the Brig. On the south side the swirl of the Don dug deep its bank. On the north side in the shallows he watched a heron, its dull beak pointing down. Several lorries passed him, heading north.

The beak darted in the water and flashed up – a silver-barred T. It could be a good sign.

Spermy turned from the parapet and stuck his thumb out. There was plenty traffic, though none would stop for a scruff like him. Then a fag van pulled in.

    – Gaain far, laddie?

    – Broch.

    – I'm gaain tae Peterheid first. Dae ye bide in the Broch?

    – Nuh.

    – I've fifty cartons for the Blue Toon. Fit a billies tae smoke.

    – Aye.

    – Far dae ye live then?

    – Toon.

    – Sae ye'll miss Christmas wi your folks—?

    – Nuh.

    – Dae ye smoke?

    – Aye.

    – Well ye shouldna. Ye winna hae ony puff left for fitba.

    – Dinna like fitba.

    – Or tennis—

    – Fa plays tennis?

    – Fit does your Ma say aboot ye smokin?

    – Ma Ma's in Cornhill—

    – O. Right. Check ahint ye. I think there's a burst carton.

the way

Two hours later he was sitting on a bollard by the wooden drifter *The Way*, smoking his way through a hundred Capstan.

    A grocery van braked to a halt with stuff and the guy began disgorging it, strung cardboard boxes and netting vegetable bags.

    – Gie us a hand, then.

    He did so, dizzily.

The van had spewed its boxes of stew and Carnation milk, its lumpy sacks of swedes, tatties, cabbages and carrots.

– Is she sailing noo?

– If they get their skates on, they'll catch the tide.

– But I thought it was comin up Christmas.

– They have their ain wey o Christmas on *The Way*. A different calendar, ye ken.

– Are they allowed tae dae that?

– I wouldna argue if I was you. The skipper's affa religious.

They came down the pier in ones and twos, eventually nine or ten. Clean-shaven, small and squarish black-shoed men, they launched their kitbags from their shoulders on to the deck below. They wore caps – flat and blue – and oiled wool ganseys.

– Far's that dashed cook?

– I doubt he couldna get the bend oot o his elbow—

– Fit a sotter.

– O, hello, hello, that's nae you again is it, young Jed? Fit are ye daein here sae far fae hame?

down the companion

An hour later he was with his Great Uncle Sprag in the galley, his knuckles white round the pan-guard, as *The Way* cleared the harbour, catching the ebb, and rose to the first of the northerly swell.

– Ye're lookin a wee bit peely-wally. Are ye nae supposed to be at the school?

– There's impetigo.

– Ye dinna close a school for a twa-three spotties.

– There's impetigo, eczema, Black Death an leprosy.

– Sae they're nae as weel as they were—?

– And a load o nits. An I'm nae one o them.

– Aye, your Da was a smart arse an aa.

– Far we gaain?

– Just alang the Moray Firth.

– Are ye huntin for kessocks?

Kessocks were the small herring he'd heard them speak about in the summer.

– Nonsense. Ye winna get kessocks this time o year. We'll just try alang the coast a bittie. If there's nithin much daein, well next week it's the West Coast for us. Alang to Inverness and through the Canal. Then up the Minches. That's where the big shoals are, they're sayin. Just sweemin aboot waitin for us. Noo whit aboot a cuppie o tea?

– For you?

– For aabody, there's ten o a crew. Ye've made a cuppie o tea afore—?

– Nuh, there's nae tea in our hoose.

– Nae tea?

– Ma mither jist drinks coffee. Coffee an reid wine.

– Well tell her ye'd like tae try tea.

– I canna.

– Why nae. Has the cat gotten your tongue?

– She's in the Asylum.

– O, richt— Well she winna get fancy coffee in there.

– She doesna. They gie her electric shocks—

– That's nae vera nice.

– In her heid.

– Fit would they dae a thing like that for?

– Tae stop her bein depressed.

– An why is she depressed, like?

– Because they keep giein her electric shocks in the heid.

– Vera smart.

– Na. Cause naebody speaks tae her.

– O, come on, surely, fit wey would naebody speak tae her?

– Cause she's a big hure.

– She's nae that big a hure—

– She is though.

– Hurry up wi that tea, or else naebody'll speak tae you neither.

Uncle Sprag lit the gas for him.

– Ye must have heard aboot ma mither?

– Fit ye hear an fit ye believe's twa different things. Now see an dinna stew it.

When the kettle of tea was ready, he poked his head up the hatch, and shouted.

– Tea-o!

They came piling down the companion.

– Pour it oot then, cookie. We're sittin here wi empty mugs.

– Whaur's the milk?

– God, it's affa het.

– Have ye nae put oot a biscuit wi this?

– Wee twat. I widna have taen him on. He's far ower young.

– I'm nae.

– Fit age are ye?

– Fifteen—

– Aye and I'm ninety-seven.

– Gibby, dinna be sic an aggressive bastard, said one of the men.

– I'll hae nae language aboard ma ship, said the skipper, as his arse swayed down the companion.

– Foo many tatties will I hae tae dae?

– Ten men, five big tatties apiece – if they're to haul aa nicht.

He peeled fifty-one tatties with a clasp-knife and bled his palm, when the boat lurched and he'd no spare hand.

And how was he to know you had to fry onions before sealing the mince? Half the mince landed up as a round cinder in the bottom of the pan.

– For what we are about to receive, may the Lord make us truly thankful.

– Serve it up, then, cookie.

– Is that aa the tatties ye've cooked? It's nae wartime, ye ken.

– Is this supposed tae mind us on the Bible – a burnt offerin?

– I'll hae nae blasphemy aboard ma ship, said the skipper, cutting a pat of butter for his tatties.

come astarn

Two hours later, still at the decoke, he got rousted up. He had two jobs – cooking for ten, and leaping about the deck to order. The crew were redding the nets, shaking and tisking out any long-deceased herring, and firing them over the side. The redding was finished, the nets prepared, night was falling.

Boat well out from the land, in their ordinary clothes men went to their places.

Somebody yapped an order at him

– Haud the buoys oot fae that cage – then fire awa fan it comes their turn.

He stood in a tangle of rope and wondered which one he should start with.

First an old anchor was dropped with a mighty splash. Then, as the boat motored slowly downwind, cable and nets and strops began to stir on the deck, began to pay out.

He felt a tug under him and grabbed the strop of a white canvas buoy, as nets went hissing over, into the water.

Uncle Sprag poked his head out of the side wheelhouse window, and looked back.

– Nae that ane, ye tattie—!

The rope whipped up round his right ankle, and rived him along foot first, up and over the gunnel's edge, riffling at the buttons on his spine, rapping his skull like a planet-burst. He heard *Astarn*!

238

as he gulfed in a shock of bubbles, boiling, cold. *Astarn*! *Astarn*!

Puppet with its foot in a string, he slewed along somewhere under the surface, ocean forcing at his nose, big curtains brushing down past him—

Bang! Thunderous bang as the prop hit reverse – now he'd be sucked back, slashed to bits, in the huge cross-wave of water.

But as the strain slackened, his stockinged foot slipped from its trap. He jack-knifed up for a gulp – and hung, pyochering, on the traitor buoy.

– Fit an abortion, said Gibby, when they hauled him back. Fit are ye? Ye're a fuckin abortion.

99.999% of history

It wasn't easy, the thought of Amande coming home. The red marks from her temples were long faded, but the scars weren't healed, Dinah could see that. The Frenchwoman walked and smiled but it was as though she wasn't in, she'd flitted. Maybe the real Amande had already gone, to her long home. All that fleeing, loving, betrayal and death, just another footnote in the 99.999% of history that never gets written. That was what had bothered Billy so much: even the 0.001% of history that was written, you couldn't connect to.

So what if Walter Drake was guzzling lampreys when Canute said he'd need a hand to stop the Armada, and then some one-eyed guy blew up the cakes just as they were signing a big document in a meadow, what was it all about, Billy used to rave on. It told you nothing about why he was living in Leith in a smelly flat, where he had come from, and what guide he might have to the future. As history it was a caricature, as myth it was irrelevant.

He'd written that, something like that, on his paper, and it came back *0% – re-sit*. When he'd told her, she'd sympathised, it was quite brave, he'd need to knuckle down a bit, but in the re-sit he'd done the same, to show consistency, and that was him out, cooling his heels on the dole, till they strongly suggested a job with the Cleansing, a bucket man, humphing the galvanised ten gallon buckets which folk put out once a week full of clinker, ash, peelings, unburnables.

Billy had started to hang on her more. He needed kind words, her to be there, a regular cuddle. But her work was hard, she saw a lot, and she needed more from a man. One night she offered him to come to her place, a couple of flatmates but they'd be in bed, yet he said he'd better not. Next night, after a bottle of Spanish, in he came, and they tore the relevant garments off or down. He tried to roll a Durex onto a shy lump of flesh that filled and ebbed, without ever stiffening. He couldn't talk about it and she daren't.

– He likes to sleep, he said.

– Is he tired? she said. He's done fuck-all, she thought.

They lay on the carpet, keeping their bare hurdies off the linoleum. By a concerted private effort he got the rubber on again in a concertina'd way. He applied for entry – to what, in what direction, why and how he didn't seem to know. She thrust up her hips as strongly as she dared, consistent with passivity. He felt the heat of her womanhood and melted, a semi-spasm, as the door moved, and a flatmate pushed right in, against his feet. Dinah caught her pal's smirk as the shrivelled sac dropped off on the lino. She was glad there was no chance of a male analysis, a going-over.

From then she knew that the way ahead was out. They'd spoken before about her parents, her father's deep knowledge about the pits, of Billy coming to Fife for Christmas. But he was becoming no more than a lapdog, and her lap was the last place she wanted him to be.

She could do with a man. Now instead Amande would come home, for Christmas, maybe for good. Mad fucking Amande.

They made him his tea, Spermy. Sausages with plenty runny egg to dip in. And a pint of tea, which he absorbed gladly, warm in his big borrowed gansey and dungarees.

– Ye're your faither's loon, said Spraggy.

– As muckle eese as a paper dirk, said Gibby.

The nets had been reshot and, after their snooze, it had come time to haul.

– Dinna think ye're staunin up on deck wi us.

– We're nae volunteers in a fuckin lifeboat.

– The only thing I'll staun for is this— said Gibby, rising in his seat to let rip a fart.

He was taken forrard to the cable locker and introduced to a black anaconda.

– Try and mind, we're nae shootin this time, we're haulin back in.

– The winch taks in the boddom rope, the bush, the messenger.

– Which ane first?

– It's aa the same thing. Different names. Aa ye've tae dae is coil it doon. Got that? Coil it.

For the next five hours he reached up to ward off the anaconda as it swayed down into the hatch, hissing its waters down the back of his neck, swaying out of reach. It was stiff enough in all conscience, and it took him all his strength to bend it into an enormous greased coil. It was mad. He stood in the coil's middle and fed the rope from over his shoulder onto the crescent snake. Soon he wouldn't be able to see over.

It came slow after a time, the messenger, the steel deck-winch creaking then halting, invisible overhead.

He was still only a delegate from the galley though, and when the haulers stopped for a mug of water, he had to dash to dice the veggies and fire them into the lentil broth.

– Is that fuckin soup bilin? said Gibby

   – Aye, it's better nor bilin.

   – Well let it cool doon, ye hure's twat. An let's see ten mugs and ten shaves o loaf up here in five minutes.

He propped the wide tray on each step of the companion in turn, and inched his feet up. He lifted it over the coaming and laid it on the heeled and streaming deck.

   Ten lips of soup ran over onto the tray.

   – Cunt, ye hinna even spreaden the loaf.

   Spermy withdrew his head and spoke to himself.

   – Last thing I dae, I'll spit in that bastard's tea.

   The skipper kept his window shut against the language of his mate. There was no need to reproach men when they were working.

From that haul onwards, Spermy spat in Gibby's tea religiously, under cover of Carnation milk.

   Next day he managed to boil the tatties, the Golden Wonders, through the bree to a watery mush.

   He got the bird for his home-made custard as he dolloped it out in sulphurous lumps.

The last of the week, they took him off both cook and messenger, put him up on the deck-hatch and set him there to haul.

   Before headering into their yellow smocks and up on deck, some grizzlers cut a slice of plug, rolled it in the sweat of their palm, and rammed it down into silver-lid pipes. Then lit it, with spills, from the fo'c's'le stove.

   Spermy popped two tabs of Beech Nut gum.

They swayed side by side, green hand and old hand, like a bank of daffodils.

– Fan I tell ye tae haul, fuckin haul, said Gibby.

That would be clear enough to a deaf gull.

– An fan I tell ye tae shak, fuckin shak—

The boat heeled towards them, they took in slack.

The boat rocked away, they held it.

They braced and shook the flat of the net like a prickled blanket, and a score of herring bounced in curves on the deck, and twitched in the scuppers.

After eight hours the last white buoy was aboard, plus the mudhook tail of the anaconda. Gibby joined the skipper behind glass. He lowered the window on its strop.

– Redd that scuppers. Get mobile.

And he slammed the window up again.

Spermy had braced himself to dip his bucket over the heeling side, then sluice each silver scale from the deck-planks, winch, mast, bulwarks and wheelhouse casing.

Shaken scales had flown and stuck like transfers to the wheel-house window. Spermy slooshed his final bucket upwards, just where Gibby's face—

The lights went down as she surged ahead. *The Way* swung hard for the Broch.

a tassie o thé

Amande was now putting on her best smiley face for the asylum. She went about humming, songs about larks and bridges, that even the Scottish knew. She went about speaking French Scots, to make them feel at home, in their white coats. All day her appetite had been amazing.

– Could I have mair potage?

– Surely.

– Pass to me that ashet of boeuf, if you please. And the big canife.

– It's fine, we'll easily slice it for you.

– May I have a tassie o thé to finish, trois-three sucres?

– Remarkable adjustment. No reason she shouldn't be allowed out, for a trial period, of course.

– It's whether she will show proper care for the boy.

– And seek stabler employment, perhaps assistant in a shop, she has so few skills, cultural bridging-points—

– A wine and spirit merchant?

– Cake-shop I was thinking.

like yir faither

When they got into the Broch, they found Spermy sleeping on top of the unredded nets.

– Why dae ye think God invented bunks? said Uncle Spraggy.

– It's better under the stars.

The fug of Black Plug and old men's farts was getting him down.

– Ye ken fit ye'll catch oot here? Ye'll catch yir death.

They lifted a hatch and chose a sample, then Spermy accompanied his Uncle Spraggy up to the saleroom.

– Why did ye nae jist choose aa the big anes?

– Because it's got tae be a fair sample, loon.

– Why did ye nae gut them first?

– We've a hunner thoosan herrin aboord. Ye'd chap at least twa o yir fingers aff afore ye'd gutted aa that. This is nae the white fish, ye ken, like yir faither—

– Ma faither? Fa wis ma faither?

– Why, Cherlie, of course.

– Cherlie wisna ma proper faither. Cherlie wis ma suppose faither—

– Cherlie was yir faither. A guid man, saft-hertit a bittie, mebbe. But ye were caad eftir his brither, Jed.

– I wis caad eftir ma faither Jed, ye mean.

– Na, na, lots o fowk get cried eftir their uncles. That's aa wattir under the brig. Wheesht, in here, noo. Plonk yir sample doon, next tae the *Girl Mina*.

Spermy laid the half-basket of criss-crossed silvery fish down on the auction room floor.

a day for close relations

The sister at Woolmanhill had been a bit surly recently, so Dinah just asked for a day without pay. The sister was totally against, what with staffing, Christmas and all.

– Is it a wedding or what?

– It's for somebody close, Sister.

– You can only have a day for close relations.

– I ken fine. I said I wanted it wioot pay.

– It would be much better for us after New Year.

She tried *force majeure*, and it worked.

– My old boyfriend died, down south.

– Killed? An accident?

She nodded.

Well she didn't say when he died—

i didna ken hens liked herrin?

They got 50/- a cran, home market.

– Fit does home market mean?

– It's sellt fresh.

– But it's aa fresh, we just caught it.

– Aye but the *Girl Mina* went for klondykin, an the *Boy Duncan* for fishmeal. An afore ye ask, that means it'll be Russkies eatin the *Mina*'s herrin, they're sma and nae sae fat—

– Fa, the Russians?

– Na, the herrin. And the *Boy David*'s herrin will hae tae be aa heated an squashed, an dried an poodered, like I dinna ken fit, an either thrown tae the hens or bagged for spreadin on the fairmers' land.

– I didna ken hens liked herrin? Fit teeth hiv they suddenly got?

– A hen wid eat a whale – if ye but ground it doon sma.

amande's bed

She got the fire going first, a good strong blaze, with thin broken boxes that the butcher put out. Then she stripped Amande's bed, which hadn't been slept in for months. There wouldn't be time for a washing, not and dry it indoors. Yet the sheets were dank, cold cotton and dank. She would like to buy new sheets for Amande. But paying the rent on her own, she had no savings, apart from £5 in the Trustee Savings that she daren't touch.

She looked at the sheets again – they weren't too grubby overall, just the odd stain. She trailed them over to the sink and worked on the stains for ten minutes with a damp cloth, some red carbolic, the big wooden scrubber. She twisted the wet parts up in a screw, like the salt you got with crisps, until the drips stopped. She went back to the fireside, and from the wall-hook, unlashed the pulley rope and lowered the drying trestle. Then she took the sheets one at a time. She flung the first on top of the trestle, and it swayed against her breast, so she tugged it, teasing the wrinkles out till it lay over the left two bars, and hung down awkward, with an air space between. Then, over the right two bars, she repeated the dose with the second sheet, the whole thing balancing eachy-peach. The hems were about touching the worn Indian hearth-rug but, when she hauled the pulley up, they were damply brushing her cheeks.

Then she got the green quilt off Amande's bed, for she had no blankets. Coarse chicken feathers stuck through the fabric, their quills making porcupine patches. If she pulled the quills out, the quilt would deflate to nothing – Amande might as well sleep under an *Express*, or a *Press and Journal*. Dinah pushed odd quills back in with a thimble, and joogled them about, so that they didn't immediately protrude through the same holes.

She didn't have a pillow, Amande, just a great long bolster. She took off the bolster-slip and washed it through. There was a wee saucer of flat Lux crystals, supposed to be gentle. At least the bolster would smell nicer. The pulley rail was full and Amande didn't have a fender to protect from coal jumping out. So she fetched two chairs to the fireside, face to face and a bit apart, and bridged the bolster-slip over them, airing it to be warm for Amande coming home.

Dinah realised that the fire was too high for her to risk going out shopping: but if she let it die down the bedding wouldn't dry. So she wouldn't have time to get stuff for next day's Christmas dinner before Amande got out. She was due at the back of 1 o'clock. The asylum always liked to give their inmates a farewell lunch. But by the time she'd welcomed her home, and settled her, Amande probably wouldn't want to be left on her own, so how could she get away shopping? Anyway, there'd be nothing left in the food shops by mid-afternoon.

It was a bit of a quandary.

nae bad

When Spraggy and Spermy got back down the quay, *The Way* wasn't there. She'd moved along to a better-like berth and her appointed lorry was already backing into position, past all the clutter of boxes on the pier.

– How many lorries will we fill?

– O, twa should dae us. A hunner cran, fower hunner boxes.

– How much is that?

– Money? At 50 shillins a cran that comes oot at £250 exactly. Nae bad, fan ye share it oot.

– Dae I get a share—?

– C'mon, get the wark deen first. Awa an fill some baskets in the hold.

daily worker, is it?

Just after 12.30, there was a rap at Dinah's door. It was Andy.

– *Daily Worker*, I suppose? she said.

– Aye, well, that'd be the twa o us for a start, eh Dinah?

– Come in—?

– No, I'll just stand here. I've just taen the Panther hame for lunch. Dinah, Madge is nae vera weel, but she was wonderin, Madge an me was wonderin, actually, if ye'd like tae come for your Christmas dennir the morn, for auld times' sake. There'll jist be the sax o us, plus Uncle Hugh and his lady-frien, Bridget, well nine coontin Grizel, an yersel like. It winna be nithin special, just the chance o a meal thegither.

– O, that's very good o ye, Andy, but I was plannin Christmas dinner for Amande. She's due for release at 1 o'clock.

– O, I see. Well, Amande can easy come an aa. Fit aboot her bairns?

– Haze bides wi her auntie in Torry, we never ever see young Georges, an Jed's ran awa tae sea or something. That was his threat tae his mother, onywey. I havena seen hide nor hair o him aa week.

– Anither fisher, eh? Well I suppose ye winna see fishermen fan they're warkin, nae mair than miners. Foo's your ain folks ye were tellin me aboot?

– I havena see them aa year. We write – on an aff. They're fine.

weigh!

You had to jump on the herring, dead and slithering in the hold. Spermy felt their litheness jiggle underfoot as his seaboots wedged, to the knees and beyond in pervasive silver.

Jackie chucked over a spare scoop, and the two of them set to serving a wicker basket. It took about five good scoops, till the herring skited over the brim. Spermy keeked up in time to see a hooked yoke descending, like a mobile gibbet, fit for the pair of them. Jackie hooked the lugs smartly on opposite sides of the basket, yelled *Weigh!* and up it flew, clear out of sight.

Jackie fetched a second basket from the wings, and they bent with their scoops. Before they finished filling, the first basket swung back into view, scaly and red.

you make me bite

Amande sat at the table for the Christmas Eve lunch. Dr Arbuthnott came and sat down beside her, and poured out some orange juice for them both from the galvanised jug on the table, the one with the bash opposite the handle. He'd taken his white coat off and left it in the office or somewhere, it was very informal.

– Madame Demaison, I give you a toast. À votre santé.

– Merci, Monsieur. I give you the same. I hope your mental hospital is better soon.

– You have turned out one of our easier patients, certainly in the last few weeks.

– Because your method appals me, Doctor. My brain is still shocked that you do that to me.

– But that's exactly the point. It does seem to have worked.

– You make me bite on a rubber bone, like a chien.

– To save you biting your tongue off.

– Do you know, some things taste wrong here. Your jus d'orange. It tastes of foul metal.

lighter duties, shorter hours

It was five to four, he'd been waiting a couple of hours in the ante-room.

– Ah, come in, Andy. You wanted to see me.

– Mr Hall, I was hame at dennir-time. Ma wife's nae well, and I wondered if there was some wey we could wark things oot better.

– Sorry to hear that. We were just discussing something ourselves – lighter duties, shorter hours. Would that help?

– But I still need aa ma pay!

– Maybe you could make that up elsewhere, working for that party of yours—?

– I'm nae in the Party. I'm nae in nae party—

– All that Russian gold going to waste, ah well. In any case we were planning to switch things, right after Christmas. Gordon Burns, you've brought him on well. He'll be electrical maintenance charge-hand.

– Ma ain job tae ma auld apprentice!

– Yes. But this is not as simple as it seems. This is a chance to let a younger man bed in.

– He's hardly served his time!

– But an excellent worker. You'll have three full days deployed on the safety side. You've always been strong on safety, and head office in Leith appreciates that. They've set aside a pot of new money. The progress this past year has been good, and now that the First

Aid boxes have been established, I think we can move on. Safety gloves at all times, compulsory helmets before too long. The men respect you, and we must go with the legislation. What do you say?

There was a rapid knock, the door swung open. Gordon Burns kept one hand on the handle and leaned his body in.

– Sorry tae butt in, Mr Hall. Sulphuric's shorted-oot.

– Again?

– Aye, again. Andy, can you come doon an gie us a hand? The back-up genny is on the blink, we're in some sotter.

the gulls' fee

They worked right through the afternoon, discharging to the lorry. He got to swap jobs for an hour. Up on the back of the lorry Spraggy and him were reeling the baskets in hand-over-hand as they swung up from the hold, surplus plopping atween boat and pier, the gulls' fee.

– Throw that ane oot, said Uncle Sprag.

– Fit wey?

– Machrel, said Spraggy.

– Machrel? said Spermy. Can ye nae eat it?

– Devil's fish, said the skipper as he was passing on the pier on the way to the agent.

– Gaes aff quick in ony heat, machrel, said Spraggy.

– Heat? Fit heat? said Spermy.

They cowped each quarter-cran basket into an oblong whitewood box. *Return to Lochinver* it might say on the side. Or *Return to Wick, Buckie, Arbroath, Pittenweem, Granton. Return to Lochinver* sounded good.

His uncle cast a spreckle of flaked ice over the bloody-nosed silver darlings. Spermy plunked the next empty box on top.

And on they went, making a cold rich tenement.

a magician

When Dinah looked out the window for the tenth time, Amande was coming out the back of the ambulance. She'd just that minute got the big bed made up.

– Jed? said Amande, looking over Dinah's shoulder. Jed?

She opened all three interior doors in turn.

– Where does he go?

Dinah tried restraining her by the upper arm. Amande shook her off.

– Ou est-il?

– It was you that said he said to you he was aff tae the Broch.

– *You said, he said* that isna use – I want to see him now. Jed?

– Well, he's nae here, Amande. I'm nae a magician.

– Get me to drink.

– I'm sure he'll be back sometime.

– Get me to drink, I say.

– Ye dinna want tae rush intae—

– Armagnac.

– Armagnac? Fae Mutch the Grocer's—?

– Inutile, Aberdeen. Inutile.

– It's nithin but a corner shop.

– Aberdeen, oui, a corner *shoppie*—

Dinah put her hand to touch Amande's arm, but Amande shoved her off hard so that she stumbled on one of the chairs left in front of the fire.

– And my petit Jed is off drowning himself!

– No, Amande. Jed's got his heid on straighter than that.

yet didn't collect

Normally, and there were many norms, they would only have hen once a year, at New Year. Nobody called it chicken, a fluff of a thing with a tiny wishbone. But this year, because of the difficulties, maybe because of Grizel, they decided to have a few friends round. Dad had roared home on the Panther at lunchtime, had roared off again without enjoying.

– Go and get a hen, Mum said when Peem got back from school.

It was a last-minute decision. Then she curled down in the easy chair, and tried to shut out Tammy's skirling.

Peem went panting along to McGruer, Quality Butcher, half way along Urquhart. But McGruer said he had only a bird that some teacher ordered as early as April, yet didn't collect. A white, soft-necked goose draped over the counter. It was like a lady's white stocking – in an orange sandal.

Coming out, he nigh-on tripped over Jobby's three-wheeled pram. The pram was half-capsized and empty. From inside his stained gaberdine Jobby handed Peem a leaflet.

COAL
Use Coal carefully
Be glad of any Coal
Don't worry about the kind
Your merchant will supply
the best he can
Issued by the Mines Department

– Thanks.

– *Finished*.

– Nae yet, surely, Jobby?

– It is *finished*.

– Merry Christmas tae you an aa, I'll have tae dash—

Peem raced back to Guffie's. Dad said he was a *tink*, but things were desperate. *I wouldna trust his mealie-jerkers, far less his fowl.*

In the blue-lit window the chrome rail was empty, with S-hooks.

In the doorway a single dove was pecking at the invisible. It scuttled to the street, and crapped as it flew away.

Rooketty-doo.

Peem went in, things were desperate.

The sawdust on the floor was scuffed and heaped in many unreadable patterns. There was nobody there. No customers. No butcher, or butcher's assistants, and no meat, not even a dough of mince in a tray, nor a little huddle of deep purple kidneys.

The scales were still bloody though, and on the downside there were three brass weights. Little greaseproof packets of dripping sat on the tiles. There was a ball of string, a blade or two and a cleaver. Peem didn't want to shout *Hello*, they never shopped there, he didn't know them. He began to hum, quiet at first, thinking the words

> *Gonna lay down my sword and shield,*
> *Down by the riv—*

Guffie came through. He was obviously drunk. He scooped up the five packets of dripping.

– Everything's in the chiller, loon. Plenty o lamb.

– I wonder have you a hen.

He disappeared and reappeared and began rearranging the heavy chessmen for Hogmanay.

– Is there a hen, though?

– How would I ken, ye'll have to look.

He bundled up the spikes and knives and sharpening files in his bloody apron, missing only the cleaver, and disappeared to the sink in the back shop. Peem looked at the tall door and peeled chrome handle of the chiller. Guffie came back, breathing heavily, for the final tool.

– Have ye looked?

– No.

– Well, you look then. An if ye see a bird ye like, tak it awa an latch the door ahint ye, I'm late as it is.

– How much will it be?

– Ach, tak it. It's Christmas. There's plenty mair auld hens.

– Thanks.

– Dinna forget the door, I'm oot the back wey—

Peem pulled on the big chrome handle. A click and the door hauled slowly to him. Sawdust flittering off his shoes, he stepped into the stench. There were horrible buckets of giblets and offal, one with a single tongue.

Hung high at the back was this hen, string round its psoriasis legs, its wattle red and floppy, its eye enraged—

a scaly man

It was getting dark up on the lorry when back down in the hold he had to go, chasing the last couple of herring, pulling them out of drains and board-slots.

– Ma back's killin me, said Spermy.

– Wait till ye're my age, said Jackie.

– Fit age are ye?

– Twenty-eight.

– Na, I'll invent somethin better. Some kind o hoover, tae sook the fish oot o the hold.

– A hoover wid jist clog.

– A watery hoover then. Keep the herrin in a tank o icy water.

– Ye're awa aheid o yersel. Ye've only jist catched the first o yir herrin.

– Wait, I've gotten somethin—

Spermy raxed up his oilskin smock, raised it up to his hips, and reached down. At the top of his left boot, sizes too big for him, lodged a slim silver fish.

– There's luck for ye, said Jackie. A scaly man.

dead vipers

As Peem swung round he banged his shoulder off a side of marbled beef. It swung by a tendon, its rough-sawn backbone, its layery pallid fat.

– Christ!

Dead vipers of sausages he shoved from his face as he ran at the door.

– Guffie, Guffie— somebody—

He might as well greet for wee Tammy to come.

a fry

The skipper spoke to him on the pier, after the stern rope, bow rope and spring were all tied.

– Ah well. I see ye've gotten a fry.

– I got a dozen, is that okay?

– Every fisher is due his fry. And here's a pound tae yersel.

– A pound—?

It was a fiver.

– Dinna waste it now.

– Can I come oot next week?

– That aa depends. A hunner cran's a passable shot, but a poorish week, we maun try ower on the West side.

– I'll get ma mither tae teach me tae cook. She's French.

– Fit, mushrooms an garlic an fried frogs' legs? We'll mak a richt sicht o wirsels steamin intae Stornowa wi berets on! Awa ye go, we'll see ye Monday.

– Skipper, thanks!

– Eight sharp, mind.

– Can I—

But the skipper was making his way over to the *Girl Mina* and was out of earshot.

that needy u

His forehead banged, he banged his forehead. He reckoned all the subtractions to hope.

– Why did ye leave the back way, Guffie?

Under rags of breath.

– Bastardin Guffie, I'm spikkin tae ye!

He punched a haunch.

– Wi ten mair pints, asnore in yir bed—

The unplucked hen glared at him.

His forehead he laid on the alloy door.

The bulb in the chiller shone cold.

He changed his absent audience.

– Dae ye nae even luve me?

Then quoted himself.

– *Luve me. LUVE me—*

Luve wi that plunging, expulsive, needy *u*.

The smooth *o* of English *love* did not approach the case.

regairds tae yir mither

– An see ye get yersel a fisherman's knife, said Gibby, in case ye gang ower the side in anither daft rummle.

– An dinna forget tae gie ma regairds tae yir mither, said Great Uncle Sprag.

He slid the single tongue out on top of the offal and giblets.

Like that cartoon in the *Sunday Post*, he upturned the slimy bucket.

Its rim cut into his bum as he slumped and jerked in lost and broken dozing—

Annie was holding a dolly by its plastic leg, selecting from three possible dresses.

Hughie was bent over a manual.

Hughie was sitting on Grizel's bed. Her hand in a grey stocking, she was withdrawing the soft body of a tangerine.

A home-made washing machine was being bumped in from the lobby, under a green cloth. Dad whipped off the cloth like a conjuror and out popped Tammy. He passed Mum up a bar of chocolate, *Five Boys*, but the *Five* had been scored out, and *Two* inserted.

On Peem's undented pillow sat a slim hinged box.

A gold-nibbed Parker pen.

And they all listened to carols on the walnut wireless.

> *I saw three ships come sai-ailing*
> *On Chrisumuss Day, On Chrisumuss day.*
> *I saw three ships come sa-ailing*
> *On Chrisumass Day in the mourning.*

On top of the wireless was a newspaper cutting.

City Boy Chills.

He woke and got up on a long stiff hobble, round and round the pallid carcasses. Did you die first of cauld or hunger?

First—?

He fetched three puddings off a tray while he had the chance, the lights would maybe go. A black pudding, *darkie's walloper* Tarry christened it, had dauds of fat. It smelt of peppery blood. It was cold and horrible. He sucked a bit and spat it out.

He slotted the two mealie puddings, *mealie jerkers* his dad aye called them, in his pockets for later.

Khrushchev had dropped his bomb

He was the better of his sleep. He kicked at the door to save his hand. He didn't know was it night or day. For all he knew, Khrushchev had dropped his Bomb and gone home again.

Then he saw a broom.

He got up on his *Oor Wullie* bucket and began to dunt on the roof of the chiller in time to the motto, listening for an echo.

Oor – Wull,
　　Your – Wull.

Oor – Wull,
　　Your – Wull.

Aabuddy's Wullie.

blue pomegranates

Amande had been quieter in the evening. She seemed a bit slower, a lot slower if the truth was told.

Dunt – Dunt.
　　Dunt – Dunt.

– I think I go back soon.
　　– Where to – Cornhill?

– Non, non.

– To Torry?

– Non, to Brittany. My time is up for Scotland. I don't make much more staying here.

– Surely ye'll stay till ye're a wee bit better?

– Non, young Jed is gone now.

Dinah reached to pour herself a third dram. She put the bottle of Bells back in her duffel-bag.

Dunt – Dunt.

Dunt – Dunt.

That racket from below, probably shifting furniture for relatives coming. Aye a long time since she'd seen any of those. Or maybe parking a ladder to get decorations up. Her stepdad she thought of, down in the pit—

She woke from her doze, her mind in a start, not used to the whisky.

Wait, there were no neighbours underneath, it was only the butchers—

She went through to the other bedroom. Amande was lying on top of the quilt, in a pink negligée, curved into herself, face to the window, back to the door.

– Amande, wake up – réveillez – somethin funny goin on doonstairs.

They put dressing-gowns and knickers on, and made their way down. What would ye break into a butcher's for? Cash. But they never left cash in a till overnight, surely.

Beef. The dunt of them unhooking sides of beef? A bit obvious, though, Burke and Hare lugging cow-corpses through the street—

They got downstairs, and opened the front door a crack. The fizzling gas was wan, yet there was brighterness from Guffie's. Dinah stepped onto the threshold and tried the door – not locked. Their slippers scuffed in the sawdust of the empty butcher's.

Dinah yanked at a chrome handle, and the white statue of a boy fell forward. It struck Amande on the hip.

– Dinah, congelé, look!

– Peem—!

– But it's Jed's ami—

– Whit a state—

– Frozen, absolument.

– Go and phone an ambulance.

– I havena gotten phone, you know that Dinah.

– Somebody must hae a phone. Knock on somebody's door.

– I don't know who has phone.

– Hurry up!

– The sleepyround woman banging on houses?

– I'm goin tae try an humph him upstairs.

Dinah ran to the till drawer, and took some brown pennies from a wooden bowl.

– Go up to the junction wi King Street, opposite Marchetti. There's a phone there. Stupid me, ye winna need money – 999, neuf neuf neuf.

– I ken nine, Dinah.

– Vite, vite, Amande!

Dinah used a lift on Peem she'd seen her stepdad demonstrate. He called it the miner's lift, it used to be the fireman's lift. Well now it was the nurse's lift. God he was frozen.

She felt his cauldness steep into her shoulder. She humphed him up two flights of stairs, the polar breath lunging out of him. The door was still open. Her hands were starting to numb. He needed a good warm bath soon, like they did in the navy, her Mum had told her. Not too hot, a bittie above blood heat. But there was no bath. She heaved him into the nearest bed, Amande's.

She was pressing her palm on his forehead, waiting for the kettle to sing, when she heard Amande's feet.

– The phone isna workin. Coupé, cut-off—

Dinah rolled up Peem's eyelids. The pupils were smallish.

– C'mon, we'll hae tae sponge het water aa ower'm. Get his arms oot o that jerkin, I'll untie his shune.

His laces were like brambles in winter, his jerkin a cement bag after a starry night. His shirt, his vest. His breeks were pipes.

– Isna warkin, Amande. There's nae sign o'm.

– We must have to heat him.

– We've only a silly kettle. The het wattir's finished fae the back boiler, an the fire's lang oot.

– I read about German pilots in the Manche.

– This is nae the time for war stories, Amande.

– Take from you your clothes off, Dinah.

– Whit—?

– Look, I take mine.

– I'm nae takin ma knickers aff.

– Fine. Guard your knickers with your life. Now roll him under, under the sheets, dépêche!

– I see your game—

– One side me, you another, climb.

They had barely touched him when they shuddered, Amande with her small melony breasts, she with her sweet lemons, they went to blue pomegranate swiftly, pressed against such skin. His chest unmoving.

Amande reached out, across the boy, a fine long arm.

– Dinah.

She gave her a stroke on the shoulder.

262

Dinah took that cue, and reached her own arms above and
below the frozen neck, as the women pulled towards each other,
out of some instinct, the boy like honour's sword between them,
they'd warm him yet.

mangrove

A distant motorbike was heard, coming.

Far? Far am I? The best of him seemed way up in the ceiling.

– I love you, Dinah.

The older woman was stroking her hair. She'd stroked her
shoulder and her back, and now she was stroking her hair.

– O.

– Ça va—?

– Aye.

Dinah gave her an answering squeeze.

Quit squashin me! I'm haein a fine dream. He flowed along one
plaster crack and changed to another – Amazon tributaries.

– Dinah, I have to go soon.

– O.

– Scotland is nae my country.

But I want ye tae bide, she thought.

– But I want ye tae bide, said Dinah.

Stop bletherin! Women aye pester ye. Just when ye want tae be
a free log on the Amazon.

– He is rewaking!

– Are ye sure—?

– Oui.

Strange to feel belly and back again, lodged between whale and
dolphin. Some fingers, his, came off and floated, through a warm
mangrove, into a sea.

– I think he isna non-conscious now, Dinah—

– Good!

– We cuddle him.

With warmth renewed, they slept far through the darkness.

a wee bit sticky

It was almost getting light. There were boots on the stairs, and the door of the flat opened.

– Ma, far are ye?

My Holy Christ, thought Amande.

– Far are ye, Ma? I've somethin for ye—

Dinah and Peem began to unslumber, fast.

The bedroom door swung wide and Spermy stood in the jamb, bag in hand. Peem and Dinah shrunk under the prickly quilt.

– Fit's this, Wee Peem, fuckin communism—?

– Jed— said Amande.

– Bit late hidin noo—

– It's pas du tout, not what you think—

– Welcome oot fae the madhoose, mither. Here's yir fish.

There came a *rat-tat* on the door of the flat.

– Taissez-vous, hissed Amande.

The door went again.

– Onybuddy at hame?

– O, god, it's ma stepfaither— said Dinah.

She tried to squeeze lower in the bed, her breasts brushing the submerged Peem. She put a hand over his mouth, kissed his flushed forehead. They snuggled down.

– I'll get it, said Spermy.

– Les habillements—!

– Onybody hame—?

Amande reached for her dressing-gown, as Spermy grabbed the promiscuous tangle of clothes from the threadbare carpet and fired it, wad after wad, under the bed.

Amande was sitting, sheet pulled to her shoulders, knees fetched up, rumpling the quilt between them in an artful manner.

– Shoogle in— said Dinah.

Amande motioned Spermy to the door.

– Closer—! said Dinah.

Amande made last adjustments for her brood.

– Hello, said Arthur, as the flat door opened. Sorry tae roust ye up sae early.

– Should think so, said Spermy.

– Have we gotten the wrang address? Does a Dinah Wylie no bide here?

– Fa wants tae ken? said Spermy

– We're her Ma and Stepda, pet, said Gladys.

– Eh, haud on a minute—

– You've gotten some scales about ye, laddie, said Arthur.

– Aye, an I've gotten a shillin for every ane.

– Rich at your age! said Gladys. Well – Merry Christmas by the way – can we just come in?

– As lang as ye ken she's nae here— said Spermy.

– Hello, said Arthur. Sorry tae come here unannounced, like, but we thocht we'd gie Dinah a big surprise, eftir aw the disappointment o last year.

– Disappointment—! said Gladys.

– Ye'll be Amande, I take it. A Merry Christmas.

– Noël, said Amande. Bon Noël.

– Is Dinah, whaur is she, oot on the lavvy—?

– I'm Gladys, said Gladys.

– Enchanté, Gladys. Dinah is under some pressures today. You know, emergency?

– Even at Christmas, eh, said Arthur, the good auld NHS. Weil we'll jist dump her presents an go for a daunder for hauf an hour, let ye get decent.

– Décente—? said Amande.

– Dinna worry aboot us, we'd a kipper on the early train.

– I just had scrambled egg, said Gladys. Far, far too early for kipper. Michty, that's a richt bonny quilt.

Amande tried to move her knees tighter.

– Did ye mak it up yersel?

– No, I'm not a how-you-say seamstress.

– Seamstress, said Gladys. Nor me. But it's aye handy if ye can stitch something up.

There was a sort of cough from under the covers.

– Pardonnez-moi—! said Amande.

– Bless— said Gladys.

– Gie Amande a break now, wumman, come awa. We'll be back in twa ticks for a cuppie o tea, said Arthur. Cheerio—

– Au retour, said Amande.

Spermy disappeared with them to the outside door.

– And fetch a loaf, shouted his mother. From the shop. Of thé also!

– Things got a wee bit sticky there, said Dinah. Eh, Peem? Ye look fevered.

– It's okay, he said.

– Okay! said Dinah. Hark at him! It's a lot better than okay, whaur ye were dodgin aboot!

– Sorry—

– O it's far too late for sorry, isn't it Amande? Just fire me up that slip frae under the bed, afore I die o shame.

Peem snaked modestly across the quilt and hung over to hunt

for Dinah's gown.

– Monkey, wee wretch—! she said, with a skelp at his bare bum. He turned to see her neat breasts bounding.

– Bon! said Amande.

the vera bottom o the bed

– Eh? She's some heicht o a woman that Amande, said Arthur, as they got into the raw air of Urquhart Parade. An whit a terrible limp.

– Limp? said Gladys. I told ye that kipper wouldna agree. How dae ye mak that oot?

– Your bletherin blinds ye, wumman. Did ye nae see keekin oot, at the vera bottom o the bed, her baith feet twistit—?

we'll make it together

Peem came back into the house.

– Far have ye been? said Hughie.

– Jist oot, I was checkin the hen—

– Checkin the hen? Excuse me, wee brither, ye hinna been in the hoose since yesterday eftirneen. I thocht ye'd been run ower by a bus. Or emigrated—

– Fit did they say? Far's Dad, far's Mum—?

– Dad nivver cam hame till four in the mornin. Overtime. Meanwhile Mum's been taen intae hospital, Dad turned straicht roon an went up tae see her—

– O no, Mum— Is she okay?

– Aye, I had tae run for the doctor, she wis greetin wi that much pain. The doctor rushed her in, in his ain car. But she's gotten some injection, and she's oot for Christmas.

– O, good. So did naebody even ken—?

– That you were oot aa night? Just me an Grizel. Dinna tell me ye were oot ridin!

– That hen took some gettin—

– Pull the ither ane, it's got reindeer-bells on. Bet it was thon Haze—

– Na, too young for me.

Hughie aimed a swipe.

– Dinna come it. Well it's eleven noo. Dad went back tae his wark an hour ago. He'll be hame at the back o five, Mum's due oot at six.

– Did Dad ken I was oot aa nicht?

– Mebbe aye, mebbe no. He nivver said nithin.

– Sae fit are we daein for Christmas tea? said Peem. Christmas dennir.

– Search me, said Hughie. By the time that pair comes hame it'll be Christmas supper mairlike.

– No, said Grizel. We'll make it together. I'll get Tammy's bottle made up, then I'll help you.

– Well, the hen's hingin in the shed, said Peem. I went back intae – I went intae Guffie's an got it.

– The shed? said Hughie.

– Aye, ye dinna hing hens in a coal-hoose, ye ken.

– Richt, Grizel, said Hughie. Never mind the professor. Let's mak a plan. How mony is there?

a fuckin ostrich

The table was an extender so that was okay, but the biggest problem was going to be chairs.

– Well Tammy's got his ain high chair, said Hughie.

– So that's four o us big fowk for a start then, said Peem.

– Shurrup, shrimp, said Hughie. Four—

– Five, said Annie. Five of us.

– Okay, good countin, five, said Hughie. Plus Grizel, of course, six.

– Dinna forget Dinah, said Peem.

– O aye, she got an invite, didn't she, said Hughie. Seven then.

– And ye ken Amande's hame, did I say?

– Amande? I thocht she'd lost her marbles, said Hughie.

– Hughie— said Grizel.

– Well she's mair than found them again— said Peem. An if Dinah's comin here, Amande can hardly hae Christmas dennir on her ain. Nae straight oot o Cornhill.

– Randy Mandy, eight, said Hughie.

– Nine, ye mean. Because Spermy's hame fae the sea.

– I thocht ye didna get on wi him?

– He's better fan he's nae at school.

– It's a bit ower mony, said Hughie.

– Sae nine— said Peem.

– Wait though, said Hughie. I saw Uncle Hugh yesterday. He's comin alang later an aa. He's got fags tae drive up tae Banff the day, but he says he wants tae see his sister.

– His sister? said Annie. In Banff?

– No, yir Mum, said Peem, is yir uncle's sister. Will Bridget be wi him, I wonder?

– Fa kens, said Hughie. Ye never ken wi Uncle Hugh.

– Sae, eleven at maist, said Hughie. I'm drawin the line at eleven.

– Dinah's Ma and Da arrived this mornin, said Peem.

– Excuse me! Fa—? Dinah's fa—? said Hughie.

– Dinah's Ma an Da, her Stepda. Her Ma was in the Wrens wi Mum. They havena seen each ither for ages.

– Is it a hen ye've gotten, said Hughie, or a fuckin ostrich?

– I'll write the menu, said Grizel.

– That's easy, said Peem. *Hen*.

– Look in the lobby press for me, Hughie dear, said Grizel.

– Dinna caa me *deer*. I hinna got horns, have I? Brussel sprouts, tatties, carrots, neeps.

– What's neeps again? said Grizel.

– Dinna tempt me, said Hughie. Apairt fae brithers that bide oot aa nicht, neeps are turnips.

   – Turnips are not very Christmassy. Fetch the rest out, though.

   – Yes, boss, said Hughie.

   – Now stuffing, did you get stuffing, Peem?

   – No, he never gave me nane.

   – Hmmph, said Hughie.

   – Wait a minute though.

And he slid the two mealie jerkers out of his pockets.

Between them they managed to wash the hen, discard the giblets, stuff it with the fatty, peppery oatmeal commandeered from the jerkers, baste it with butter, and place it on a metal tray. Hughie lit the gas oven, with its serried burners, a hall of blue. Peemie wanted to position the hen ceremonially, but Hughie just clashed it in.

   By the time the tatties were peeled, the carrots scraped, and the sprouts trimmed, the top of the cooker was three-quarters full of veg sitting in cold water. So they cubed some neeps as well, to be on the safe side.

   – We grew all that, said Peem to Grizel. All of it.

   – Pity you didn't grow some pudding as well, said Grizel.

   – Mum always makes clootie dumpling at Christmas.

   – Clootie how many—?

   – Clootie dumpling. Her recipe book's in the sideboard drawer.

Oatmeal, flour, suet, sultanas, currants, bicarbonate of soda, cinnamon.

   – But it says here buttermilk, said Grizel.

   – Or sour milk, said Peem. If there's yesterday's milk still in the press, it's bound to be aff by noo.

   – It is, said Grizel. Tammy turned up his nose at it. It's smelly and lumpy.

   – Ideal. And we can use a big dishcloth for the cloot, said Peem.

   – Okay, cleverclogs, said Hughie. Far are we goin to boil it? The cooker's completely booked up. Four veggie pans waitin on top and yir mervellous aa-nicht henorama in the oven.

– That's right, said Grizel. We can't have three hours between the main course and pudding. Our customers will never come back.

– Good, said Hughie.

– The wash-hoose, said Peem.

– Eh? said Hughie.

– Bile it in the boiler.

– Boil it in the biler— said Annie.

– Bile ees heid sae far as I'm concerned, said Hughie.

As the afternoon progressed, fires were lit under boilers, hens were checked, carpets were hoovered, sideboards dusted, and tables laid. Chairs were still the problem.

– Eleven did we say? said Hughie.

– Thirteen, said Peem.

4 kitchen chairs, plus 4 spaces on the arms of 2 easy chairs, 2 hard RAF toolboxes, with cushions, one low pouffé with 2 added pillows, Volumes A-J of the *Children's Encyclopaedia*, Volumes K-Z ditto.

Plus one chair from Jehovah Morrison, begged from next door. Black horsehair was bursting from it.

– They dinna celebrate Christmas, said Hughie. That's their story.

– Save themselves for Easter, divn't they? said Peem. The Resurrection.

– God kens—

– Is there enough cutlery?

– We've some lyin somewey fae fan Gran died—

– O that's lucky.

– Right, are we ready? Brilliant, it's still only half-past-four. Let's check that hen.

In came Spermy.

The hen was a sore letdown. Carbonised for three hours, it seemed to have shrunk, and large squidgers of oatmeal lay expressed from the area of its arse.

Spermy took on the lead for the prosecution.

– Hen? Hen! I've seen bigger spurdies faa oot o the trees in winter.

– It's nae even an apology for a hen, said Hughie.

– Fit does a hen hae tae apologise for? said Peem.

– Keepin ye awauk at nicht? said Hughie.

– That's cocks, said Annie.

– Annie—! said Peem.

– Clap it atween twa shaves o loaf an gie it tae the bairn for a sandwich, said Spermy.

– Hey you, keep oot o it, said Peem. Ye're supposed tae be a guest.

The door opened.

– Hello, aabody, said Dad. Ye've been busy. Was that the only hen ye could come up wi, Peem?

– Dad— said Peem.

– Well I hope it wasna fae that tink Guffie! Ye were lang enough aboot it. Foo much was it?

– Free.

– My certie, said Dad. We winna need communism eftir aa, if there's free hens.

– They should have peyed ye tae tak it, said Hughie.

– Onywey, Ludwig's here, he's just gettin his leathers aff. I'm glad ye've put oot plenty places. One thing though.

– Fit—?

– Mak sure aabody brings one item o fool washin the nicht.

– Fool washin—?

– Fool washin.

– Foo fool—?

– As fool, dirty, an barkit as they can possibly manage.

only a king edward in the pan

– Will ye help yersel tae anither sausage, Gladys? I canna begin tae tell ye foo pleased I am tae see ye. Your dochter's turned oot grand. It's good tae hae a nurse—

Peem keeked at Dinah across the table. Fork in tattie, she glanced at him, shushing her lips. He dived into his greens.

– Thank you, Madge, said Gladys. It's richt fine, these chipolatas. Mind the sausages we got in the war. Drippin, sawdust an I dinna ken what—

– Craturs killed aff the road, said Madge.

– Stoats, rabbits, foxes, said Andy.

– Wi bombs? said Peem.

– No, said Arthur. Wi GI jeeps.

– An RAF motorbikes, said Andy.

– A peety ye never got pigs on the road, then, said Hughie.

– Sorry—? said Madge.

– Better for sausages.

– Roadhogs, said Peem.

– Aye it wasna safe. Nae heidlichts.

– Why no?.

– Tae stop the bombers seein the cars, said Arthur.

– Sorry, Ludwig— said Madge.

– No, it's okay, said Ludwig. We know the war now, it's not a surprise.

– A surprise for thae stoats an badgers, though, said Hughie.

– You're very cruel, said Grizel.

– Hiv tae be cruel tae be kind, sometimes.

– When are you kind, tell me?

– Ach, stop *grizzlin*—

– Noo, said Madge. There's a coupla tatties goin abeggin. Dinah, are ye game for another tattie?

– Fit aboot Uncle Hugh? said Peem.

– God, ye're richt, Uncle Hugh. I hope he got on okay the day on the road tae Banff.

– I dinna think it was too bad, said Andy. Fan I was oot tae the shed last there was just a skifty o snaa.

– O, you— said Madge. Ye're back an fore tae that shed aa the time.

– Well let's get the dishes cleared, said Andy.

– What aboot pudding—! said Grizel.

– The clootie dumplin's needin aa its time, said Peem. It took ages tae heat the water, that biler.

– Aye, the days o the wooden biler, eh? said Andy.

– Well, gie it its time, said Madge. There's nae panic.

– Nothin worse than a hauf-cooked dumplin, said Gladys.

– It clogs up your guts, said Arthur, for days—

– We could never get proper clootie in Cornwall—

– But biled properly, there's nithin better, said Andy. Amande, would ye nae agree?

– O, I'm sure Amande's had plenty tastier dishes, said Madge.

– Crêpes, said Amande, Suzettes. Pavlova—

– I thocht that was a dog, said Arthur.

– Nithin would surprise me in that department, said Madge.

– Richt, said Andy. Hughie an Peem, come oot wi me—

– Fit's aa this, suddenly? said Madge.

– Haud your horses, ye'll ken soon enough.

They wheeled in the washing machine. It was kinda awkward, wrapped and taped in ten sheets of buff paper, plus two with holly.

– Merry Christmas, Mum!

– Merry Christmas, ma dears. Ye shouldna have gone tae aa this trouble for me.

– It'll mak things a bit easier.

– Foo dae ye get the water in?

– A few basins.

– An oot—?

– A pan. A big pan.

– A pan—?

– Or you could siphon. We could rig a wee hose an ye could sook fae the sink end.

– Till the fool water cam throu in ma mou? said Madge.

– Aye, roughly—

– Dae ye nae like it? said Hugh.

Peem saw his Dad blink a couple of times.

– I'll do the ironin, Mummy, said Annie. I can stand on the pouffé.

– Annie! said Mum, and pulled her and Peem into a double cuddle. She stretched all the fingers of her left hand out to Hughie, who held three sheepishly.

Andy lifted Tammy from his high chair, stepped in behind her, and kissed the top of her head.

– O-oh, said Gladys. You're right lucky. Arthur never makes me washing machines.

– I've got a flooer for ye, said Annie.

And she gave Gladys a Christmas rose. But most were caught a bit on the hop. There wasn't a present for everybody. Hughie gave Grizel a calendar, with a Snark rocket, from America. Grizel gave Hughie a wallet inscribed *London*.

Spermy said, Mither, ye ken I already gave ye yir fish.

– Merci, mon petit. Come and I will give you a kiss. Viens—

– Gad's— said Spermy, refusing.

Dinah turned sideways, to give Amande a consolation on the left cheek.

Peem gave Madge one end of a little parcel, done up as a cracker.

– Fit's this?

– Pull, Mum, he said.

The cracker tore, and a blue stone fell out.

– But is that nae your special stane—?

– Right, said Andy, that was fine, aabody. Noo for the main event. Fetch oot that dirty washin ye were aa tellt tae bring.

They trooped out into the lobby and came back with their offerings, as Andy part-filled the drum from the immersion heater above the sink.

Spermy had a pair of grey seaboot stockings, their tops sequinned with scales. Grizel took through her sheet, a bit stiff-like. Megan's Christmas dress had gravy spilt on it, apparently. Dinah had a nurse's pinny.

– An fit have ye got, Amande?

– Une brassière.

– That's braw. Hughie?

– An ily hankie.

– We'd better let that steep for hauf an oor.

– Dinna forget the Christmas cloot, said Madge.

– Nip oot tae the wash-hoose, Peem, and get the dumplin fae the biler, said Andy. It's surely ready by noo.

– I'm not the big fanatic of machinery, said Ludwig.

– Well that's aa very well you sayin that, said Arthur, but it's a big help doon the pit. I'm nae Luddite tae chuckin his clog intae the cog—

– It was not my clog. Look—

– Aye, thon must hae been gey sair, but that's what ye get wi a poor outfit. I tell ye, we're workin on a 65° slope just noo in the Seafield, an if we didna hae hydraulic rams tae haud the roof up, I dinna think I'd be here. When that cutter's breengin alang the tap o the seam, the coal fair rummles doon, lumps ten times as muckle's yir heid. Withoot hydraulic rams tae coory ahint, ye'd be cairried awa—

– Jings— said Spermy.

– Naebody's in a hurry to hear aboot hydraulic rams, said Gladys.

– Spermy's been tae sea on a drifter, said Peem.

– I wish Jed would not go there— said Amande.

– A drifter , said Arthur, a drifter. Is that nae vera hard work?

– Go on, tell us, Jed, said Madge, fit's it like at the fishin? I've aye wondered.

– Nae bad, quite good— it's great!

– The fish luve it.

– Shut up, Hughie, said Grizel. She moved a trace closer to Peem.

Peem looked across. Dinah had laid her hand on Amande's, Arthur was sketching on his decrumpled napkin, Ludwig sank his chin in his palm, and Gladys was shaking her head.

– Just tell us aathing, said Madge. Fae the minute ye left the harbour—

Peem watched Annie deliberately slip off her Eiffel of encyclopaedias, and push them back before they became a Pisa. She hopped in Dad's lap.

And Spermy told the story of his week.

Uncle Hugh and Bridget came about eight.

– It's good tae see ye, Madge, said Uncle Hugh.

– I'm sorry, there's only a King Edward in the pan, an twa Brusselers.

– Did ye hae hen?

– Nearly. But never mind, ye're just in time for the clootie dumplin.

– Champion, said her brother.

– Mair than that, ye're just in time for the big switch-on, said Andy.

Now that the dumpling lay in a steaming mass on an ashet in the centre of the long table, he dropped its stained, suety, cinnamon-coloured cloth on top of the rest of the inaugural wash, and clapped on the loose lid.

– It winna wash itsel, said Madge.

Andy lifted the lid and put a fair sprinkle of Persil to lace the brew. He dried hands with a dish-cloth, bent to the wall, and inserted the plug.

– Noo for the big switch-on. Flick of his finger and the belt was set whirring, a whooshing got up from inside and some foam lipped through.

– Gee whiz, said Uncle Hugh. Wonders will never cease.

– Sorry it's sic a racket, said Andy.

– Well, Hugh, foo far were ye oot the road the day? said Madge.

– Sorry, Madge—?

As she leant closer to her brother, she winced.

– Foo far, I said, did ye get oot the road the day—?

– O, oot the lenth o Banff. They smoke a ton o Senior Service oot in Banff.

– Tippies?

– Na, they're for the full reek.

Grizel nudged back towards Hughie. The machine shoogled and rattled.

– But alang the road in Buckie, it's funny, it's aye Woodbine wi them. A shorter drag.

– Amazin the differences across Scotland, said Arthur.

– Across Buchan even, said Uncle Hugh. Because it's Black Plug in the Broch, for choice. Terrible stuff.

– Would that be the same across Germany? said Arthur.

– Black Plug? said Ludwig. The same. Black Plug in Dresden, Black Plug in Hamburg.

– Arthur— said Gladys.

– You hadna nae alternatives, said Ludwig. That's history. You had to kill my family so's I could sit here with yours.

– O, my! That's an affa wey o puttin it, Ludwig, said Madge.

– It's the gods' truth. I was greetin for my family ten year. As soon as it got dark, every nicht, just greetin. They didna come back to me, Sonia, Wilhelm, Eva, for a million years greetin. I live here now. It's the same people – two arms, two legs.

– Aye ye'll hae tae change folks' herts first, said Madge, afore ye change their institutions.

– Mebbe so— said Andy.

– Nivver thocht I'd hear ye say that, Andy! said Uncle Hugh.

– No. Incorrect, Andy – too simple, Madge. It is Nazi that is evil, not German heart. Tory that is cold, not the heart of Scottish.

– Fit aboot Russia? said Madge. Fit aboot Nikita Khrushchev wi his thoosand missiles?

– He is on his road, said Ludwig. Better nor Stalin. You need a Scottish government, that's your road. A small country doesna go bombing.

– A Gaelic government, said Bridget. Housed in Portree. A government that knows how to sing, I'd rather. Forget your Edinburgh. Hugh, where's that accordion of yours? Madge would like fine to be hearing a tune now.

– An aa I've got is this washin machine racket—

– Madge— said Andy.

– Well. It's like a joke.

Andy switched it off at the skirting board. He lifted the lid. The water was irrefutably murky.

– See, it warks fine.

With wooden tongs he lifted up stockings, pinny, hankie, cloot, tight-tangled. The bra was wound in a strip round the impeller.

– Fit a snorl, said young Hughie. Auntie Betsy's Hotpoint gaes baith weys.

– Whoopee, said Peem.

– Madge— said Andy. Madge?

– C'mon Bridget, said his Mum, let's get a bit o Peem's clootie inside ye. Brither Hugh, will ye try some?

a big lot o time

– Is it a lang operation? Dad asked.

– Depends. Whit did the surgeon say? said Dinah.

– Nae much. Depends fit they find.

– Aye, that's it, said Dinah. They'll dae their best. Wha's the surgeon, dae ye ken?

– Mr Carruthers.

– Aye, he gets a good name.

– And I suppose they winna let her oot in a hurry.

– O, she'll need a big lot o time.

– I ken, tae come tae hersel.

– Dinah, one thing?

– Aye, sure.

– Can ye get on the team, for Madge's sake. Somebody wi her, that she kens?

– I'm new at Foresterhill. Mebbe on ward, no in theatre. That's way beyond me.

– Dinah—?

– I'll try.

fit a bonny woman

Madge was high on the trolley.

– I was hopin—

– I want ye to count to ten, said the nurse.

– O, please. This is bad enough. Dinna treat me like I'm daft.

– Sorry, Mrs, eh, Endrie. List me aa the names of your family then. Is that better for ye?

– Fine.

– Well fire awa.

– Tammy, Annie, Peem—

She felt the prick. And heard, from submerged, the nurses speaking over her.

– Hugh, Hugh ma brither—

– Fit a bonny woman she is still.

– Ros, Ros an Bet, an Andy—

– Aye it's a richt shame.

for a dove it could have been whiter

She was about falling out of the bed with her two sisters. In the single they were, head to toe, toe to head, nibbling water biscuits. Ros had pinched a couple from the tin high up, standing on a chair. Betsy spoke in laughs and splutters, trying to round up flakes with her lips. Jacob's Cream Crackers, there wasn't any *cream*, and *where did Jacob come in?*

Ros wiggled a toe in Betsy's face, *who am I?* and Betsy bit at it, with spittly crumbs. And boys were daft, *huffing and puffing* and telling their lies in your lug and sliding a hand either down or up, to your body's hot amazement. With your sisters arrived in the lobby too, you could hear *stop!* and pliant noises. And you'd take his peck, and give him a smoorich, and slide but slow along the wall, till you clasped your hand round the wobbly knob, you had to go in.

And on the knob you felt their hands pile. So you pulled yours out from underneath. *On top* said Ros. *On top* said Betsy, anything for a game.

And a voice crackled out from high in the gas meter *We are at war, report to your unit* and soon that horrible Haw-Haw accent *Where is your Ark Royal? Where is the Repulse?* So you ran in the street and down to the Vicky, to crouch behind a line of privet. They came axing along, stripped to the waist and two to an axe, o they knew where you were alright. And a rude head of sycamore came toppling, slowly.

So right up the street you ran, and at the top was a tram climbing Rosemount. It dinged to a stop and hundreds of passengers came out from the paper-shop to board. Girls in triangular cotton frocks and boys in bracered shorts. A man had a cloth steaming with tatties and a string of peapods over his shoulder like green boats, they were off to the country. Madge was shamed she'd no food to share, so she clambered under, for all to see but nobody looked, in behind the cowcatcher, wedged akimbo in the underside struts.

The tram clacked on, the points sent sparks, the rails glowed hot, the driver racking up speed. Past mansion and bungalow at such a rate, the sparks flew up her nose – if nobody cared, they'd go up in a whoof at the terminus. She tried a hankie at her mouth, to hold any blood, it was far too small, no, it was a big man's hankie.

Bugger it – terminus! shouted the driver, on trams they pretended to be in charge. But the wheels went off the tedious rails – they whined on to tarmac, and then away cross country, singeing the springy heather, quenching themselves in wet peat.

Madge nigh shook from her perch, as all sorts of beasts came bounding now, a fox and hounds she could see through the bars, and thundering quarters of it looked like ponies, a black mamba weaving between their thighs. She wiped off the blood with her hankie and cheered and whipped at them, for a short while – why?

The *Rosemount* leaned against the sky and they were away up a brae, she keeked at the marker stones that said *Devil's Prick, Angel & Dick*, and the last *Fit a Swick!*

My stop, Mister! she yelled to the driver, and the driver shouted down through his slats *Sorry, lass, didna ken ye were doom by.*

She felt a sharp go into her, the usual flint, and flinched *Stop, driver!* and he shouted louder *Haud on, we're awa for the ither side.* And it wasn't fair, all the others would be snoozing on the upholstered green of the tram, clean oblivious to boulder and mountain. *Stop at the Atlantic, then!* she yelled, but the driver had small enough clue about that, he was only used to the Rosemount run. He'd done his shift, they'd paid no fare, she could hear him snoring on the curly stair.

And the tram flailed on dry sand, the wheels being thinnish, and then it got lower where the sand was wet and sliced up starfish, you could hear the hearts of cockles break on either hand.

So the tram was lovely and buoyed as it hit the water, they knew how to seal a tram, she was proud of them, she wanted to climb up aboard and congratulate, but that was hardly for her, she had her orders to look out the cowcatcher. No foe would be gulled for long by a seagoing tram. *Rosemount, where is the Rosemount?* She was glad it was green and white, in the rough northern waters.

And seals came ranging, and looked across anxious with bubbles. And seahorses stood as outriders, momently, while jellyfish pulsed, with great long pulsings, and eyes on top of their head. And jellyfish seemed watery violet, like lovers, until they suddenly fled.

Locked now, they moved through the sea, a cold metal T. Where did that hard sub come from? Its lid upflipped, and a flag with stripes billowed way out and blinded her cowcatcher. Up on deck she went at last and Peem was there and his pal Spermy, holding the only course possible, they'd rammed the sub fair and square.

Hello, Madge said Peem, he must think something was wrong, he was awfully formal. *Spermy is getting the net out now, we're going to catch her.* She wanted to squeeze his arm but he was busy. The men in the conning tower flung buckets of glittering star-shapes, tinsel or tin, that flew past their faces like cowboy spurs.

Water poured off both ends of the sub as it forged sideways, and Spermy began to swing the black net round his head, while the men on the sub poured drums of ketchup into the water, to hide their purpose or emphasise trail.

And long jettisoned cargoes foamed past the tram on either side, torpedoes, probably, you didn't need to see stars fly to see how fast they were going. *Stand by to come astarn* shouted Spermy. *Ower much electric for a Rosemount. Come astarn!*

And Peem ran along the deck and kicked off the boarding and hollow panelling, it wasn't a tram, no more than fly in the air, all along she knew it was more than a tram. And the lines of the good ship *Gardyloo* shone clear, and she cleaved the water, and the net was flying. Spermy was whirling the net wider. *Enough for the lot o them* he shouted. *Yanks away!*

All over the sub black hatches popped up like mousetraps, and the men on board came running along her deck to bait the springs. *Use new!* shouted the commander. *It's too strong, sir!* shouted one of the men. *Blow them into Kingdom Kong!* shouted the commander. And they put barrels of something in every trap.

Let's go home, for pity's sake said Madge, but the boys looked ahead, their hair growing long, against the wind they knew was coming.

Each pair of men had a big axe, poised. Until they hit the rock of

Rockall, and the men toppled, and brought down axes slowly as they fell. Deck mashed, the sub smashed upwards red – look away – glowed white – look, nothing at all. The sea rose in an instant wrath, and they rode on that swell.

Wheelhoose! said Spermy as the wave mountained. They piled in quick, secured the door – brass Yale and silly wee snib. Only when they faced forward could they see the extended tilt, their noses like mushrooms on the glass as they gawked down a huge hill of water.

And all behind them was hissing, steaming with balefire, bodysurfed by stark men, their white flesh bubbling like cheese. *Melted cheese* Peem said to her, *is that the right messages? O plenty* she said. *Ye winna hae enough money for aa that.*

And on they raced, into the darkness, pinned on the chest of the monstrous wave, along with their outriders, whose faces buried in the slope, thank Christ. Madge felt her eyeballs about bursting with blast, ride, the surfing dead, her stare into the future.

And one pin of white appeared from the left. She wished a pigeon, doo, a dove, call it whatever, and a dove appeared. It moved towards them, taking up station down below, in the very curve. And the doo sped into the dark a notch ahead, with not the slightest choice of where to go, what speed to go at. *As doos do, do as doos do* she thought.

And the dove knew its trade alright, a blessing, and there was land sure enough. A rugged shape was coming visible, down and ahead of them, in the giant trough. *I've been tae sea* said Spermy *I think that's Scotland. Dae we want tae go?* said Peem. *It was good enough for Ludwig* she thought.

Soon monstrosity and its prisoners were speeding high over baffles of dunes, and meally hills and well above steeples. It was a big gun ride for the *Gardyloo* alright, poised high, locked on the turbinous wave.

And flicking up from the quick-drowned clachans and whelmed homes came small brass cylinders, flying up the face of the wave. Each hit a surfing body with a puff of foulness, so that it sank away. Peem hung out of the starboard window with a butterfly net and plucked at them and ladled them in. Brass cylinders, with felt at each end so they sat down softly, till you swivelled the inner chamber open and took out the short receipt. *It's some dividend* she thought. *Dividend!* she said.

And the minute she turned the first one over she recognised the writing, it was Frankie Groat, and the heading was *Leverburgh*. She scanned it quick and crumpled it up and tried to mind what Frankie had said.

And *Leverburgh* was just a place that was deliberately planted, the people were poor and lived on tatties and oats and fiddly lobster. So Lord Lever gave them a pier and a shed out of his own bank account, and the next thing they were hauling dead whales ashore and boiling strips of them at a time to make margarine, till the place stank to high heaven and was fair an abomination. But it was progress and Lord Lever took his green leather seat in Parliament and not just that, in the Labour Cabinet, and the place soon closed and the folk slunk off to live in Glasgow, in the depth of the Depression. But they couldn't pawn their whale-stunk clothes, whether Sabbath bonnet or Saturday waistcoat, the smell of the whales was in them and wouldn't go.

And the second one, that shot up the wave and punctured a foul body, the writing in the tube was from Billy Mill, and it said *Rodel*. She glanced at it quick and scrunched it.

And *Rodel* wasn't much of a place, just an old kirk that they trapped folk in one Sunday, and stuffed the windows with hay and smoked them to death, because they were completely the wrong clan, from the next glen, and there was always cattle or catechists wandering, and what could you do? So now they had done up the kirk and made it public, so folk could drink and ease the pogrom, and consider some beauties of the football. It had a very high bar, and nowhere to sit, so you got drunk quicker, you poured ferment and distillate straight down your throat.

The third one Theo had mentioned once, she recognised. *Dunvegan*. She uncrumpled the message to read it clear.

Dunvegan was just a castle nonsense, all turrets and draughts, and the laird was thinking of selling a few mountains so as he could get the masons and plasterers in, slaters too, she was sore in want of a roof. So maybe he'd market some Black Cuillinn and then, if he needed carpet or what, he could sell off the Red.

Mad for a country the lot of it, no doubt of that, and all the better of a good sweel-oot. But she saw no more brass cylinders come whizzing up the face of the wave, they must be crossing one of the bleaknesses, like Rannoch Moor, no muckle to tell of a place like that.

We'll catch no fish at this speed said Spermy, as he and Peem quartered the wheel, holding the spokes of her grimly as the wave raced on, neither slower nor faster since the submarine blew. But they never looked at the compass, what was the point?

And the second night came down, just a few stars twinkled below them, reflected off the bottom of the wave, or they might have been herds' shielings, or climbers' bothies, or country retreats, at their final twinkle. And what must their last thought be, Madge wondered, as the wave came roaring on them beyond enduring, and even the breath of its nearing bent in the windows like Cupid bows. Did they hear the dove speed past? She was sad for them, them that were wiped from geography – without so much as space for a kiss.

Then dawn came in, angrier than ever, and she knew at last what a mess they were making. Blood, and not of the skies, was swimming before her eyes, the wave was boiling brown and as she looked out the stern, she saw the great ripped purse-net, trailing and fizzling like a failed and empty scheme.

And all she could see zooming towards them was a great bridge, made of hollow red diamonds. Their ship could no way get under that. Faces of folk she saw, behind the glass of a train, pressing and pointing up. She shrugged her shoulders. The *Gardyloo* sped above them, light as a craft, while the wave swiped carriage and brig, like Tammy swept rusk and plate from his high table.

And then she saw a big white on the eastern horizon, moving fast their way. A big white and brownish wave, maybe it had come from Russia the way. *Hold on!* she shouted to the lads, as she hauled the wheel down right. They didn't have much to say for themselves these days.

And she carried their ship through a maze of stacks, belching black to the sky, and the net was wrenched from her so she could have gone faster but the wave seemed slower, and she could see a city before her, not her city by any means, but she knew odd things about it. And she knew she didn't have long.

She turned from side to side in the wheelhouse, but the boys were gone – all that pain of boys – then they were gone.

She was entering the city now, it didn't have gates to split asunder, just tracts of tenement houses, a rough castle, a black monument like a filthy rocket. She swerved as needed, with a lean of her hips, and coursed along a glen of gardens. The Russian wave reappeared out of a side street, they crashed and met, and up they went for a good long while, and down the length of High Street in vortices of brown.

I'm Madge she said, as she stepped from the subsiding ship, onto and into the muds of Scotland. But it wasn't as easy as that. The dove was circling, the mud was thrashing, there was a spatter of books, and heads amongst them, churning. They seemed to need the look of her eyes.

Up bobbed a timber – *Haly Rude* – which the doo sat on and gripped at with rudimentary claws. For a dove it could have been whiter.

She tried to stand, but slipped on the muddy glass. She tried, and skited again. A curved half-acre, an architecture, curved like an upturned boat.

They winna let me rest she said, and closed her eyes.

morn

to feel history blister

The news came up from Constitution Street. It was the Constitut-
ioners that heard the trams, slipping down towards the beach in
the dead of morning. Lord Provost Rust had said the trams would
be respected, and thousands had turned out the night before, to
cheer them through the streets, some leaping off and on, a pipe
band up on an open-top, and the streamlined ones with plenty
bunting. Then they'd turned into the tall tramsheds, the cream
would be off to Museums, the Provost said, and a nice sum turned
for the rest, for scrap.

Spermy had been down at the docks when the scrappie ship came
in, the SS *Vulcan. Vulcan? It's Vulcan ridiculous* he'd said to Peem.
They'll never fit a tram on that. Right enough the scrappies were
only up for mangled metal, whole trams an anathema to them.

A surreptitious dawn procession was therefore heading down
towards the Beach, towards the Prom, and swinging back round
and filling the Boulevard. But from Constitution, right up Park Road,
past Lemon and Jasmine Streets into Rosin and Urquhart, the news
soon spread. Doors were banging helluva early, and what was going
on?

    – The trams— said Dad.

    – What? said Peem.

    – C'mon, there's something afoot they're sayin. Trams.

    – I canna be bothered, said Hughie, wi measly auld trams.

They were still in Park Road when the plume soared up, and by the time they turned beachwards, the first half-dozen were roaring ablaze. There were folk flowing towards the Beach, converging from all over, running with their coats half-fastened, hauling sleepy kids by the hand.

– O this is affa, c'mon, we mustna miss this—

– Dinna scuff yir shune, ye vratch—

– That souvenirs'll aa be gone afore we even win doon.

You could smell neither Scottish Fertile nor Gasworks for the niff of burning paraffin and paint. Their faces were well warm as they overtook Tam Clunie.

– Aye aye, is that you, Tam?

– O hello, aye, it's you, Andy.

– Bad business.

– Aye. We used the like as barricades in Barcelona.

– Thanks by the way, Tam, for the flooers, lilies, ye sent— I should hae written ye back.

– Ah, well, it was wrang that we missed the funeral. But we were doon in Ayr at Congress aa the week.

– Na, we understood. It was good o ye tae send flooers.

– We'd hae taen them oot tae the grave—

– Ah, but the point is, Tam, there isna a grave. Ye ken Madge. She didna want tae mak a nuisance o hersel.

– She was aye a guid-hertit wifie.

They walked on, the heat getting fiercer.

– Ye ken Scottish Fertile's oot on strike next week? said Andy. At least the sparkies.

– Aye, we heard. Your reinstatement dispute.

– Nae doot the Party thinks it's a bit individualistic—

– The Party hasna taen a line. It's nae an issue.

– Nae an issue—?

– We'll hear how ye get on.

All the trams had been fired now, by the Corporation guys, mufflers round their lower face like guisers. Thank goodness they'd taken the glass out first, cannibalised windows and mirrors, for the future tribe of buses. The crowd was standing about twenty yards back, wanting to feel big heat on their faces, feel history blister them in this auto-da-fé, sacrifice of the past, this Council blitz.

Smoke whoomed from eyeless windows, a bright handrail went straight to liquorice, floor-slats flared and fell on the Boulevard, like brands that could have raised clans.

The only thing raised was a black Labrador, Peem had seen its spit down here before. Somebody was lobbing a rubber bone nearer and nearer the long conflagration, getting the big dog to race in daft and fetch. Heidcase Casey's dad, Casey the Conductor.

– Mad, eh? said a voice at Andy's elbow.

    – Hiya, Theo. Hello, Marcie.

    – Hi, Andy.

    – Sae what dae ye think o this, Theo?

    – Politically or sculpturally?

    – Either.

    – I think it's a brainless mess.

    – We've got some books, said Marcie. If Peem would like tae come roon, would ye Peem?

    – Uh-huh.

    – Weekends are usually good.

Andy spotted Conal and Abe, two of the baggers, and went over.

    – Far's the rest o the team? Ye're surely nae hopin tae bag somethin here?

    – Never mind that, Andy. The baggin shop voted on Friday tae come oot in support.

    – Ye're nae, are ye, boys? I never heard. Fan did ye vote?

    – Jist at the hooter.

– That's brilliant, that's really good o ye.

– Well, it's a stitch-up, isn't it. If they can pile a guy like you on the rocks, fit could they dae tae the rest o us?

Peem saw Tarry and Raymie slinking around on the outskirts, but they didn't wave. Pinners was standing with a small stocky woman, you didn't expect teachers to come gawping at public bonfires. Not when they could have feet up at home, parroting parts of speech, or the spelling of *Mississippi*.

Andy felt a prickle as somebody suddenly bumped him.

– Aye, aye, Mr Royston.

– Mr Endrie—

– This'll be your wark, nae doot. Prood o it, as usual?

– You Commies see the world in far too simplified terms.

– Aye, ma wark's fair been simplified. Doon tae three days a week, an a faimily tae feed. Time-an-Motion, dinna mak me puke.

– Sorry to hear that—

– Yir tears widna weet muckle—

– Over-reaction can be as bad as no reaction.

– An ye're just happy tae be the reactionaries' tool?

– There's a dialectic. In passing, you should know I argued all thru for trams. Their inherent predictability and fuel efficiency have been abandoned for the appearance of freedom, to wit the bus and car.

– Aye, well, ye lost that ane, then. Sae far are ye aff tae noo?

– Hell, Glasgow.

– Well I hope thon case is genuine crocodile.

– Alligator. Why—?

– Ye'll need it.

Peem had edged away from the Rosin and Urquhart folk, there were lots more folk coming streaming now, along from Fittie and

Torry. The fisherfolk, that his Dad misdoubted, were coming to pay their respects to the trams. They didna have a piper, and they didna have an accordion. But a woman first, the men following, they struck up a song, another of these songs he'd never heard. The woman had blondie hair, and a three-quarter camel coat linking down to her black cowboy boots.

Fareweel to Tarwathie, adieu Mormond Hill,
And the dear land o Crimond I bid ye fareweel,
I'm bound out for Greenland and ready to sail.
In hopes to find riches in hunting the whale.

Strange to live in a country sae lang and still be hearing new sangs.

Adieu to my comrades, for a while we must pairt,
And likewise the dear lass wha fair won my hairt;
He saw Dinah alang the crowd a bit, but couldna see who she was with.
The cold ice of Greenland my love will not chill,
And the longer my absence, more loving she'll feel.
She was with Amande.

The cold coast of Greenland is barren and bare,
No seed-time nor harvest is ever known there;
And the birds here sing sweetly on mountain and dale,
But there isna a birdie to sing to the whale.
He wondered where Spermy was – and didna listen to the rest.

Annie was standing real close to Dad. He should go back now and join them. But he could see Dinah and Amande coming towards him. He pretended not to though, and next thing they had crept up behind him on either side and slipped gloved hands round his waist, to cuddle him in.

– How's our special boy today? said Amande.

– Good tae see you, Peem, said Dinah. Ye're getting sae tall now!

– How is your father to care with the baby and all? said Amande.

– Tammy greets every nicht, it's nae easy—

– He needs a maman.

– An we dinna aye hae money so much. Annie was hopin for a new dress for her eighth birthday, but she just got butterfly transfers tae stick in a book.

– Amande's got wark at the fever hospital, said Dinah. The City.

– I must have so many injections first, said Amande. Just to wipe floors.

– I was in the City once— said Peem.

He wanted a controller, the brass ratchet that determined electrical resistance and tram speed. Annie was needin her breakfast, so he told Dad he'd stay on by himself for a while.

After the great affair, they were down to chassis and bogeys pretty quickly. But a burned-out tram takes a time to cool.

Dinah eventually got it for him, with her leather glove, and gave it to him with a peck on the cheek. He put the knob in his pocket, warm, a sort of thing.

It was not a souvenir.

easter

the air show

They were sitting at breakfast, a Saturday.

    – Dad, can we go to the Air Show?

    – Ower muckle tae dae.

    – Dad, though, can we?

    – Bedroom tidy?

    – Nearly.

    – Swept the lobby? We've swapped days wi the Morrisons—

    – Fuckinchrist, breathed Hughie.

    – Fit! Fit wis that? said Dad. Well, nae Air Show then.

    – I'll do sweeping.

    – Ye want tae come, Annie?

    – Better her nor me, said Hughie. I'm bidin here.

    – Wonders will never cease. Wi Grizel I suppose, said Andy. Right, one o the pair o ye, pit the fire on, it's still far fae summer.

Peem dashed out and unlocked the coal bunker with the worn-barrelled key, set the hackstock on the black concrete, and fetched down the small axe.

    – Set them up, bartender, he said.

He took from the stack a small irregular clog and sat it on the hackstock. Legs out like a colossus, he brought the axe whanging. The clog coggled, dust rose.

At the second stroke the axe bit better. He hoisted the hooked clog and boinged it, as Wallace clove Edward's skull—

Aunt Betsy had pâté sometimes, like squeezed brains, when they went over these days.

Good, they were taking the Panther. His father had fitted a sidecar to it, one he'd haggled for at the scrappy, re-welded and licked with paint.

– I want to go in the silver sidecar.

– I thocht a big girl like you would want tae drive?

Dad wedged an olive haversack in behind her, probably sandwiches and a thermos, leant down and gave her a kiss. Then he skirted round and kicked the Panther into life.

Peem was palpating the stiff stain on his helmet. He stopped. He threw his leg over and gripped his Dad by the belt. Dad was wearing his RAF greatcoat, more a grey-blue, thick as felt.

– All aboard for Dyce!

Peem trawled in his pocket. He didn't have the blue stone any longer. He did have the molten tram-knob, though, that Dinah gave him.

Hughie was standing behind Grizel at the front bedroom window.

– Onwards an upwards! Dad said, and rotated the throttle.

Grizel waved.

whaur once there was human beings

Just before they got to the aerodrome, Dad veered and stopped the bike on a cast-iron bridge.

– What are they, Daddy?

Plump and black, heads catching the sun, angry knoblets over their beaks.

– Muscovy.

– What covey? said Peem.

– Russian ducks. Bonny, eh?

Probably exiles.

– Gie them some bread, Daddy.

– Na, we're nae divin intae haversacks yet.

They roared up to the RAF entrance gate. From the deep side-pocket of his greatcoat he drew out his demob papers, and showed them to the chilly guard.

– Not current, sir.

– Current! I'm still demobbed, amn't I? The peace is current.

– Lost me there, sir.

A couple of flight lieutenants were passing through.

– Well, if it's nae yersel, Freddie.

– Andy! Comin back? You joining up?

– Fit in hell would I dae that for?

– Sort out Nasser.

– Bomb the Sphinx?

– Lost face already.

– Exactly. Na, I'm jist tae show the kids roon, ye ken, look at whatever, maybe get a turnie up in a—

– Well, when you're finished, pop doon the mess.

The Lancaster's wings were thick, each with two engines, big as cars. When Peem climbed through the hatch, it was all hollow, echoey, with perspex pulpits.

– This is where the bombardier lay, said the guide. Look down through the cross-hairs. See that red hotel and the four green houses I've put on the tarmac?

– O, Monopoly.

– Now a Lanc like this carried ten ton of HE, high explosive – it never did to get hit before release—

– Wi flak?

– Or Messerschmitts.

He rejoined his Dad on the ground. He hadn't come up and he wasn't speaking.

The three of them walked towards a different plane.

– Have they not got an engine today, Daddy?

– I didna think ye thocht aboot engines.

– It's not a butterfly, it has to have an engine.

– But it's a glider—

– I don't want to go.

– Safe as houses. It's a bonny fine day, I'm sure Megan'll enjoy it.

– She willn't.

– Has she ever tried it?

– Megan's dead. I need the toilet.

Peem and his Dad walked back to the Nissen with her, let her go in herself.

– We'll just have to go back.

– But it's free.

– We canna leave your sister ahint, she'll be up tae high doh.

– Dad, why did you not climb up in the Lancaster? Tell me properly, I'm big now.

– Nithin tae tell. I used to work wi Lancs and Hudsons. That was eftir they posted me awa fae Beaus. When I screwed up the radar, they suspected somethin. But I wasna goin tae see twa crew court-martialled for an honest error.

– Ye were brave then, Dad.

– Ye see the reason I couldna go in that Lanc an hour ago is well, ye ken – afore we could ever mend a radar, electrics, or R/T, we had tae deal wi the effects o flak.

– How?

– Hose oot the fuselage wi a pressure hose, an sweel oot through the bomb-doors. When we were finished, the tarmac aneath the plane had changed colour. And it wisna black nor grey ony langer. Far once there was human beings, noo there was just bits. Watch, here's Annie comin. Sae never forget what I tellt ye afore – there's nithin glorious aboot war.

– I want to go in the glider—

– Anniekin? Really? We were jist ready for hame.

the speckled slope

They walked out towards the bare-winged glider, its nose hooked to a cable that lay lank to a tug-plane beyond.

– The baith of ye, a word aboot the pilot. He's caad Lewis, but he canna hear ye.

– Is his helmet too thick?

– Na, he's deif-an-dumb. That's why they caa him Lugless Lewis.

Dad helped Annie up, then slung his haversack in between them. When Peem got up into the co-pilot seat, Lewis crinkled at him. He had white creased skin on his left cheek and a bit of red moustache. Lewis handed him a pad and a pencil. On the pad it said *Hi!*

Peem wrote *Hi!* and handed it back.

Lewis placed the pad on his overalled thigh and wrote *How hi?* Peem smiled up into his left eye, under the bushy eyebrow. Lewis pointed at Peem's helmet, and gave him a thumbs-up. He reached across Peem's body, with a strong reek of pipe tobacco, to help him with the clasps and webbing.

Peem could see the prop whop on the plane ahead, then whirring. Then the cable between them was up like a mamba, bar tight, and – jerk and two shimmies – the glider was off, an orange windsock flashing by, going the other way.

They passed into air, silent, hissing. Lewis pointed at the altimeter, one thousand, two. As soon as its tongue flicked at three thousand, he pulled a lever, the tug dived off, and they had the sky to themselves.

– It won't even fall, said Annie.

They followed ribbons of roads, hives of roofs, to the city centre, dirty, sparkly, castellate.

– Hey, Dad—

Green roofs, weaving and bunching on Union Street.

– Dae ye see oor hoose?

– No, Dad.

Look there's Pittodrie. There's the gasometer, grey circle. There's Trinity cemetery. An there's Rosin.

– I canna see our number.

– Ye can sut. Look there's the concrete shelter oot the back, and look, somebody's got a washin oot—

– It's Mrs Hird's day.

– Aye, pink sheets, odd towels, an look – there's her teensywee bra hingin—

– Dad!

– And quick, that seventh rose doon, there's a coupla greenfly. Divvels!

A slow reach of the lower river fed past bollarded docks, and quickened seawards to Girdleness. On the last of the ebb slid three trawlers, punching over the shallow bar.

– Aye, but oot there we'd be buggered for thermals, drap like a stane. Lewis'll circle for inlaun noo.

Indeed Lewis swung the whispering miracle of balsa and flesh west then north, sweeping over the groyned beach, the tiny Bumps – no sign of Mary – the sluggish Don.

Lewis's gloved finger reached out and tapped the altimeter. Nearly four thousand.

Perched on a hill were sky-tilted scallops. It must be the things Spermy had seen, on his way up to Fraserburgh. With funny aerials and fal-de-rals.

Lewis wrote on the pad and showed *Mormond Hill*. Of course – the place in the song. Then he wrote *Yanks*, and wrote *listening and watching for Russkie subs.*

Mostly it's whales they hear wrote Lewis. *Official secret – whales sing!*

Dad began diddling.

Fareweel tae Tarwathie, adieu Mormond Hill,
An the dear land o Crimond I bid ye fareweel,
Deedle ee dee dee deedle—

The saucers were getting bigger. He hadn't a clue on the middle verses.

Adieu to my comrades, for a while we must pairt,
And likewise the dear lass—

They banked soft left. Probably Lewis didn't even know his dad was singing.

All along the sky in front of them were a series of flattened cigar-shaped clouds, like long lenses: they were rising towards the first one now, altimeter at five thousand.

For Bennachie, the Mither Tap, the glider slanted. Her warm pap sent them high over a land abead with dykes – ribbed and breathing with plough – here and there hairy with larch. Buoyed up past Foudland – a grey tractor crawling its geometry – they swooped away to Huntly.

Upon that hill there stood a doocot;
It's no there noo, cause some sod took it.

– Dad—!

– Aye, that's whaur I used tae live as a loon. Start at the river bend, follow that piddle o a burn, in past the routh o trees, and intae the Haugh o Glass.

They had lost height now.

    – Will we hae tae choose a field? said Peem.

But Lewis caught the wave, the rising air, and headed towards the next high lens, and on to the Cairngorms.

– Heave me up that haversack, Annie.

    – What's in?

    – Ye'll see.

    – M'hungry.

Two webbing straps buckled the haversack shut. Andy unbuckled them. He slid out a fat brown polythene jar, it would be about a quart.

The glider was high above the Lairig Ghru now, just thinking to sink.

Lewis pointed to the bulwark of a huge corrie.

    – Ower there, that's our target, said Dad. Braeriach.

    – Riach?

    – Speckled hill, speckled slope.

The glider tilted down.

The thin dark line of consciousness, flaring over the edge.

    – I canna get this bugger o a lid aff—

    – Fit is it?

    – The polythene's flamin mated.

The glider was swooping towards Braeriach's plateau.

    – Sorry for shoutin at ye. Ye ken we didna exactly bury Mum?

    – Why? Why didna we?

    – Because she said *I dinna want tae be holin aboot in a cemetery in Aiberdeen, wi fowk comin gypin, an ma flooers gettin foosty.*

    – Sae she went tae the Crem instead?

– Because up here's far she loved. Tak a wee haunfu, look, and I'll slide back the winda.

– Ooh, they're greasy.

– Canny.

– An crinkly.

– That's aa the potash.

– Far's the rest? said Peem.

– That's the lot.

– Got some, said Peem.

– Right, trail your haun oot the winda. Let go, quick, let go!

– O—

– Look, there she goes, flutterin doon on the snaa there. Annie?

– I hope mine goes in the wee river, Daddy.

– Well tak a good helpin—

– Cause I can see her in the Dee in Aberdeen.

Andy gave the base of the jar a couple of dunts with the heel of his hand, and hung it out of the cold rushing window.

– Are ye gaain tae drap the jar as weil, Dad?

– Fit, an litter the bonny hills for aye? Na, it'll come in handy for somebody else.

The glider was skiffing the summit snow, when she hit the wave on the western side.

Up she went, and up, like the lift in the Co-opy.

ᜰ